SHERYL NANTUS

"If you're a fan of strong female characters
and mysteries with a paranormal twist,
this is a real winner."
—*Reflections on Reading Romance*

"The story moves at an even pace and the mystery
is slowly revealed as the romance of Rebecca
and Brandon develops. All in all, Sheryl Nantus's
Blood of the Pride is a shifter romantic mystery that
paranormal fans should find quite satisfying."
—*Love Romances & More*

"An enjoyable mix of mystery, action and feline
shapeshifters. Tired of werewolves? Try this instead."
—*Goodreads* Reviews

"Well-written urban fantasy
with a strong, appealing heroine."
—Nicole Luiken, author

SHERYL NANTUS

BLOOD OF THE PRIDE

CARINA PRESS™

ISBN-13: 978-0-373-00209-2

BLOOD OF THE PRIDE

Dear Reader,

A few years ago I signed up for National Novel Writing Month, or NaNoWriMo. This writing exercise is attempted by thousands every year with the goal of writing 50,000 words in only 30 days.

But what to write? I loved detective stories and enjoyed reading paranormal novels but couldn't think of a way to make them merge and be different from what I'd seen before.

I thought over what qualities would be most useful as a private investigator. Enhanced smell and excellent hearing came to mind, allowing my woman to get the job done faster and more efficiently than others in her field.

Enter Rebecca Desjardin. Canadian, Felis (cat shifter) and a private investigator.

And a misfit. A genetic throwback of sorts, unable to shift into her feline form at will. Outcast from her family, she's been forced to make her way in a human world while keeping her secret from everyone.

Toss in a handsome tabloid reporter determined to work his way into her heart and life and I knew these two would be trouble.

I hope you'll enjoy *Blood of the Pride* and come back for more adventures from my fearless Felis P.I. and her main man.

Sheryl

For my husband, Martin, who doesn't mind hairballs on the bed; AD, who has the patience of a saint; and the real Jazz—still miss you, my sweet little fuzzaloid.

BLOOD OF THE
PRIDE

SHERYL NANTUS

was born in Montreal, Canada, and grew up in
Toronto, Canada. A rabid reader almost from birth,
she attended Sheridan College in Oakville, graduating
in 1984 with a diploma in media arts writing. She
met Martin Nantus through the online fanfiction
community in 1993 and moved to the United States in
2000 in order to marry.

She loves to play board games and write haiku,
although not usually at the same time. In her past she
was a Guardian Angel—no, not *that* type. She also
spent over fifteen years in private security, working at
hospitals and high-security sites.

A firm believer in the healing properties of peppermint
and chai, she continues to search for the perfect
cuppa.

She has published multiple books. In 2011 she
won two second-place Prism Awards from the
Fantasy, Futuristic and Paranormal chapter of RWA.
Blood of the Pride is her first book with Carina Press.

ONE

"Our character is what God and cats know of us."
—*Thomas Paine*

I SMELLED THE blood before I had a chance to look for it, the tangy, dense scent landing on the back of my tongue. Forcing the familiar taste to the back of my mind, I opened the office door and studied the man sitting in the chair opposite my desk. He was clean, dressed smartly in a white dress shirt and dark blue pants. He didn't get up as I approached the desk, walking around the chipped wooden edges I had unsuccessfully tried to hide with walnut oil.

"Ms. Desjardin." Harry Cloches bobbed his head up and down as I sat down in the old oaken chair. "Sorry for being early, but I wanted to get the information I requested as soon as possible." He waved at the door. "Your front door was open when I arrived, so I thought I'd come into your office and wait in here." Beads of sweat appeared on his forehead. "I hope you don't mind."

My nose twitched as I rocked back, urging a creak from the worn old wood. A small box rested on the left side of the desk. It hadn't been there when I had gone upstairs last night after locking the doors and checking the windows. The brown paper wrapper encased the palm-sized box fully, but moisture was already beginning to fight through the paper.

I picked up the file folder from the top of the small pile to my right and opened it up, spreading the black and white photographs across the desk in a half-circle display. Cloches leaned forward, his pink tongue darting out across dry lips as he squinted to see the images.

"Your wife is not cheating on you." My finger tapped the image of the brunette exiting a coffee shop, latte in hand. "She's actually working a second job."

His forehead furrowed. "A second job?"

"Your ten-year anniversary is coming up in a few months. She's saving up for a cruise." I could smell the nervous sweat on him, mixed with the scent of another woman. It took a concentrated effort to stop my nose from twitching.

"Oh." He pulled out a handkerchief and wiped his face dry. "I just thought…"

I sighed, trying not to show my disgust with the man. "She's not having an affair, Mr. Cloches. Your fears were unfounded and your marriage is secure." At least on her end.

I pulled the typed invoice out from the bottom of the file and pushed it across the table. He stared at it while as I gathered up the photographs and closed the folder. "This is my bill. Please send the balance due within thirty days."

The bald man mopped his face again, the damp fabric barely able to contain the moisture now. It stank of fear. I spied a small trace of lipstick just below his right ear. "It was…It looked like…" He shook his head, trying to grasp the reality I had tossed in his face.

I got to my feet and motioned toward the door, urging the overweight man out of his chair. He staggered to his feet, staring at my bill as if I'd tossed a live cobra into his hands. "She's not having an affair, which is what you contracted me to investigate. If you wish to engage my services for another matter we'll have to discuss it later." I glanced at my watch. "I'm sorry, but I have another client due any minute." My cloying smile accompanied him into the hallway toward the front door. "You understand, privacy issues and all that."

Cloches nodded, tucking the damp cloth back into his pocket. One hand tugged at the tie threatening to strangle him, pulling it loose. "It just seemed like…" The fingers waggled in the air as if he were trying to summon fairies to carry him away from this existence. He glanced down at the page in his hand, his eyes widening as they hit the bottom line. "Oh my." The pink tongue flicked out again. "I didn't know it would cost so much."

I pressed my lips together tight, suppressing the urge to start smacking the moron around. What he had wanted was for me to justify his own infidelity so he could obtain a quickie divorce and I hadn't done so. Still, if he didn't pay the bill I could and would drag him into court. I wasn't wealthy enough to let welchers get away with it, and certainly not this bastard.

"If you have any questions please have your lawyer contact me." I moved closer, herding him out the door. "Good day to you."

I closed the door behind him and snapped the deadbolt across, locking both my office and my home. Some may find it awkward to live and work in the same building, but to me it was sort of comforting. There's nothing like padding downstairs in your big fuzzy bunny slippers at three in the morning when you have a good idea and want to get to work. Or breaking early for the day when there's a rocking matinee down at the retro cheap theaters.

I sat down at my desk and stared at the box. You don't just rip a cryptic box open without inspecting it, especially when there's something dead inside.

The brown paper covered the box with enough clear tape securing it to cover the CN Tower and then some. It wasn't enough to stop a small leak in one corner, just beginning to work through the tape and paper to spread across my desk. The crimson stain had begun to travel upward as well, edging toward the top of the box. What wasn't there was as important as what was.

No return address. No stamps. The person dropping it off managed to carefully pick my front door lock before sneaking in and placing it on my desk. Quite a feat considering I had been twenty feet away in my bedroom at the top of the stairs and I don't sleep that soundly.

It sure as heck wasn't Cloches. He wasn't smart enough. All he had wanted was validation of his affair. The guy couldn't break into a loaf of bread without a chainsaw.

I opened my desk drawer and pulled out my Mac-Gyver knife—well, technically it was a Swiss Army knife, but it had enough gadgets and things hanging off that I had renamed it.

The blade slipped easily under the paper and sliced clean around the box as I peeled away the wet covering. When it fell away I stared at the cardboard box and the larger scarlet stain by one corner. It wasn't human blood. I knew that scent intimately.

I flipped the lid up, holding my breath as the stagnant air escaped into the room. It stung my nostrils, bringing back old memories of early-morning hunts and of fresh-cut grass wet with morning dew.

A rabbit's foot lay on a bed of paper towels, the white fur stained with fresh blood. This wasn't your regular rabbit's foot, clean cut with a dainty little chain secured at one end and nothing at all to remind you this once was a living creature.

This was a fresh kill. The nails were dirty with soil that smelled of fresh grass and hay, the foot suddenly shattered by a hatchet that cut through bone and sinew with a single blow. I sniffed the foot instinctively, placing the rabbit. It wasn't a wild one. It had been born in a hutch and died in a barn. I knew exactly which barn.

The farm. This was a call to come home.

Great. As if my day hadn't started off with enough bullshit.

I flipped the blade shut and stuffed the knife into the front right pocket of my jeans. The cell phone clipped onto my belt, sliding against my white blouse. It was as cheap a model as you can get—I didn't need internet access or the ability to watch music videos.

The stairs up to my living area took only a few seconds to climb as I leaped over the rickety top step masquerading as a cheap alarm system. I grabbed my black leather jacket off the coat rack then started back down. My roommate paused at the top of the stairs as I descended, trilling her curiosity.

"Jazz, you're in charge until I get back." I waggled my index finger at the thin white street cat. "Don't let in any strangers."

She began to wash her face with the usual haughtiness I had come to expect from a younger sister. I shook my head and checked the lock on my way out. Miniscule scratches on the metal spoke of a darned smooth hand, a professional. I locked it behind me, pushing once to make sure the deadbolt worked.

My red Jeep Cherokee sat in the small parking lot behind the house, hidden from casual pedestrians strolling by on the street. I liked it that way—it kept the car safe from idiots who figured that if you were stupid enough to leave your car on a Parkdale street you deserved to lose your CD player. It was a narrow and dangerous alley to get out of, however, and the numerous scrapes and dents on the brick walls and the matching ones on my car illustrated how many times I had miscalculated.

The traffic leading out of Toronto was light. I skipped onto the Gardner Expressway parallel to Lake Ontario and out to the northbound 400 Highway with ease— a good thing, since my mind wasn't on driving and I really didn't need any more stress. Weaving out from behind a slow moving tractor-trailer and sliding into the slipstream of a black Porsche that saw the posted speed limit as a suggestion rather than the law, I tried to figure out why I'd been summoned.

I had been forced out of my home more than two decades ago and now they had sent the equivalent of a draft notice, calling me back. That couldn't be good. The Pride was adamant that no contact be made with outcasts and I hadn't seen a whiff of that rule changing over the years, twenty years with nary a hint that just outside Toronto a whole community existed in secret for generations, long before I had come on the scene. Now they wanted me back. That smelled worse than the rabbit's foot.

TWO

THE FARM WAS pretty far off the beaten path. I pulled off the main highway and slid along gravel roads for a good half-hour into the Ontario hinterland. As I got closer and closer my muscles began to tense, my body getting ready for a fight. I owed them nothing. Still, they had called me and if nothing else, I was damned curious as to why the Pride had broken their code of silence.

I slammed on the brakes and spun the Jeep down the side road that could have easily been mistaken for a bike trail. If you didn't know where to turn you could easily shoot by, ending up at Wasaga Beach with no idea of where you had gone wrong. I hadn't been down this road in years and it was as if I had never left. The same rickety mailbox sat at the entrance with Hammersmythe's name on it. The same long drive up the dusty road that had never been paved and probably never would be. The same farmhouse with the same ugly paint job—a dark red that was peeling in more spots than it wasn't, showing off the numerous coats that had been applied over the years by delinquent kids doing penance.

It looked like any other farmhouse in North America.

It held more secrets than the Pentagon's deepest bunkers.

I pulled into the gravel parking lot. The SUVs and tricked-out trucks made my little Jeep look like a Hot Wheels toy. I picked the spot closest to the road in case

I needed a fast getaway and then got out of the car. The scents charged into my consciousness—freshly cut grass mixed with the ever-present manure and straw, and more than a single barn cat seeking out mice. And, if I wasn't mistaken, an apple pie or three cooled near a window, making my mouth water even though I had just eaten.

"Reb?" Karen stood on the porch, shading her eyes from the noon sun. "Rebecca?" Her face was suntanned to the point of becoming leather, her white-and-gray hair pulled into a short ponytail held back with a rubber band. She untied the apron around her waist and neck and tossed it over the back of one of the rocking chairs as I approached.

She opened her arms wide. "It's been such a long time."

I accepted the hug, holding back just a bit. My aunt hadn't objected to my being declared an outcast due to my "disability" and, while two decades had taken the edge off of the pain of being rejected by blood kin as well as by my family, it still didn't mean I had forgiven and forgotten. Karen hadn't aged well and I smiled inwardly, taking a bit of pleasure in that fact.

"They're inside waiting for you." She released me, a worried look on her face. "I guess it's something really bad."

"Bad enough to call me." I gave a low chuckle. "Yep, I figured that one out."

One dirty running shoe scuffed the wooden deck. "You're looking good."

"Thanks." I didn't return the compliment. "Excuse me, I think I better get inside before they call a hunt on me."

The older woman flinched, a gesture so minute

most people would have missed it. I didn't. I opened
the screen door and walked through, turning my back
on her. "See you later."

I was lying, of course.

"Stop in the kitchen first. Get yourself a drink." The
shout carried through to where I stood in the hallway.
A series of light jackets hung on the old wooden pegs
set into the wall. I didn't add mine to the stack.

The smell of cooked apple, cinnamon and way too
much sugar grew stronger as I stepped to the left into
the kitchen. On the spacious table sat five cooling pies,
the steam still escaping through the slits in the light-
brown dough. Next to them stood a row of bottles—
rum, vodka, whiskey. Picking up one of the empty
glasses, I filled it halfway with rum, adding some cola
from a nearby fresh can. The pies were tempting but
there wasn't a fork or knife in sight and I didn't think
I had room to shovel the whole thing into my mouth
quickly enough.

"Good God." The woman's voice spun me around,
my lips on the glass.

Ruth Huckleton stood there, cradling a baby in her
arms. Her dark red hair hadn't lost any color over the
years, nor had she lost the sparkle in her eyes that made
all children love her. "I heard they had called, but…"
She gestured toward the living room with a nod. "I
didn't expect you to answer, never mind come all the
way out here. Not after…" A squalling cry came from
behind her, invoking a deep sigh and a knowing grin.
"And, as usual, David can't keep himself dry for a minute." She turned around and walked briskly into the
living room, bouncing the yellow-haired baby on her
hip. He responded by grabbing one of the loose tails of

her apron, stuffing it into his mouth and chewing on it with the enthusiasm I would have reserved for the pie.

I followed, taking another sip of my drink.

The cribs were set up just as I remembered, the clawed and scarred wood bearing the marks of children either trying to break out or in. Wooden blocks, trains and planes spread out over the floor created an obstacle course Ruth navigated with ease, pushing the old-fashioned toys to one side or the other with her feet. Plastic might have been lighter and easier but wooden toys tended to last longer with Felis babies.

"Got quite a few visitors this week so I'm running the daycare again." Ruth put the baby she had been holding down into one empty crib, covering him with a blanket as the child rolled over and began to fall asleep. Right next to him, David, a rotund bundle of dark hair and attitude, gathered another lungful of air to scream again. Ruth picked him up, cooing in an attempt to divert the tantrum.

"Healthy little bugger." I glanced at the other cribs. A small calico kitten romped around in one, pouncing on a small stuffed tiger he had tossed into the corner. Another held a pair of tortoiseshell kits, snuggled against each other while they slept.

"Those are Art and Edith Brill's," Ruth offered by way of explanation as she put the fussy baby down on the changing table. Neatly folded fabric squares were stacked next to the mandatory wet wipes, diaper rash cream and a plastic box holding safety pins. Expertly she whipped off the cloth diaper and dropped it into the nearby disposal bucket, talking all the while. Her hands showed the results of years of caring for kits, covered with hundreds of small scars and scratches, including more than a few from yours truly. But they were still steady and for a second I envied the children around me receiving the undoubting love of a woman who had been unable to have her own. "The calico's Dennis Bucknell's son. Married Jem Luchness a few years ago." She paused, holding a safety pin in her mouth. "You remember her, I think."

"Maybe." I watched as the calico kitten rolled onto his back into the center of the crib, stretching his paws out in all four directions. Slowly he began to Change, the fur shrinking and receding into his skin as his body remolded itself. The claws retracted, disappearing between his knuckles while his green eyes flashed from the familiar feline slit to a more acceptable human circle. Within a minute there was no kitten, just another baby who stared up at me with wide curious eyes and a small pink tongue sticking out.

"He's got pretty good control." Ruth placed David back in his crib, shushing the child as he rolled into a corner, cradling a stuffed lion. Putting her hands on her hips she looked directly at me. "I'm serious. I didn't expect you to come."

"Jess called." I shrugged, taking another deep swig of my drink. "Board calls, you answer." Even with every effort to make it sound casual, I knew she could see through the façade.

The older woman shook her head. "You always were too forgiving, Rebecca." A tear broke free, rolling down her cheek. She stepped forward and took me in her arms, forcing me to put the glass down on the changing table. "Damn it, girl—I missed you."

Closing my eyes, I relaxed into the embrace, inhaling the familiar scent of an old friend and den mother. After a few minutes she released me, stepping back as she wiped her face with both hands.

"You better get upstairs before they come down here and start making a fuss. Don't need them to wake the kids." Ruth smiled. "I'll see you later."

"Probably." I walked into the kitchen, refilling my drink before heading toward the staircase. "Just don't let the kits claw you too much."

"Won't be the first or the last." Her words drifted up behind me as I climbed. "And you were the worst, I recall."

"I only bit you once." I grumbled, walking onto the second floor where the walls had long since been knocked down and cleared out to form only one room. The varnished hardwood floors were immaculately clean. A large round table took up the majority of the floor, a series of chairs scattered around the outside. A few beer bottles and glasses sat on the table, adding more rings to the numerous stains dotting the surface. Stacked against the far wall were cheap steel folding chairs for when larger meetings were called.

"Welcome." Jess Hammersmythe's voice boomed out of the shadows at the far end of the room where she sat behind the table. She lifted a bottle, waving me closer. "Glad you could make it."

"You called." A lump formed in my stomach, threatening to kick back the mouthful of booze. The last time we spoke she hissed curses into my ear, pushing me down the lane outside with a few dollars in my pocket and the clothes on my back. "You called so I came." I took another step into the Hall, my knuckles white from gripping the glass. Keeping my knees locked, I nodded to the two men sitting on each side of Hammersmythe.

"You're looking good, Reb." Dennis Sommalier nodded, the cigar hanging from his lips. I couldn't remember a time when he didn't have one in his mouth. Freud would have a grand old time with my family.

"She always did." Old enough to be my grandfather, Davis Konnerburg smiled as he lifted his own glass toward me with a sly wink that made my skin crawl. "We appreciate the prompt response."

"I'm sure." I walked up, grabbed one of the chairs and flipped it around, sitting down and resting my arms on the wooden back. "So, what's the crisis that you gotta call in the misfit?"

This was not how you were supposed to address the Board. Protocol was that you stood at attention until invited to sit. Then you placed yourself at a discreet and proper distance in the chair with your hands in your lap while keeping your back ramrod-straight and not speaking until spoken to.

Jess leaned forward, out of the darkness. An ugly scarlet scar dragged down across her face, starting just above her left eye and ending down at the left edge of her mouth. The dead eye glared, catching me in its glass reflection. "As I said—glad you could make it." She pulled the label off her beer bottle and tore it into little pieces, pushing them around the tabletop. "We have a problem and want your opinion on it."

"Bullshit. You don't do democracies." I took another mouthful of rum and cola. "If I recall correctly you don't usually ask anyone's opinion on anything. Now you're asking me?" I stared at each of the Board members until they looked away. "What's the big secret?"

"You understand, of course, that this is not to be repeated outside of this room," Davis droned in his authoritative voice. "Your oaths are still valid."

"You kick my ass out into the street and then ask me to play your game?" I snorted. "I don't think so." It was a weak attempt at a bluff but I had to let them know I wasn't going to be bullied into anything. "I go by my own oaths these days. I don't owe the Pride anything."

The group hiss crackled in my ears with the sudden shift in their bodies—the scent of fear. This wasn't a game. Something big was going down and they needed me more than I needed them, and we both knew it.

"You called, I came. Now state your reasons or I'll be on my way."

I was halfway up from the chair when Dennis spoke. "We want to hire you." The cigar bounced up and down while he spoke. "Janey is dead."

The rum burned my throat as I sat down and chugged the last of the drink. "Really. Old age?"

"Don't be a smartass," Jess snarled, pushing the label flakes into a small pile. "She was murdered."

"Then the police should handle it." I got to my feet and put the empty glass on the table. "I'm not a cop."

"No. But you're one of us." Dennis unfolded a rolled-up paper resting in front of him and slid it across the table to me. "And you understand what this means to us."

It was a two-page spread in the center of a tabloid, the picture taking up the majority of the space with weird trivia and a few ill-placed advertisements for weight-loss products and cheap herbal drugs surrounding it. There was a short article next to it but my attention went first to the photo.

The black-and-white photograph depicted a dead woman, sprawled on her back with her arms and legs at odd angles, as if she'd suddenly fallen to the ground. The tufts of fur around her face and on her hands suggested she had died in mid-Change. My eyebrows rose, prompting a comment from Dennis.

"She was killed two weeks ago. Her neck was broken." Dennis replied in a flat tone. His thick, meaty fingers pressed down on the table.

"That takes a lot of strength." I frowned, scanning their faces. "Up close and personal." I glanced at the article before flipping the paper over to see the headline.

"The Toronto *Inquisitor*? No one takes them seriously." My fingers rapped on the postage stamp-sized black-and-white image advertising the centerfold. "This reporter, for lack of a better word, has us digging through trash cans in High Park, ready to pounce on unleashed dogs. It's nothing but rumors and lies, and badly-written ones at that." I looked at the tabloid headline. "Although 'Dead Cat Woman Found!' does seem a bit tackier than their usual stupid quips."

"Extremely," Dennis replied. "Regardless, Janey is dead. And whoever took this picture set her up to be exposed." He stabbed the tabletop with a finger. "Set us up to be exposed."

"In a media rag. With pictures that could have been manipulated and changed by any kid with a computer." I looked up from the page. "Why didn't they post it online if they were serious about exposing us?" My mind kept bouncing between using "us" and "you/them" as I navigated my feelings about being back.

"Ever look online for reliable information about the Felis?" Dennis chuckled. "Or any?"

I chewed on my bottom lip. "You keep that offline?"

"As much as we can. Right now, according to the search engines, we're running far behind the reptilian overlords." He exchanged glances with Davis. I wouldn't put it past them to hire hackers to crash any sites coming close to the truth. "And if he or she had posted it we'd be able to track it back without any trouble."

"So he gives it to a real person, an investigative reporter in the lowest sense of the word, and hopes he takes the bait." I traced the blurry image with my index finger. "And he produces nothing but crap."

"Picture, thousand words," Jess said. "The article isn't what's important. The picture is what we're worried about."

"What did the police say?"

"Aside from investigating the murder they're trying to find out who took the picture. The question of the extra fur was simple to take care of. Just a medical ailment. Not pertinent to the investigation." Dennis shrugged. "We had one of our own who works on the inside make sure the emphasis was placed more on the murder than the condition of the victim."

"As it should be. Murder is murder." The Pride had friends in high and low places, ready to tweak things to keep us safe. I flipped through the cheap newsprint. "And she's competing with 'Bigfoot going on dancing show.'" My left eyebrow rose. "Going to have to set the tape machine for that one."

Jess shuffled the shredded pieces back and forth. "The problem is that she was murdered and left in an alleyway." Her dark eyes caught mine. "This is a danger to the Pride. In more ways than one."

"On the first front, her death. Yes. On the second, the matter of the photograph—maybe. But no one's going to take this seriously. I mean, the *Inquisitor*? We're not talking a major newspaper or a television investigative report. I wouldn't put money on the hack pursuing the story past what you have here." I shook my head and pushed the tabloid back into the middle of the table.

"I agree that it's a problem. But I don't see why you called me."

"Jess has argued that Janey's murder warrants a professional independent investigation." Davis picked up his own glass. It was filled with a clear liquid, probably vodka.

"The police are already looking into this. I can't just walk in and take over the case." I spun my empty glass around. "That's not how things work."

"We want to know who killed her and why they felt the need to show the world who she was." She pushed the pieces into one hand and curled her fist up, crushing them together. "They only have part of the puzzle, a dead woman. You have a different perspective."

"Amazing how now I'm now able to relate to Pride matters. How the times have changed." I let the sarcasm seep through with a touch of anger.

"Your point is acknowledged." Dennis glanced at Jess, a stern look on his face. "We have two problems. First, the photographer must be found and all copies of that image destroyed or discredited."

"A good smack about the ears, in other words."

"Give us the name and we'll take care of it. The second and more important is that Janey Winters is dead. Killed by either another Felis or a human strong enough and fast enough to match our skills. He must be found and brought to justice."

"Pride justice?" I shook my head and got up from the table. "I've had enough of that for one lifetime." Unbidden I rubbed the small of my back with one hand, trying to banish the phantom pains.

"Reb…" Jess opened her hand, letting the small paper ball fall onto the tabletop. "We can't change the past." She took a deep breath, the scar flexing across her skin. "Janey had two children and a husband. They deserve the truth. The cops won't be able to catch this guy." Her cheek twitched. "You know they're over-worked and likely to just write this off. She deserves better than that. She's family."

I closed my eyes for a long while, then opened them. "Five hundred dollars up front for a retainer, fifty bucks an hour plus expenses." It was double my usual rate.

"Done," Dennis replied.

"And I get full access to Pride records." I put my hand up as I saw Davis's mouth open, ready to object. "I'm not stupid. You're calling me in 'cause you want someone to chase down this jerk and you don't want to do it yourself because you might make a mistake and make an even bigger mess." I glanced around the table. "I'm assuming that while we've got 'friends' in the cop shop, no one's willing or able to run this solo. But that's going to handicap me from the start. If you're going to get me to do this, you have to give me full access to find out what happened." I gave the glass one more spin and put it down on the table. "If it's a Felis I'll need that ac-cess. That's not negotiable."

"Agreed," Jess growled, flicking the paper ball across the table toward me, "but you answer to us, and us only."

I picked up the tabloid paper, folding it and placing it under my arm. "I'll be in touch. Send one-week ad-vance payment. Let's call it for forty hours for a grand total of twenty-five hundred dollars in my account by the time I get back to my office. I'll provide receipts for the expenses later. Email me the files if you don't have them here." I raised my right brow in a hopeful man-ner. I had rent due and a car payment this week—and I might even be able to buy food for Jazz and me. And I knew they could afford what I was asking.

"We'll get the information to you later on today. And we'll be waiting for your updates." Jess nodded, dismissing me as if I were a child waiting for the principal to let me out of detention. The three of them got up from the table and walked past me in silence. I remained seated, waiting until they had gone downstairs, staring at the ball on the table.

I reached over and tossed the paper into the far corner of the Hall, watching it disappear from sight. "Bastards," I whispered to the empty room.

Ruth met me in the kitchen while I filled my glass with water. She wiped her hands on her apron, shaking her head. "Those kids. You'd think they were the first ones to ever discover their toes."

I smiled back. "Wait until they start chewing on them. As I recall it took me until I was five to let those nails grow to anything respectable."

"And you claimed they tasted like sugar." Ruth laughed, a low rumble that settled in my heart. "You look good. Keeping the weight on, finally. I thought you'd be one of those anorexics by now." She touched my arm, a wistful look on her face. "You have your mother's eyes."

"And my father's temper." I drained the glass, putting it in the sink. "Tell them to remember that." I kissed her on the cheek. "I'll talk to you again. Right now I've got to get to work."

"I'd like that. Seeing you again, I mean." She squeezed my arm. "Janey was a good woman. She didn't deserve this."

"No one ever does." I moved to the door. "But that's the way it happens sometimes, eh?"

I walked out onto the porch. Karen wasn't there. She had probably wandered off to avoid another awkward moment. Better for both of us.

I trotted down the steps and took a deep breath, drawing in the scents and sounds from my past again. In my mind's eye I sorted and catalogued each, identifying three Felis in the woods just to the north, most likely hunting some wild rabbits. Two more worked one of the fields that provided the farm with an income. With the rise of organic products, the local farmers' market had become a popular and profitable place for the breads, pies and vegetables the family churned out—with Ruth's help, of course. Not that the farm needed the money to survive. The tithing of all Pride members made sure those who lived on the farm had a comfortable life.

A fat lazy barn cat sprawled across the hood of my jeep. I opened the driver's door.

"I need to get to work."

The cat raised his head and yawned, displaying an impressive set of teeth.

"Seriously." I jerked my thumb back behind me at the house. "Don't want Jess getting mad, now...do we?"

The black cat leisurely rolled off the jeep's hood onto the gravel road, stretching out his legs one by one and flexing his toes in the air. He arched his back and let out another yawn before strutting back toward the barn, tail held high.

"Snob." I got in behind the wheel and turned the engine on, tossing the tabloid onto the seat beside me. I sped back down the dirt road to Toronto and my real life.

THREE

I PROBABLY SHOULD have stayed and asked for more details on Janey's life, but I had little faith in the Board's ability to give me the actual truth. Better that I find out for myself what exactly made this woman, only a few years older than me, a target to be murdered and then made into a centerfold.

I pulled over to the side of the road, out of sight of the farm and grabbed my cell phone. I wasn't fool enough to think I could drive and talk at the same time.

"Attersley." He sounded like he was situated in a deep, dark hole, which he probably was, given it was Station 14 deep in the bowels of west Toronto.

"Hey, Hank—it's Reb." I checked my rear-view mirror out of habit. The road was clear.

"Don't tell me you want another loan. I can't afford to support two ex-wives and you."

"But I'm so much more fun." I picked up the tabloid rag and flipped to the page. "Besides, who else is going to put up with your crap? Not to mention that I wouldn't invite you into my bed on a dare."

"If that's your way of sweet-talking me, you need some work." A rolling belly laugh sounded across the airwaves. "So, what can I do for you?"

"Murder case. Janey Winters. Left in an alleyway near Queen and Spadina two weeks ago." I squinted at the grainy photo. "Got a photo in the *Inquisitor,* of all places. Family wants me to check it out." It wasn't a total lie. No matter where you were and what you did, the Pride considered you family.

"Hmm." The sound of scratching and banging signaled a search of his desk, with rapid tapping on a keyboard. "Case's not mine. It's down with Martin Huffington." A minute's pause. "They're set to mark it down as cold, no real leads at this point. No witnesses, no obvious enemies. Sorry to say, but it looks like she was in the wrong place at the wrong time. Coroner says her neck was broken, one fast snap. Bruises are full and nasty-looking. She put up one hell of a fight but wasn't able to throw him before he got a good grip and twisted. I'm thinking druggie, personally. And what's with the fur?"

I tucked the phone against my shoulder and stared at the paper. "Ah, costume party stuff, I think. Family's not as worried about that as they are about the picture in this trashy paper. Have your boys already been out to interview the family?"

"The detectives have already been there. Don't feel that you've got to hold back for fear of my boys racing in and jacking you for information. Looks like just another crackhead jumping the girl for her purse, if you ask me. She fights back, he freaks and kills her."

"Possible. But the photo's another problem. Family's worried that the photographer's got more shots and is going to spread this crap around." I glanced at my rearview mirror again. A dust storm appeared.

"They could sue but as long as the tabloid blurred her face enough that she's unidentifiable it's not going to fly. Not to mention the reporter's not going to give up his sources. Even the *Inquisitor*'s got some morals. And highly paid lawyers to keep them on the edge of the law without falling off." The last few words were said in a choking laugh. "Reporter's name is Brandon Hanover. Used to be a good journalist years ago and now he's printing trash like that. Huffington's pissed that it looks bad for the police but what can you do? It happens all the time, fellows looking to make an extra buck. When they get a juicy crime scene photo, they sell it to the press." I could almost hear him shrug. "It's the way of the world these days. With cell phones and everything but your underwear able to take pictures I'm surprised more crap doesn't get online that shouldn't be."

"Thanks, Hank. I'll drop you a check in the morning." The dust cloud resolved itself into a small car speeding toward me. I flipped the phone off without waiting for a response and tucked it back into my pocket.

The dark blue Ford Taurus slid in behind me, the engine dying away in a shudder and snort. I stepped out and then stared at the driver with my hands in my pockets.

Jess's long, lanky body uncurled from the seat like one of those clowns from the little clown car. Rubbing the back of her neck, she strode toward me with a sheepish grin on her face.

"Didn't mean for you to run off so quickly." She leaned on the hood of her car, arms crossed. "Figured I'd catch you chatting to Ruth or snatching one of her pies."

"Sorry. Didn't think I was welcome for lunch. Or dinner." I slammed my door shut and then moved around to lean on the back of my car, facing her. "So, what brings you out to talk to me outside of the Board?"

One finger moved up to trace the scar on her face. She had never mentioned plastic surgery and no one had dared to bring it up. "Dennis didn't want to call you in. Davis had a fit."

"And yet you did." Spreading my hands, I shrugged. "However, I do have a phone. Could have just called. I have an answering machine."

"You'd have hung up. Or deleted the message." She stuffed her hands in her pockets and scuffed the dirt with a dark-brown cowboy boot. "We know you too well. You wouldn't have come out here on a dare."

"So you send up the freaking Pride Signal?" I pointed at the sky. "Get a searchlight next time and toss up a cat's head or something. It's going to take days to get that aroma out of my office." I wrinkled my nose at the scent memory.

"We wanted to make sure you'd come." She bounced on the hood of her car, stressing the thin metal. "Brought you the records on the Winters family."

"I was going to wait a day or so and see if they showed up before I made a fuss." I didn't move. "Figured you'd want time to black out what you didn't want me to see."

Jess stood, shaking her head. "Reb, it's not all about you. Not this time." She looked out at the farmlands around us, over my head. "I thought you figured that one out."

We stood there quietly for a second, old memories running around us. When I had arrived in Toronto years ago, I had been terrified by the closed spaces, the small rooms and the narrow roads keeping me away from the wide-open sky and the fields I had grown up in. My legs tensed, daring me to whip off my running shoes and sprint along the road with bare feet as I had done for the first few years of my life. Damn, I'd missed being out here. Then a shiver of pain ran along my right shoulder blade and I remembered why I wasn't out here anymore.

"Point taken." I walked past her, opened the back

door and plucked the large brown envelope off of the seat. "Thanks."

"We think it was an inside job." She didn't move when I sat on the hood beside her.

"I thought we had resolved that was a likely scenario. Not too many humans able to get the jump on us." I didn't open the envelope.

"No, a real inside job." She tapped the edge of her nose, a serious look on her face. "I'm thinking Dennis, to be truthful."

The hairs on the back of my neck began to curl up. "You think a Board member killed her?" My fingers tightened on the envelope. Good thing, too, otherwise I would have been gouging my palm with my fingernails. "What the hell has been going on since I left? First you've got blood killing blood and now you're saying it's Dennis?"

"Things have changed, kit." I clenched my jaw in automatic response to the gentle admonishment. "You never got into the internal politics and all that. It's a pain in the ass, but it's a fact of life."

"For you." I bounced off the hood and walked back to my car. "Sorry I didn't get a chance to find out how much fun backbiting could be among family." I opened the door and tossed the envelope inside. "Just out of curiosity, why Dennis?"

Jess looked out over the fields. "He likes them young. He divorced Cindy a few months ago, and he's been making trips into Toronto. I figured he was just finding companions down on Lakeshore. Now, well…" She shrugged. "Men. They're all animals. Keep him on your radar, that's all I'm saying."

I rolled my eyes and got inside the car. "I'll be in touch. Thanks." The last word grated against my teeth, but it was only good manners. My mother had always insisted on good manners.

Jess remained where she was as I pulled out, growing smaller and finally disappearing from my rear-view mirror as I headed back to the highway. The traffic was light, the afternoon commute from Barrie back into the downtown chaos of Toronto just beginning.

I pulled off at the first opportunity to get coffee. The shot of booze hadn't given me a slight buzz, but it had been stupid of me to take it in the first place. I didn't need to get into an accident or worse in my current state. Between the alcohol and grinding my teeth in anger I needed a chance to calm down.

The Tim Horton's employee smiled when she passed me a double-double and a small box of Timbits. I sat down at a table far enough from the counter as not to draw attention to myself but close enough to keep an eye on my Jeep, and opened the sealed envelope.

Janey Winters had only been a few years older than me, but she had taken quite a different path. She had married Mike Winters when she was twenty, approved by the Board without any concerns.

The Pride kept genealogy records that would make the Mormons blush. Every birth, every death was recorded and each branch of the family tree dissected and analyzed to make sure there was no way there would be any sort of genetic damage to new members. Still, there were always those who found true love outside of the family and decided to marry a human. For them, the rules were strict.

Secrecy was mandatory. You couldn't tell your new human husband or wife about your family history. Nothing about the kittens, nothing about the Changing, nothing at all. We couldn't breed outside of our own, so there would be no kids. For some it was a heavy price to pay for true love but they went and did it anyway.

I popped a donut hole into my mouth. The chocolate mouthful was chewy and covered with plenty of glaze, perfect. Flipping the page I read on, eyeing the cinnamon dough ball next.

She had gone on to earn a Bachelor and a Master's in English, obtaining her teaching certificate and a nice little job teaching English in downtown Toronto at the Upper St. Clair Girls Academy. A private school, it was the favorite of Pride women and an automatic guarantee of acceptance into whatever field you wanted to go into.

Her husband had managed to wrangle a good living out of managing a corner grocery store, the type that charges you double for milk and triple for bread at midnight on the weekends. No franchise, but I knew there was Pride money behind it. They kept their fingers in everything you did, said and owned.

Which led to the children, Michael and Fiona, both teenagers doing well in school. Perfect children, perfect little life with a townhouse in Cabbagetown and a good time for all involved. Except now the kids were without a mother and the husband without his wife.

I went for a plain glazed instead of the cinnamon and washed it down with another sweet mouthful of coffee. The Pride had no reason to be pissed off at the Winterses. Both were registered as full Pride members, meaning they were able to manifest the same abilities as the others and were able to keep the family secrets.

Whoever had trapped Janey in an alleyway and killed her was good, good enough to kill a Felis in her prime. And whoever had taken the photograph had hated her enough to try to expose her as a freak to the public. That wasn't someone who was just ticked off at their daughter getting a low mark or something.

The coffee had grown cold. The box was empty, chipped pieces of lonely glaze scattered around the bottom. I flipped the pages back and forth to see if I had missed anything.

The police had called Mike. He had called Jess. Jess had called the Board together to manage the emergency. Dennis told Mike the Pride would take care of him and the kids. It was more symbolic than anything else. They would be fine financially. Mentally, there wasn't much that could be offered other than sympathy. And the promise that Janey's killer would be brought to justice.

This would not necessarily be in a court of law, which is where I came in.

After draining the cardboard cup of every last drop I picked up my cell and dialed Mike Winters. A young girl answered the phone, her whiny nasal tone signaling I had called at an inopportune time. Which, if I recalled my own teenage years, was any time.

"Dad!" she screeched, pulling the receiver a few inches from her mouth. "Somebody for you!" The crash of the phone on the tabletop rang in my ears.

"Yes?" The man's voice sounded tired, as if he'd been running a marathon.

"Mr. Winters, my name is Rebecca Desjardin. I've been asked by Janey's family to help out with the investigation." There was a sudden intake of breath on the line. "I was wondering if I could come by the house and talk to you."

"Sure. Now is as good a time as any." A loud crash sounded in the background, breaking glass. "Do you have my address?" Mike shouted into the phone as a rap song threatened to overwhelm us both.

"Yes. I'll be there in about an hour or so." I hung up the phone and shook my head, trying to clear the ringing from my ears. The stress in every word was like nails on a chalkboard, scratching a new wound. I flinched inside, wondering how I'd cope if I were in his place.

It's one thing to lose your mate, another to lose her to a killer. The crap from the *Inquisitor* wasn't helping any.

By the time I got back on the road with a refill of coffee the rush hour was in full effect, commuters racing home to the north of Toronto and the workers racing south out of factories and businesses toward their homes in the city. Years ago it had been reversed and it would probably reverse again in my lifetime as the cycle continued with people emigrating from the city and back in again as prices shifted and it became fashionable, not to mention affordable, to live downtown.

The Gardiner wasn't bad, for once, and I managed to slide into a parking spot not far from Mike's home just before dinnertime. The row of houses had been there for decades, many of them built back in the day when having street after street of identical houses had been all the rage.

The front of the house had a postage stamp-sized lawn, the grass brown and torn up by more than just animals. On the porch sat three stacks of plastic containers filled with board games and books, wedged up against the bay window looking out onto the street. I trotted up the steps and rapped on the front door.

A stiff breeze shot up the street, carrying the sweet smell of dishes originating in a thousand countries being placed on a plethora of plates for people to eat, talk over or just savor.

Mike Winters opened the door. He stood about six feet tall, with dark hair and a set of bright blue eyes

that could talk you into anything, except now they were
bloodshot with deep, dark bags giving his face a skel-
etal look. He gestured me in without talking, closing
the door with a strange gentleness.

"Fiona. Michael. Upstairs." The quiet command had
the two teenagers racing up the stairs, but not before
a scowl attack from the pouting girl. Michael gave me
a glance over the screen of the PSP in his hands as he
disappeared from sight.

Mike led me to the living room, sitting down on the
faded red leather couch as I took the matching chair to
his right. The table held a variety of papers, all open
to the obituaries with a few clippings of Janey's death
lying near a pair of scissors.

A coffee mug on the table didn't contain coffee. I
could smell the whiskey without having to concentrate
too much. Mike gave a half-hearted sad smile with no
hint of an apology.

"It's been a rough couple of days." He picked up the
mug. His fingers gripped the ceramic so tightly I was
afraid it would shatter. "We're just…It's been a shock."

"I'm sure." I pulled my notebook out of my right
pocket and flipped it open. "I'm sorry for your loss."
The words were trite, but true. I glanced at the photos
spread across the walls between flower arrangements.
Kids on horses, kids on hay wagons, kids at amuse-
ment parks with silly grins on their faces. One wed-
ding picture with an ungodly number of people in the
background, probably family and friends on both sides.
"How are they holding up?"

"Mad. Sad. Angry." He glanced at the level of whiskey in his mug and frowned. "I'm thinking of sending
them up to the farm for a few days and letting them

run free, work it out of their system. After the funeral, of course."

I nodded. "Might be for the best." A pair of wild cats dashing out and about on the estate wouldn't be noticed and Ruth would probably welcome the chance to mother them to death. "Kids are pretty resilient. You'd be surprised what they can work out when they're on their own." A stray lock of blond hair flipped across my face as I spoke, forcing me to tuck it back behind one ear.

"I guess." He finished his drink and put the empty mug down on the table beside the cut pieces of paper. "Guess this is a little morbid, eh?" The man waved a hand over the clipped newspapers with a nervous chuckle.

"Not really. Give the kids something to remember her by." I picked up one of the obits. "You had her cremated."

"As per the rules." He let out a low squeaky sigh, startling me. "I wish it didn't have to be that way, but…"

I nodded my agreement with the statement.

"Tell me about that night, if you don't mind." I dropped my voice to what I hoped was a low, comforting tone. "I know you've told the police, but…"

"But you're kin." A weak smile settled on his face. "She was working late that night, said something about making sure the school projects were graded before she came home. It was a bit of a mess at the school. Some jokers had scribbled crap on the walls the day before and everyone was out of sorts." He glanced at the black-and-white photograph at the top of the obituary. A contented light-haired woman beamed back. "Kids."

I nodded, encouraging him with my silence.

"She called me at about five, said she was leaving the school. Turns out her car wouldn't start. We'd been having problems with the Toyota for weeks, nothing new there. She would have walked to the nearest street-car stop."

"On Queen." I filled in the gaps. "That would have been the quickest way home."

He nodded, staring at the tabletop. "Except she didn't make it for dinner. Then I waited and waited." A deep sigh echoed around the two of us. "By nine I knew something was wrong. Then the police showed up at the door." Mike let out another pained sigh, huffing in stages. "I could smell their fear about giving me the news, can you believe it?" His eyes darted up to meet mine, suddenly feral. "Cops, afraid of me. Like I'm a bad guy. Hell, the worst thing I've done is keep stale bread on the shelves a day too long."

"It's a tough thing to do." I felt strange standing up for the police. "Delivering bad news, it's hard to predict how people will react. Some cry, some lash out at the messengers." I extended a finger to tap her picture with my nail. "She'd probably have ripped them to shreds if it had been the other way around."

A choked laugh came out. "Oh, for sure. Janey, she never liked to let go but when she did…" He reached over to scratch the back of his shoulder. "I've still got scars from when we were dating." The sheepish grin disappeared in a second as his focus returned down to the papers. "And now the cops are saying nothing and it's all going to go away without anyone paying."

"Someone's going to pay." I stood up and put the notebook in my leather jacket's right pocket. "That's why they sent me." I hated to make promises, but this was something that needed to be taken care of. Any-one who could slip behind a woman like that and kill her couldn't be left on the streets whether he was a Felis or not.

"He broke her neck, you know." He rubbed his hands together. "I'm not stupid. That takes a lot of strength to do, to do that." The weary man shot me a sideways glance. "I think it was another one like us." He wouldn't even say the name aloud. Another point for the family's secrecy.

I nodded. "Board thinks that too."

Mike shook his head. "I don't understand. We don't…" His hands shook from side to side. Couldn't blame him.

"I'll find out the truth. Promise." I didn't know what else to say, as if anything I could offer would blunt the shock and the pain. "I'll let you know as soon as I find anything out."

"Thank you." He got to his feet and looked at me, biting his lower lip. "I just don't understand. Who would do something like that, send a photograph like that to the news? What sort of monster is out there?"

I didn't even try to answer.

Loud music played upstairs as Mike escorted me back to the front door. Some sort of rap-pop slop stuff. Mike shrugged with a lopsided smile. "I can't stand that crap."

"Kids." We exchanged one of those knowing aren't-we-wise-for-our-age glances. "I realize this is a pretty silly question, but did Janey have any enemies you know of?"

"She was a teacher." Mike opened the door. The dying sunlight was bright and intrusive as it split up between the houses, sliding between the buildings and cutting through the shadows. He put his hand over his eyes and squinted as I stepped out onto the porch. "Probably every kid she failed and every parent she pissed off by failing their kids. Standard."

"Well, that narrows it down." We shared another set of awkward glances.

Now for the toughest question. I couldn't avoid it any longer. "There wasn't any…" I waved my hand in the air in some vague shape. "Problems in your marriage, was there?"

He stared at me for a minute before responding. "Nothing. Nothing at all." A scowl appeared. "What, you think she was having an affair?" His hands began to shake, his entire body following as he gritted his teeth and continued to speak. "You think Janey was…"

His eyes began to narrow, the backs of his hands beginning to fur up slowly. His lips started retracting from his teeth as he let his breath out slowly.

"Stop." I put my hands up and advanced, moving to let my jacket fall open as wide as possible, highlighting my weakness by showing my belly. "I didn't say that. I was just pursuing a possible angle."

His breathing became more labored as he stared right through me, his fingers flexing back and forth. His face began to change, the faint orange fur shifting to cover his cheeks and his forehead, the nose beginning to retract just a bit.

I sighed once and then moved into Mike's personal space, face to face. "Mike Winters." I dropped my voice down as low as I could and snarled his name again. I flipped my jacket down my arms and off, showing my white blouse. I'd done this before, calmed angry males by moving into a submissive mode. It didn't have to extend to rolling on my back to offer my bare stomach. The slightest aspect of appearing vulnerable would do. The leather jacket landed behind me as I lifted myself

up on my toes and roared into his face, hoping the jux-
taposition would be enough to jar him out of his emotional state.

"Mike! Snap out of it!"

His eyes caught mine and locked, the irises already
spinning into feline mode.

"Do not do this. In public? You remember the rules."
I glanced around. The street was empty but that could
change at any minute. "Would Janey want you to get
into a fight with me? With kin? Would Janey want you
to help me find her killer or not?"

Evoking her name stopped him. Suddenly he blinked
once, twice, the pupils returning to normal. I remained
in his face as the light hairs retracted and he drew deep,
gasping breaths as a full human again. He stepped away
from me, surrendering the space, letting me win.

"I'm sorry." He sagged against the front door and for
a second I thought he would faint. I grabbed his arm
and pushed him upright.

"Don't worry. Perfectly understandable." I forced
a smile, hoping to reassure him. "I was out of line. I
apologize."

"No, no." He waved me off. "You have to ask these
types of questions, I know. It just caught me off guard,
that's all." Taking deep breaths, he stared at his hands.
"Close one there."

"You have no idea." I rubbed his back in small circles, feeling the muscles relax. "I hated asking that,
you know." Clearing my throat I turned the conversation back to more important topics. "I'll be in touch if
I find out anything. Just don't leave the country, 'kay?"
I smiled, encouraging him to return it with a chuckle.
"Hey, it's a classic line. Can't blame me for using it."

Mike stared down at his shoes for a second, shuffling

the pristine sneakers back and forth on the thick woven floor mat. "You think you can find out who did this?"

"I'll try my best." That much wasn't a lie. "We take care of our own."

While I walked back to the car I rubbed my stomach, trying to quell the nausea threatening to burst out and have me recycle the coffee and donuts. Even if it had been a random killing, which I didn't believe, it definitely stuck a giant pin in the bubble of security the Pride had built around themselves. Ourselves. We had been told from birth that we were special, a whole world apart from the rest of society. That we had to stay separate and secret in small packs around the world. Now in a single swoop, that secrecy had been stripped away. Either we had become so weak a regular criminal could stalk, trap and kill us or there was a killer inside the family. Either was unacceptable.

I would probably end up screwed no matter what happened. If Mike had attacked me I'd have been down in a second under those claws and teeth. He had forgotten but I hadn't. I couldn't.

FOUR

As I UNLOCKED my front door my nose started to twitch at the blood scent, still strong even though I had double and triple-bagged the damned foot. I slammed the door behind me, picked up the stack of mail from the floor and headed upstairs into my living space, flipping through the envelopes. An offer for a magazine subscription, an offer for a book club and an offer for cheap cell phone service. But no offers to take this mess off my hands or hand me the answer in three easy payments.

My computer was an old beast, so while it went through the ancient ceremony of booting up I wandered back downstairs.

I picked up the television remote, flipping around the dial while mentally cataloguing the contents of my pantry. The channel stopped on the Food Network. Bad idea. My stomach let out a growl at seeing a display of obscenely large hamburgers.

"Yep, Ramen noodles it is." The cupboards offered up a package of instant noodles caught between a few cans of vegetable soup and three cans of tuna. Within a minute I had the water waiting to boil in the small pot and had turned my attention back to the television set.

The local all-news channel had moved on from Janey's death, giving it a quick sound bite about the investigation continuing, which was a nice buzzword for saying they had stalled. Not that I was complaining. Having the cops around wasn't going to help.

Finally settling on Animal Planet I dumped the contents of the packet into the boiling water and ran back up to the computer.

I had two targets to hunt down. The photographer and the killer. I figured the easiest spot to start with would be the scum who took the picture and sold it to the tabloid. With any luck one would lead me to the other. At the least I'd be able to give the name of the photographer to the Pride and let them decide what to do with him or her.

There was also a chance the photographer was the killer. It'd make things easier to a degree but I couldn't assume anything at this point.

The front page of the *Inquisitor* website had the current issue displayed with poor Janey Winters taking up a small square at the bottom with a thumbnail photograph and the tag "Cat Woman found dead!" It wasn't a good shot, intentionally blurred to avoid anyone identifying the face. Some of the fuzz had been added electronically but it was still disturbing as all hell. I skipped over the article excerpt and headed for the information page. Sure enough, Brandon Hanover's picture was there with a link to his email address.

Of course I wasn't going to just email him. I didn't like doing business without seeing or hearing a person. It was much easier catching a lie when you could see a person's sweat or hear the tension in his voice.

After a few minutes of internet searching I had his cell number. I dialed it while slurping up noodles and nibbling on slices of old, old cheddar retrieved from the back of my refrigerator. The cheese helped cover up the smell of the blood but the aroma still danced in my nostrils, sending me back to early morning hunts and urging me to get a nice rare slab of meat for a snack later.

"Hey." The tone was jovial and mellow.

"Hey, Hanover."

"Who's this?" The voice dropped from friendly and cheerful to less than welcoming. "Who's this?"

"I'm looking into the death of Janey Winters. You know, the dead woman you got pictures of?"

"Oh, right. The cat woman. What's it to you?"

"Like I said, I'm looking into the case. Can I meet you and discuss it over a beer?" If I knew something about reporters, I knew they would never pass up a free drink.

"You got it. Handy Andy's on Queen in about an hour. I'll be the hot stud hanging out at the bar." The line went dead.

"Modest, ain't ya?" I set the plate down on the kitchen table.

Jazz slithered onto my couch and rolled onto her back. I sat down beside her and began to stroke the thin hair.

"You're on guard duty. Don't give away the place."

With her answering trill in my ears I snagged my jacket and headed out to the main street. There was no way I was going to try to find a parking place downtown then deal with having a drink or three, depending on how the meeting went.

I knew Handy Andy's from years ago when it had tried to establish a niche for itself as a Goth bar, failing miserably because the owner figured Goths couldn't count and wouldn't know when they were being ripped off for drinks. It had passed through a variety of owners since then, finally settling on a nice dark place serving beer, good pub food and a set of pool tables in the back beside the oldest pinball machines I had ever seen.

The bar was still half-empty when I arrived, tripping over the clearly marked step despite the yellow fluorescent tape. A series of giggles and guffaws welcomed me into the pub. There was a single empty table, set up against the plate glass window looking back out onto Queen Street. I sat down at the circular wooden platform and waited.

The waitress was the first to arrive, an older woman with more wrinkles on her face than a grumpy Shar Pei. She put a photocopied sheet of paper in front of me and smiled, almost a sisterly grin.

"What can I get you?"

"Molson's Dry." I wasn't even going to try to guess what they had on tap. The woman nodded and then disappeared into the small crowd standing around the bar.

The customers were the usual afternoon fare. Businessmen trying to avoid going home to their wives and children, and businesswomen looking for businessmen. Or businesswomen. The meat market may have shifted and evolved, but the game never changed. I flipped the menu, drawing my finger down the coffee-stained type.

The waitress returned with a bottle and a glass. "What can I get you to eat?" Her tight white blouse had a blotch of ketchup on one sleeve.

"Asian steamed dumplings, please." I handed her the glass. "I'm not that much of a lady." We exchanged saucy winks and then she walked away.

I spotted a few fellows giving me the once-over before continuing their search. A place like this threatened to overwhelm my senses—the rush of different scents, images and noises almost deafening me on all fronts. My nose couldn't stop twitching, hardly making me look approachable and certainly not all that sexy. Which, again, was fine with me.

Turning my attention back toward the window and the street, I took a swig of beer while watching the sun dance away between the office towers and small shops dotting the skyline.

The dumplings showed up, little packets of pork happiness with a small dish of soy sauce on the side and, God bless them, a dash of wasabi paste. I dipped the tines of my fork into the green stickiness and mixed it into the soy sauce before spearing one of the dumplings and letting it swim in the sauce. I began alternating sips of beer and spicy bites, my mouth exploding with a delicious heat.

Pub fare had changed from when I was growing up. Back then if you got a decent hamburger you were lucky. Not to mention luckier if you didn't get E. coli.

The waitress put a fresh bottle of beer on my table as I finished off another dumpling.

"Thanks for the refill." I reached into my pocket and pulled off a twenty from the small wad I put aside for expenses. "I'm waiting for Brandon Hanover. Can you let me know when he gets here?"

She paused. "I can do that."

"Great." I added a second twenty. "And if you can make sure we're not bothered by anyone, that'd be great."

The waitress grinned as she pocketed the extra cash. "Sure. I'll send him your way." She paused after picking up the twenty. "I'll bring your change back from your meal and drinks."

I waved her off. "Don't worry about it." It wasn't a generous tip—I didn't want to get pegged as a rich woman—but it never hurt to help those who were in the know. She smiled and bounced away into the crowd.

While I finished off another dumpling a man in a long black leather duster strode up, taking his place at my table without pause. He stood a few inches over my petite five foot four. His flaming red hair was short, almost too short. He wore a baby blue long-sleeved shirt tucked into his jeans and just a hint of aftershave. My nose twitched at the smell. He reminded me of a pure-bred cat running wild in the street.

"Bran Hanover." He extended a hand, shaking mine with a good firm grip. "Rebecca." He lifted his other hand in the air, waving at the overworked waitress.

"Reb. And how did you know my name?"

"Caller ID." He spread his hands with a friendly grin. "Don't leave home without it." As a Heineken appeared on the table, the reporter nodded his approval. "Thanks, Eddie."

When she vanished into the crowd he turned his attention back to me. "Actually, I'm not blind. As soon as I knew it was you I called up some contacts and got a description along with some references."

"Ah." I sloshed the last of the first beer around in the dark bottle. "And you still came?"

"Never on a first date." He winked, trying to spark some sort of reaction. He was kidding and he knew I was kidding and we both knew that was about as much foreplay as he was going to get away with. Bran took a deep mouthful of beer before continuing. "So you're working on the cat woman case."

"Her name was Janey Winters. She was married and had two kids." I impaled the last dumpling on my fork. "She was a school teacher and didn't deserve to die in a Parkdale alley."

"There's not many people in this world who deserve to die." His eyes were on the doughy bundle swimming in the wasabi-boosted soy sauce. "However, it always makes news."

"I want to know who gave you those pictures." I waved the empty fork at him.

Sitting back as much as he could without tipping the chair, Bran smiled. "That's business. Photos sell the story and without a good picture there's nothing to sell. My job is to sell papers." The single chair leg squeaked in annoyance. "And I'm not giving up my source just to make you happy." Another ear-splitting twitch of the leg. "And what's up with the hair, anyway?"

"Janey Winters had a medical disorder. She didn't deserve to be immortalized in a trashy rag like the *Inquisitor* as the 'cat woman.' Your mother must be so proud." Finally satisfied that the dumpling had fully drowned, I retrieved it from the pool and popped it into my mouth.

The redhead nodded in silence, watching me chew. A single bead of sweat rested on his forehead. I had hit a nerve. Dang. And on my first try.

"Now, you know the cops aren't going to be happy about someone trashing the crime scene before they got there." I cleaned my mouth out with another swig of beer. "So, tell me who started this and I'll turn him over to my contacts, they'll put the fear of God into him and we'll all go home happy." I didn't make mention of the fact there was still a killer out there.

"Problem is, sweetheart," one eyebrow waggled at me in a seagull's wave, "I don't know. Envelope was slipped under my door while I was at work. When I saw the picture, well…" He shrugged. "Can't blame a man for doing his job."

"Sure I can." I leaned forward and plucked his bottle away. "You don't know who it was?"

"I get lots of anonymous submissions." The way his lips curled around the glass sent a hot rush through my veins. "Some people like to shine flashlights into the shadows, see what jumps out." He tilted his head to one side and smiled. "Some of us like to play in the dark and take our chances on what we'll find."

Damn. Smart, sarcastic and sexy as hell. In another time, another place I'd be buying him drinks and making sure I had enough cab fare to get home early the next morning.

Instead I kept to business. The personal angle would have to wait for later. "And he didn't leave his contact information, want any money for it."

A smile curled around the bottle edges. "Believe it or not, there's plenty of people who believe in freedom of speech and all that."

I swallowed, feeling the first bit of a beer burp threatening to break free. "It was taken before the cops arrived and secured the scene."

"That it was, sweetie." Bran leaned forward. "But I'm not sure why you want the photographer."

"Because if he was there at the right time he could have seen the killer. Or maybe he is the killer. The photo could be a souvenir of his hunt." I ground the fork tines across the plate, creating a high-pitched squeal.

"Whoa." Bran looked at me. "Don't take it out on the fine china."

"Sorry," I grumbled.

He waved Eddie over and gestured at the plate. "I'll have what she's having. And another round of beers."

Her eyebrows rose as she looked at me, trying to

figure out if I was in trouble or just playing with fire. "Sure. No prob at all. Back in a flash."

Bran reached over and touched me, a light brush across the back of my hand. "Didn't know it's more than a professional job. Sorry." He leaned back from the table. "But that's how I got the pic."

My skin tingled, as if I'd been rolling in fresh-cut grass. I tried to shake it off as just a reaction to his aftershave.

I'd gotten used to lying to myself a lot over the years.

"So, what's so special about this?" Bran shifted into reporter mode. I could almost see the pencil poised to scribble across the empty page in his inner eye. "I mean, it's horrible and all, but what's the real story here?"

"Her family is upset about a photograph being smeared across the cheapest rag in the city, including toilet paper." An order of dumplings appeared in front of him, Eddie supplying another set of napkins. "I'd have thought that much was obvious."

"To a degree." He picked up one dumpling with a fork and dabbed the end into the wasabi, smearing the hot green paste all over the tasty bundle. "But there's more to this than just finding who took the photograph. You're going after the killer while the cops do their own investigation. And don't even try to tell me you're not. I can't see you quitting after grabbing the photobug." He popped the dumpling into his mouth without flinching, chewing it slowly. "That puts a whole different spin on things, now."

I watched as beads of sweat broke out on his forehead, trickling down the sides of his face while he continued to eat the doughy bites without a single sip of beer. "Now, I'm pretty sure the police are going to write this one off. Not fair, not nice but that's the way it is.

They're overworked and underpaid and all that. So, this is how it goes." He waved the empty fork at me. "You allow me to follow the Cat woman Killer story with you and I cut you in for part of the credit when you catch the killer and I write the sequel."

I almost reached across the table to strangle him right there, damn the good feelings I'd had a few seconds before. As it was, I flexed my fingers, wishing I had kept my nails as long as some of the women back on the farm did. A good scratching was almost acceptable in polite society, if I recalled correctly.

"Look, I don't think you understand me." I pulled in a deep breath and tried to center myself, find a Zen place and stay there. "If I were going after the killer, and I'm not confirming that I am, I'm hunting a man who killed an innocent woman. I'm not looking for street cred or some version of a Pulitzer Prize for crappy rags. This isn't some reality show where you get to dash around and play the hero and drag me along for the ride."

"I get that." His face went sad and solemn, the silence falling over us blocking out the rising noise from the bar. "I've been there, done that. I know what you want. All I'm asking is to come along for the ride." He snatched up the bottle and drained the foam out of the bottom. "Besides, you need me to get started." His previous joviality returned. I wanted to smack him.

"Okay." An overpowering rush of perfume hit my nose, sending a shock through my system. Some woman was just aching to have me dunk her in the nearest body of water, even if it happened to be a toilet bowl. "This is how it's going to work. First, you're going to take me back to your place."

Bran's eyebrows shot up as he grinned. "Really?"

"Yes, you are. Do you still have that envelope the photo arrived in? Or the actual photo?"

"Of course not." He finished off the remaining dumplings in a rush. "I handed it off to the editor and trashed the envelope."

"You never wondered who took the picture or why it ended up on your table?" My fingernails dug under the paper label on the beer bottle, pulling it off in small strips.

"Honey, where do you think the majority of my stories come from?" He exhaled a mouthful of wasabi, causing my nose to curl up. "People drop off this, that and the other thing at my desk at the *Inquisitor* all the time. You should see the crap hitting my email box with pics changed around to justify Bigfoot or the 9/11 conspiracy silliness or whatever's the hot thing online right now." His fork impaled the last dumpling. "I was surprised as all hell to see an actual paper document showing up under my door. Took me back to the old days, it did."

My blood pressure started rising. "And you gave the original over to your editor?"

"Like I wasn't going to?" Bran put the fork down with a loud clink. "I had no reason to keep it at my place."

"So you sold the picture and wrote the story to go with it."

"Right." He rapped the table with his knuckles. "I did exactly what I get paid for and what the public wants." Bran smiled. "And now you've got me just curious enough to keep following this story much further than I would have taken it if you hadn't shown up. The fact that her family's pissed enough to call you in makes it much more interesting. So let's scratch each other's back and work out a deal." He pressed an index finger against his right nostril with a wide grin. "That's what reporters go on, honey."

"Right." I pulled my wallet out and tossed a few bills onto the table. "We're out of here."

Bran's eyebrows rose again as he looked at me for a minute before sliding off the chair. "I must admit, you're pretty easy."

"Don't bet on it."

FIVE

WE FLAGGED DOWN a cab right outside the bar. It was well into rush hour by this point and I had chosen wisely to not try to bring my car into this mess.

As the taxi began to maneuver in and out of the traffic on Queen Street, Bran turned to me, a curious look on his face. "So what got you into this business? Seems to me like a girl like you deserves better."

I couldn't hold back the laughter. Chuckling, I glanced out the window to make sure I knew where we were going. The smell of old cigarette ash was almost overpowering. The cab was obviously one of the last to switch over to non-smoking as the decal on the window attested.

"Gee, haven't heard that pickup line before." I rubbed the tip of my nose and saw a bit of the playfulness disappear from his face. "Let's just say that I fell into working security and then just expanded into the private arena." The traffic slowed to a crawl around us. "So how does a reporter like you end up working for a rag like the *Inquisitor*?"

"The fickle follies of life." He lifted his hands in a melodramatic display. "Either way, we're here now and that's what's going on."

"Thanks for the update." The vehicle pulled up at the entrance to a small apartment complex down near Yonge and King— one of the hot-up and coming spots for the youthful businessman in the downtown core.

These condominiums cost more than a million dollars. Not what I expected from a cheap hack.

The doorman nodded to both of us as we walked through the lobby, his eyes scanning me as a security professional would. I had no doubts if a cop came by later he'd be able to give a pretty darned good description of me with the exact moment my foot crossed that threshold. This was a pricy place that didn't hire kids looking to find a place to sleep or study on the night shift.

We stepped into the elevator, a gaudy trip of mirrored walls and gold-plated buttons screaming upper class.

Bran was silent on the trip up, bouncing back and forth on the toes of his black running shoes as if he was preparing for a marathon, quiet until we hit the seventeenth floor and walked out into the hallway.

"So, what do you think?" He fumbled in his slacks for the keys, finally hitting the lock on the third try.

"Aren't you supposed to ask that after I see the interior of your apartment?" I joked, trying to figure out who this guy was.

"I guess asking if it was good for you too should wait, then." He grinned and stepped inside, flicking a set of light switches to his right.

The condo was larger than if you had dragged my house's second story down onto the first floor. A variety of shelves stood here and there, scattered across the open space and splitting it into rooms. Off to one side I spotted the largest large-screen television I had ever seen outside of stadiums and rock concerts.

"Want a drink?" He took off his leather coat and hung it on a series of wooden knobs set into the wall, not offering to take mine. Good thing, because I hate awkward goodbyes. Bran walked into the spacious kitchen, gesturing at a number of appliances laid out on the marble counters. "Cappuccino? Espresso? Whiskey? SoCo?"

"How about just coffee?" I moved toward the kitchen, my feet light on the hardwood floors. They had been polished to a bright sheen and just screamed for a sock dance. "I think we've both had enough to drink tonight."

He shrugged and pulled out a machine that had more buttons than a space shuttle. "Whatever." After punching in codes to probably set off nuclear missiles toward Cuba, he set two matching mugs into the small recesses. "Milk? Cream? Half and half?"

I turned back from where I had been unabashedly staring at the oversized computer monitor and the top-of-the-line machine artfully hidden in a dark redwood desk. "Half and half, if you have it." My stomach began to hum in anticipation of the creamy delight.

"Make yourself at home." I didn't need to be told twice. While he mucked about in the kitchen I inspected the rest of the apartment including the double bed discreetly tucked at the far end behind a set of tall black oak shelves. He was neat and tidy, and obviously had a bigger pocketbook than I'd expected.

"Pretty good for a hack, eh?" Bran appeared, a mug in each hand. Gesturing to the black leather couch, he sat down opposite me, placing the cups on two of the small round stone coasters spread across the glass table.

"The *Inquisitor*'s paying more than I thought." The cups were black ceramic, immaculate and beautiful. He had good taste. "So, about that envelope."

"I told you I trashed it." He took a sip. "Special Columbian blend. Can't get it at Starbucks. Delivered by private courier once a month." One edge of his mouth curled up in a teasing smile. "I only go for the best."

I tried not to smirk. The verbal jousting was perfectly timed like our foreplay in the bar. He was hitting all the right buttons and playing it out like he should. Reporter trying to protect his source and investigator trying to get information. It was a finely-timed dance we'd both done before.

"Then I need to see your garbage." I put on my best smile. "'Cause I'm going to drag it all across this sweet hardwood floor and make sure you didn't keep it by mistake."

The right side of his mouth curved upward, just a fraction. Bingo.

The mug went back on the coaster. "I think you used that nice fancy scanner over there to scan in the shot and send it to your editor that way so the computer geeks could add more fur and blur her face. So that envelope is here, along with the original picture." I glanced around the apartment again. "One man doesn't make a lot of mess, so…" I stood up and walked to the kitchen, opening random bottom cabinets. "Why, lookie here. A garbage pail."

Bran stood up, his hands in his pockets again and a sheepish grin on his face. "Damn, you're good."

I beamed back at him with an even wider grin. "You'll never know." I pulled the white garbage bag out of the plastic bucket and turned it over, dumping the contents onto the floor. Old coffee grounds were mixed with limp shredded carrots and a dash of sirloin steak tips just beginning to get ripe. My nose wrinkled at the different scents trying to overwhelm each other. There, at the bottom, lay a single manila envelope.

I plucked it free and brushed off a handful of coffee grounds, waving it in the air. "Why, look what I found."

He chuckled, looking at the floor. "Guess I didn't empty my garbage as often as I thought I did."

"So there's the envelope." I tossed it onto the table. "You've got three minutes to produce the original before I move this garbage bag across your entire clean apartment to search for it."

"What makes you think I kept the photo?" Bran shuffled over toward me, an angelic expression on his face.

"Because I can smell it." I tapped the tip of my nose. "You don't get rid of anything you can recycle. That photo's something you're saving for the 'best of' volume in your scrapbook."

He let out a low whistle, crossing to the computer desk. He opened a drawer and pulled out a thin file folder. "You ever play poker?" He walked over and placed it on the marble island between us, opening it to face me. "I think you'd be deadly."

I shook my head. "Not good at bluffing." Nudging the cold-water faucet with my elbow to get the water flowing took a second. I washed my hands quickly and wiped them on the pristine dishtowel hanging from the bar set on the refrigerator side.

The shot was the same as in the tabloid but this one was untouched. Janey's blank eyes stared up at me, the slightest tufts of orange hair breaking free across her face.

Attached to the photo was a printed note, the blocky letters on generic lined paper. "What is she?" in fat capital letters.

I couldn't hold back a gasp at seeing the unmarked photograph. I'd seen dead bodies before but this was personal, this was family. It was almost a voyeuristic shot, catching her in mid-Change.

"You knew her." It wasn't as much a question as a

statement, his words low and soft. I started, suddenly aware of him standing way too much inside my personal space. The thin hairs on the back of my neck began to tingle. I had never been a big fan of letting anyone get close to me, physically or mentally.

"We didn't know each other directly. Family friend." At this distance I could smell the beer mixed with sweat and his personal musk. Dang, it was seductive. It'd been a long time since I had gotten involved with anyone. When you've had your entire life ripped away you learn not to trust anyone, not let anyone in too quickly. Some scars you just can't hide.

I reached out and touched the dead woman's face, stroking the glossy fur.

"I'm sorry," he whispered, still too close for comfort. I shook my head and spun around, breaking the contact while I washed my hands again.

"Yeah, well. Everyone dies. For most of us the timing sucks." We were back on professional ground and I was glad of it. I wiped my hands and then flipped my ponytail back over one shoulder. "Not a chance of getting prints." I leaned in toward the photograph, inhaling deeply. Scent tracking might not be standard procedure for most investigators and wasn't admissible in court, but it worked for me.

"I'd think not." Bran scratched the back of his head. "Mine are definitely on there and I doubt he'd have been stupid enough to leave his own."

I nodded, closing my eyes. Damn it. It was faint, so faint I could barely catch it, but it was there. Felis scent. I turned my attention to the envelope. The inside might have a stronger smell. But I couldn't start sniffing it like a bloodhound with Bran watching. Instead I went for the safer, more common types of detection.

The envelope was blank on all sides, the flap torn
open where the owner had taped it shut. "No chance
of getting saliva from here." I shook my head. "He's a
smart one."

"It'd take you weeks to get a DNA match anyway."
Bran leaned forward again. "That sort of fast response
only happens on television. And with you not being a
cop, well…" He chuckled. "I don't think you're willing
to wait that long."

"I still don't understand why you didn't turn this in
to the authorities." I traced the black-and-white image
with one finger.

"Because they'd haul my ass in and I couldn't tell
them anything more than I've told you." He snorted and
shook his head. "They've got the crime scene. They've
got way more information than this scrap could give
them with no prints and no way to track it back to the
owner."

I couldn't dispute his logic. If the police were running cold it was unlikely a photograph would blow the
case wide open.

Unless they could scent it like I had just done.

"So how does an old hack working for a tabloid rag
afford this?" I raised one eyebrow. "Working under the
table, maybe? Criminal attachments, maybe?"

"Inherited old money, maybe?" Bran walked away
from me and sat down on the couch, spreading his arms
across the long, leather back. "My parents were pretty
well off."

"Did they approve of your work?" I picked up both
photograph and envelope and returned to my seat, placing the two items on the glass table between us. It was
better to keep my distance and my senses clear.

"They died quite a few years ago so it's a moot

point." He avoided my eyes, focusing instead on the accusing photograph forming a wall between us. "So, what next?"

"Tell me what sort of people bring you their garbage and think that it's fit to print."

He grinned. "Well, aren't you the snob?" He shrugged, the blue shirt riding up and down across his broad shoulders. "I get the same sort of 'deliveries' as everyone else in the business—some very honest, hard-working people seeking to have their story told—and more than my fair share of wackos looking for their moment in the sun. They've got the 9/11 tapes, the Bigfoot photographs, the reason why the oil prices are so high and the air car conspiracy. All wrapped up, usually, in a brown paper bag smelling of booze and old vomit tied with twine and a handwritten letter declaring that I'll be saving the world if I just print this." His head rolled back and he stared at the exposed wooden beams of the ceiling. "Those are just the ones I can stand to remember."

"Delivered to your front door?" I jerked a thumb behind us at the entrance. "How did they get past your doorman, who seems to be ex-military?"

He frowned while he kept looking at the ceiling. "Good point there. Dan only allows private couriers to my door and that's with an escort. Everything else stays down at the front desk until I check in."

"And this guy slunk in, trotted up to your front door and slipped this under without getting caught." I leaned forward, cupping the now warm coffee mug in both hands. "He really wanted you to get it. Didn't trust Dan to hold it for you or send it to your office. Wanted you to focus on it, make it a priority."

"Why?" Now it was his turn to lean forward. "What's so special about this woman?" His fingers, long and slender, pulled the photograph closer to his side of the table. "Who was she?" His eyes went to the handwritten note. "What was she?"

"Janey Winters was a teacher, nothing else." The cup of coffee grew colder in my hands, along with my tone. I'd pointed him at the rabbit hole and the bastard was curious enough to fall in, damn it. "She was in the wrong place at the wrong time and someone wanted to make a spectacle out of her death, which you provided when you sent this to your editor and it got published in that piece of crap you call a newspaper." A growl began to grow in the back of my throat, threatening to break free. "You shouldn't have published that photo."

"Hey, back off." Bran pointed his index finger at me. "First, all I knew was that there was a funky picture of a cat woman slipped under my door and that's a story. I didn't print her name or anything and we blurred the important points, so don't get your knickers in a knot more than you've already done." His stare returned to the ceiling, inspecting every knothole. "Now all you need to do is tell me about her skin condition. It would be a great follow-up column."

"I think not." I got up from the table and snatched up the picture, stuffing it into the torn envelope. "I've got what I came here for. I'll leave you to your trash reporting and malicious rumor mongering."

He stood between me and the door. All I had to do was get by him and I could get on with my life and my investigation.

His expression reminded me of a kit on his first hunt. I wasn't getting away from him that easily.

"There's no need for name calling." Bran moved closer, still blocking my escape. "I've played nice. I've let you in to my apartment, into my life. I had nothing to do with her being murdered, so why the hate?"

"I don't hate you." The amount of emotion in my words shocked me. "I just have a job to do."

"As do I." There was a predatory spark in his eyes. "Which is why I'm working the rest of this case with you."

The words hit me like a bucket of ice water. I shook my head. "I can't. I work alone."

"Not anymore." He stuffed his hands back into his pockets, an almost childlike grin on his face. "Because if you don't, I'm going to put in another story talking about your involvement in the case."

The words caught in my throat. "That would compromise my work. I might never find the killer."

"That's right." Bran nodded with a knowing look. "So, why don't we start with me asking my doorman for a glance at the security tapes to see how that envelope got up here?"

Closing my eyes, I pinched the bridge of my nose, buying some time. "I don't have partners." I chose the words carefully, saying them slowly. "I work alone. I've always worked alone. However..." His scent washed over me in waves, sending my pulse into triple digits. I was breaking my own rules. The problem was, I liked it. "As long as you do nothing and write nothing until we finish this up, you can come along. And I want a full apology printed in the *Inquisitor* for publishing that picture." My eyes flew open, glaring into his dark brown ones. "That's as far as I'm willing to take negotiations. Take it or leave it."

"Deal." Bran reached behind him, grabbing the doorknob. "So let's go talk to Dan."

SIX

THE DOORMAN WAS actually ex-SAS, a retired officer who wanted to keep working despite receiving a decent pension. He motioned us to the back of the security station where the cameras and tapes were kept.

"They're on a twenty-four hour cycle, sorry to say." He shook his head, the few white hairs peeking out from under the pseudo-military cap. "So there won't be anything if it happened more than a day ago."

"You didn't see anyone?" Bran frowned. "Not like you, Dan."

The salt-and-pepper moustache bristled at the admonishment. "I didn't miss anything. No one gets in here on my shift." He wagged a finger at the ledger sitting atop the polished counter. "They all sign in and sign out. I don't let anyone just wander in here." He pulled the ledger around to face him before flipping through the pages. "You haven't had any deliveries in weeks, Mr. Hanover, other than food services."

"I believe you." Dan broadcast respect and authority, reminding me of Jess. Men like this didn't lie. "We were just wondering how this fellow walked in and out like that."

Bran looked at me, a confused expression on his face. "How do you know it's a guy? Why not a girl?"

Because I could tell by the scent. "I guess I just make the assumption 'cause it's likely a guy did the killing." I shrugged. "Consider it a generic term, then."

He turned back to Dan. "No offense meant. We were just concerned."

"As you should be." The thick Scottish accent grew more and more noticeable with each syllable. "I'll tell the other fellas to sharpen up their act or they'll be outta here." He jerked a thumb toward the street to make his point. "That'll be enough of that around here."

"Thanks." Bran clapped a hand on the pseudo-military uniform shoulder. "I knew I could count on you."

The veteran let out a rumbling chuckle through the moustache. "For you, Mr. Hanover, anything." His cool gray eyes searched my face. "Been awhile since you brought a lady friend home. Wish you'd do that more often. Be a pleasant sight for these old eyes." Dan threw me a sly wink, invoking a smile in return.

"Reminds me of an old English sheepdog." I flagged down a cab as we stood outside the condominium on King Street. "Sweet old man."

"Sweet enough to disarm three punks last summer who were looking to do some break and enters." Bran chuckled. "Underestimate him at your peril."

The streets were now dark, the majority of commuters having fled the downtown core for the supposedly safer suburbs. I opened the back door of the cab and slid in across the broken vinyl seats, sticking a bit on the duct tape crisscrossing the well-used cushion.

Bran sat beside me "Where to now?"

"The crime scene." I directed the cabbie to drop us off a block away from where Janey Winters's body had been found, settling back for the short drive. "Best place to go right now."

The bunched-up envelope dug into my side where it had been crammed into the small inner pocket of my leather jacket. I had the original photo, but it wasn't going to undo the damage to Janey's reputation or the danger to the group.

The cab came to a shuddering stop, the brakes screeching their annoyance. I passed the driver a twenty and got out of the car. Bran followed, scrambling to keep up with me.

The walk down the street to the alleyway was well lit and filled with pedestrians making their way to the small cafés and bars littering the area. A streetcar rumbled by, stopping at a cyber café to take on a handful of students swinging fat backpacks. This was hardly an area to grab a woman off the streets to drag her into an alleyway. She hadn't been tackled and pulled into darkness. She'd walked in with her eyes wide open.

"Hey." Brandon caught up to me, tugging on the back of my jacket. "What are you looking for? The cops probably went over this place with a fine-tooth comb."

I pulled up short, seeing a flash of yellow tape fluttering in the wind. "They might have missed something."

Something to do with the Felis.

The yellow crime tape had been stretched from one end of the entrance to the alley to the other, originally crisscrossing in a giant X but now ripped down and flying free. I stepped over the threshold into almost total darkness.

The alley was barely large enough for two people to walk down side by side. The brick walls were scratched and dented. A small trail of liquid trickled down past me into the street, stinking of urine, bleach and other things I couldn't identify.

"How can you see anything?" A bright light flashed behind me, momentarily blinding me. Bran held up a small flashlight. "God, this place reeks."

"Turn that off." It wasn't a request. As the light faded my eyes readjusted to the darkness. A scattered trail of rotting tomatoes and lettuce was spread across the concrete floor.

I knelt down, trying to recreate the scene in my mind.

Janey had ended up here, her feet pointed toward the street. I looked at the bricks on each side and the ground. It was a mess. Scratches, deep scratches. Felis nails had done those, not human. She had fought him to the end, trying to use the walls for leverage.

"How can you see anything?" Bran repeated and crouched down, resting his back against the wall.

I picked up Janey's scent easily. There had been enough of it back at the Winters house that it was impossible not to notice. But there was another one there, one I didn't know.

It wasn't Dennis. I could put Jess's theory to rest on that part. There was another Felis signature here and it was solid. It was strong, male and so thick it clogged the back of my throat as I tried to imbed it in my memory and my senses.

It was the same as on the photograph.

The Felis had not only killed Janey but taken the photograph and delivered it to Bran.

There was only one target for me to hunt.

It didn't make me feel any better.

"What are you doing?" The reporter sighed, rubbing his leather duster back and forth against the wall. "Dang, my back's itchy."

Then I saw it.

It might have just been a smattering of small hairs sticking out of a crack high on the wall but it was a whopper of a clue.

Bran followed me as I stood up to pluck it from the dirty crack with my bare fingers.

"That's not evidence, is it?" He glanced back toward the street as if he expected the police to descend on us at any minute.

"No." I pulled a small baggie from my pocket and flicked the hairs in, sealing it tight. It was Felis and not the normal alley cat kind. Thinner, grainier and coarse to the touch.

"If that's evidence it should have been collected by the cops." He shook his head, moving closer to me. "You're going to get us both arrested."

"I didn't think you were afraid of much."

Bran's hand landed on my shoulder. "I'm not afraid of much but I do dislike being hauled off to jail for messing with a murder case."

"Well, you're not. So there." I pocketed the plastic bag. I pulled out the bent envelope and salvaged the photograph. "Come here, please."

"Do this, come here. Feels like I'm your boy-toy slave." He chuckled as he moved to stand beside me. "Now what?"

"I'm standing right over where the body was." I handed him the photograph, pushing it into his hands. "Turn on your flashlight if you need to."

The small white beam sent jagged shards of pain through my eyes before I could adjust. "Does your cell phone take pictures?"

"Do they make any that don't?"

I decided not to tell him about my ancient pay-as-you-go model.

"May I have it, please?"

He handed it over and waited.

"Good." I lifted the phone to my face and looked at

the image. "This would be about where the photographer stood when he took the shot, right?"

The light bounced around the narrow alley before landing again at our feet. "More or less."

I looked through the viewfinder and pushed the button. A quick flash illuminated the two of us. I handed the camera back. "How close is that to what we have?"

"Hardly." He showed me the backlit image. "You wouldn't have caught her feet and hands."

"So I'm too short to have stood here and taken that picture, correct?"

Bran shone the light on the black and white photo. "I'd say so." The beam bounced around the narrow alley before returning to our feet. "Unless he had his hands over his head this picture must have been taken by some guy about my height, at least." The reporter flashed the beam at our feet, illuminating us in an eerie glow. "He wasn't a short one, that's for sure." He smiled at me. "I'd guess you're about five foot four, eh? I'm a bit taller than that."

"Really." I studied him for a minute. "Not by much."

"Hey." Bran spread his hands with a smile. "You know us men. Always exaggerating something."

"Hmm." I traded the photograph for the cell phone. "Well, that gives us some idea of the killer's height."

"One guy grabs her, snaps her neck. Other guy stops by and takes a photograph," Bran mumbled. "Sends me the photograph with a question about 'What is she?' Not who she is but what she is." He turned toward me. "Why would he be asking that?"

The illumination from the cell phone disappeared, leaving us in darkness. His heady scent threatened to overwhelm me, screwing up my thoughts and emotions. It was like a thick afghan blanket that started to curl up around and over me, cradling me in its warmth and rocking me to a deep, contented sleep.

"Just take a step away from me, please." I closed my eyes again as they readjusted to the dark. My senses were reeling from the musk of a Felis male, two strong Felis women and a single, very strong human male who kept muddying the waters. One of us was dead and the other the killer.

It would seem that all I had to do now was race back to the farm and hand them the hair to have them check it against the database, but that wasn't going to happen. We didn't keep records like that. There were still some things in which the Pride were woefully behind, and creating a database of all Felis DNA was one of them, or had been when I'd left.

"Right. I'm out of here." I stepped over the imaginary body and made my way out the narrow passage onto the street, pulling in a deep lungful of relatively clean air.

Something swept across my senses, a wave so overpowering it threatened to swamp me. I held my ground in the dizzying haze of food carts, diesel exhaust and body odor from the unwashed masses, turning around slowly to try and find the source. It was Felis, that much was sure, but too little to identify. Had Jess put a tail on me or was there another nearby?

"And…" Bran appeared behind me, letting out a cough. "Where to next?"

I shook off the feeling I was being watched. There were hundreds of Felis in Toronto who lived and worked every day just like I did. It wasn't impossible for one of them to have just passed me. "Me? I'm going home to sleep. You, you're heading home, as well." I waved at him as I walked away. "Don't call me, I'll call you."

SEVEN

THE STREETS WERE filling up with tourists getting out
from the stage shows or the movies, each looking for
a nice slice of Toronto to take back home with them.
As I maneuvered through the crowd I could hear Bran
swearing behind me, but his voice faded with time and
distance.

I hopped the first streetcar that came my way, pushing my way through a posse of chattering teens to grab
a seat near the back. I'd always been a fan of the Red
Rocket and used it as much as possible. The cost of gas
and downtown parking helped keep my driving down
to a minimum, thank you very much. I glanced behind
me as we lurched forward, grabbing the plastic seat
next to me for support. Sure enough, I had lost Brandon in the crowd.

I huffed when we slid to another stop, the back
doors opening to let off another gaggle of chattering kids. There was something reassuring about the
streetcar's rocking motion and it helped tune down my
overwhelmed senses. It wasn't too often that I was at a
murder scene and never that of a fellow Felis. Usually I
dealt with runaway teens and adultery accusations with
a few background searches tossed in. It wasn't glamor-
ous but it paid the bills.

We rolled into Parkdale, one of the poorer Toronto
neighborhoods. In a nearby darkened stairwell a man
rocked back and forth, clutching his arms around his

middle. Probably a heroin addict. It was a popular spot to hide in the shadows, shoot up and then go visiting the gods. My favorite reporter was nowhere in sight when I reached up to tap the bell cord, signaling my stop.

The 24/7 convenience store had a neon sign announcing FRE H COF E and DO UTS, both of which I sure didn't need. A trio of teenagers hung out in front of the store smoking cigarettes someone else must have bought for them. One glared at me through long greasy locks screaming for a shampoo and a buzz cut. I glared back and he shuffled closer to the neon sign.

The walk down the street to the house was quiet and longer than it needed to be, with my thoughts racing all over the place. It wouldn't be difficult to get hold of the Board and ask for information on all the members who were tall enough to meet my requirements—there weren't a lot of Felis over six feet high—but it was going to be a bitch to quietly investigate the suspects to find out who killed Janey. I'd end up in more challenges than I could imagine or handle. You can't just suggest that someone's involved in the killing of another Felis and not be prepared to back that up with either hard evidence or your fists.

Unfortunately, part of life in the Pride included challenges. I was pretty sure that was how Jess had received that nasty scar—probably some kit figuring he'd move up in the ranks by taking on the Old Lady. No one actually died in the challenges, but there were some injuries that could last a lifetime. I wouldn't be able to withstand a single challenge.

I walked up the small sidewalk to the house, noting that the rose bushes were blooming yet again. Unlike some of my brethren I had little to no skills when it came to gardening, but somehow these red beauties had kept on going.

The lock was firm under my fingers with the dead-bolt sliding back with a resounding thud. It refastened with a swift twist of my wrist after I stepped inside, securing the front door again.

"Nice place. Although those roses could use a little pruning…"

I spun around and whipped the taser out of my pocket. It was just slightly illegal.

"Whoa!" Bran lifted his hands from where he had been standing just inside the doorway. An impish grin spread across his face. "Plenty of space here. I'm not crowding you at all."

"How the hell did you get in here?" I glanced back at the deadbolt. "You broke into my house?"

He let his hands drop down to his sides. "No, not technically. See, I didn't actually 'break' anything. One credit card and the door gave up her secrets willingly." His hands shot back up as I took a step forward. "By the way, that white cat of yours? Not much of an attack cat. Welcomed me in and showed me where you kept her treats. She's pretty easy to bribe, that one." As if on cue Jazz appeared, winding her way around his legs with a loud, gravelly purr.

"Traitor," I growled to the cat. "We'll talk later." I returned my attention to the grinning reporter. "How did you get here ahead of me?" I kept my finger on the trigger.

"I took a taxi. Cost a few bucks, but well worth it." He waved a single finger toward the door. "I'm good with my fingers but not fast. Keep that in mind."

"How did you know where I lived?" I didn't drop my arm a fraction, keeping the weapon firmly aimed at his chest. It wouldn't kill him but it'd be a heck of an ending to the night.

"I'm an investigative reporter. I investigated." Bran dropped his hands. "Now if you're finished with the temper tantrum, I thought we'd get some rest before striking out on your next part of the investigation."

"What?" The Taser didn't move. "What are you talking about?"

Bran let out an exasperated sigh. "Look, I'm no rookie to this. You agree to let me in on the story, you dump me, you 'forget' to tell me what's going on." He shucked his duster and hung it on the ancient hat rack behind him in the corner. "You don't trust me, I don't trust you but there's a story here and I'm not going away until I get the scoop on this woman's killer." He rubbed his hands together and beamed his best smile at me. "So, how about I make us up some decaf to go to bed with and we'll continue this in the morning?" One edge of his mouth turned up in a sly smile.

A deep throbbing started behind my left eye. "We are not 'going to bed.' I am going to go upstairs to my bedroom and you are welcome to suffer down here with the cat and a lumpy couch." I lowered the Taser. "I don't have any coffee. You're welcome to some of the herbal teas, for what that's worth."

"Excellent." He strode through the living room and threw open my office door, continuing to the small kitchen in the back. "Peppermint would be great right about now, I think, unless you have some ginger spice, which is excellent for digestion."

I pulled off my jacket, closing my eyes and trying to will the headache away. "Yes, yes it would be." I hung it on the hook next to his jacket and leaned on the wall with one hand, wondering if I could hide a body as well as I did the rabbit's foot. With a nasty glare at Jazz, I made my way upstairs.

The smell of peppermint drifted up the stairs while I changed out of my work clothes into a baggy sweatshirt and sweat pants, dark gray and filled with more holes than a piece of Swiss cheese.

I put the small baggie on my desk and booted up the computer. Thankfully the files Jess had given me were up here, safe and sound and away from a prying reporter's eyes.

I picked up my land phone line, the old rotary I'd rescued from a garage sale years ago. My fingers dialed in the contact phone number Jess had given me.

"Yeah?" She answered on the first ring.

"I have something for you. For the Board." I drew a deep breath. "Janey was definitely killed by one of the Felis, not a human. One of the family. I have a hair sample here that's definitely not hers."

Jess's gruff voice rolled through the air. "And the cops don't know?"

"Even if they found the hair it's likely it'd be identified as feline and they'd drop it as a lead. No one's looking for cat people. Well, no one who's sane." I picked up the bag and studied the contents. "I also know it's a male, a tall male." I pursed my lips before continuing. "And it wasn't Dennis. I didn't recognize the scent."

"Ah." There was no surprise in the voice, no disappointment. "And Mike?"

"Mike says that she wasn't having an affair." I left out the part where he almost Changed in public and challenged me. "From what I can gather she was too busy to have one. She was a good wife who got lured into the alleyway by one of the family for some reason and was killed."

"Good work." The hairs on the back of my neck stood at the compliment. She didn't do compliments too often. "Keep us updated, please."

"The killer was the one who took the photograph."

A long minute of silence drummed through the phone line.

"Fuck," Jess said. "One of us."

"One of you," I replied. "Is there any way you can get me a list of all Felis men that are close to six feet tall?"

"That's all you got so far, that he's tall?" Jess sighed. "I'll take it up with the Board."

"The clock is ticking and every minute means this guy could be getting further and further away from us. You're not making this easy."

"Never said it was going to be." Her voice drizzled out across the line like slow honey. "Besides, that's not going to give you much of a lead. Heck, the guy could have been wearing lifts. I'll do the best I can, but you know how we operate."

It was a battle I couldn't win. "Thanks for the help. I'll be in touch when I have more."

I hung up the phone and put both hands to my temples, rubbing them as hard as I could. The headache was threatening to break into a major migraine and while I had meds to take the edge off, I wasn't about to dull my senses even for a few hours. I couldn't risk it, not if I was going to have to go up against one of my own.

The aroma of peppermint grew stronger, the richness helping alleviate the pain just a bit. I dropped my hands to my desktop and took deep breaths, closing my eyes and focusing on the pleasant odor.

The pressure returned to my temples, a light circular rubbing, almost tickling. Except my hands were still on the desk and I wasn't blessed with extra digits.

My eyes shot open to focus on the steaming hot mug of peppermint tea sitting in front of me and the man standing behind me, his fingers stroking and pressing in all the right places.

"Bad headache, eh? I can believe it." Bran leaned forward, peering at the display on my office phone. "So, who you been calling?"

I resisted the temptation to fling him over my shoulder and smash the desk with his lifeless body. His touch was just so good on my skin right now, massaging away my annoyance in seconds. "That is my client and none of your business. That whole confidentiality thing? You know?"

"Oh, sure—throw that in my face." The pressure ebbed, shifting down to my neck and shoulders where he pressed down, rotating his fingers around on the fabric. "Can't blame a guy for trying."

I drew in a deep breath, tasting the peppermint on my tongue. Mixed in there was the heady scent of Bran, leaning in and whispering the words in my ear. This was not good. More so because I had subconsciously ignored him coming up the stairs, marking him as friend instead of foe.

"Thanks for the tea." I stumbled over the words, pushing the pain back into the dark recesses of my mind. "However, I think it'd be best for us both if you went downstairs and took up residence on my couch. Sorry there's no television down there. There's a radio if you're desperate for information." A shiver ran up my spine, tickling the nerves. It'd been a long time since I'd had some nice touching.

"No problem. I've got one of those newfangled contraption cell phones that gets everything. The internet, MP3 player, the whole shebang." He stopped kneading my shoulders, now just resting his hands on my gray shirt. "You know, we'd work better together if you didn't see me as the enemy."

I held back a sigh, wanting his hands back on my bare skin. He'd triggered an itch I wanted him to scratch. If he only knew how much he had already worked his way into my system...

"Until the end of this case you are, by definition, the enemy." I exhaled the words, hating every one.

"Your call." The heat left my shoulders, sending another shiver across my skin. "I'll see you in the morning, then." The stairs creaked with his departure. "Just don't try to sneak out on me. I don't really sleep these days. I catnap."

I couldn't help smiling, wrapping my hands around the mug and taking a deep pepperminty breath. My eyes flashed for a second to the Winters file, safe on my desk away from Bran's prying eyes. Last thing I needed was some outsider trying to make sense of a Pride file.

"This case is going to kill me," I murmured to the empty room. I picked up the mug and shuffled to the double bed, tossing back the thick, light-blue comforter with one hand and dumping the two pillow shams onto the floor. The mug went onto the nightstand as I pulled the sheet back. I reached for the remote and turned on the television, setting the volume low and finding a local news channel to drone in the background.

I sipped the tea and pondered my next move. There was no way I could investigate every man who met the height requirement, even if they sent me a list right away. I could petition the Board to have a Grand Meeting, bring everyone together and let me just look across the crowd to see the tallest men, but it was only called for extreme measures.

Such as declaring one of their own outcast.

I wondered if a Felis killing another Felis ranked as high.

I frowned, pushing the memories out of reach. One hand put the near-empty mug on the night table, the other turned the light off. I snuggled down under the thin sheet and tried not to think too hard.

THE ALLEYS WERE dark, dank and smelled like fresh urine. I ran down one narrow corridor, paused at an intersection and then turned on my heel to charge down the other, feeling the hot breath of a hunter on the back of my neck. He growled once, letting me know he wasn't in a rush to finish the hunt. A claw reached out and ripped the shirt from my right arm while I charged into another alley, searching for a way out. The moon was full in the sky over us and filled the brick walls with misty shadows and distorted shapes.

He smelled like garbage, old jeans, sweaty underwear and moldy cheese dipped in turpentine. I coughed, resisting the temptation to drop to my knees and throw up. If I did he would be on me and that wouldn't be a good thing.

I skidded around another corner and lost my balance, slamming hard into the wall and falling to the ground. My foot went numb as I struggled to my feet and tried to limp away. The roar grew closer, the scent stronger in my lungs as he approached. All I could do was flatten myself against the wall and hope my first strike would disable him, maybe even kill him.

He leaped out of the shadows at me and smashed me into the wall with a near-perfect hockey body check. My shoulder popped out of its socket, leaving my arm numb as I collapsed. The hunter was on me before I could catch my breath and straddled me with little effort. I stared up into the feline face, trying to recognize it even while I strained to force myself to Change.

The mouth opened, the canines dripping with hot saliva. His tongue flicked out once to wet his lips then retreated as he pinned me effortlessly to the ground. He arched his back and screamed at the sky above us and then glared down at me, daring me to try and escape.

I had nothing. Not even a whisper of extra strength, my weak human body nothing more than a shadow of what it could be. But I still had my senses and I wasn't going to give up until the very end of this dream.

I lunged forward and smashed my forehead into the feline face. His nose, more delicate than a human's, could be a liability in close fighting.

It worked. He released my arms and brought up both hands to cradle the injured and hopefully broken nose, roaring his muffled disapproval and pain.

I woke up.

He was still there.

EIGHT

I BUCKED MY hips up and rolled to one side, falling onto the floor as the attacker pulled his hands away from his face, still feline, still Family.

Still trying to kill me.

I crouched into an attack posture, a mixture of what I had been taught as a kit and the result of a few self-defense courses. The television's dim light illuminated my assailant as he knelt on the bed for a second before scrambling to his feet to continue the attack. Jazz was somewhere in the room, hissing her defiance at this invasion but smart enough not to get in the way. My shoulder ached but wasn't dislocated. Obviously my dream state had magnified the situation.

I didn't recognize him, but that wasn't surprising. The teenager had a white streak running down one side of his nose, just enough to give him an eerie look in the dim light. His scent was the same as on the photograph, identifying him as the photo taker and Janey's killer.

He jumped off the bed and came at me, both paws in the air with claws extended. This wasn't going to be some play fight at the farm where we both rolled around like kits until one got tired and called it quits.

I grabbed the arm closest to me, the right, and yanked it past me, wincing as his left hand gouged my sweatshirt to ribbons on the way past. He slammed into the wall face-first, collapsing on the hardwood floor but only for a minute. He scrabbled back to his feet with another yell.

"What's going on?" Bran yelled from downstairs. Great. As if things weren't complicated enough. I stepped forward toward the attacker and shot my fist out toward his throat with all my strength. The Felis moved to one side at the last minute, spinning around to face me. The blood was still gushing from his nose down his black shirt and jeans, strangling his breathing and making it sound even more fearsome.

"Leave me alone," he rumbled. "Just leave me alone."

"I'm calling 911!" The panicked voice matched the pounding footsteps coming up the stairs. My attacker spat out a mouthful of blood before reaching out and grabbing me, pushing me toward the steps even as his claws dug into my skin through the material.

I began to topple, my bare feet unable to keep hold of the slick varnish. Suddenly my own claws appeared, long enough and sharp enough to embed themselves into his forearms and pull him down with me. I glared at him, a smug smile on my face.

"Let's do this," I said as we spun toward the stairs together. "Let's do this right now!" His shocked eyes met mine. He hadn't anticipated that I'd fight back with Felis claws.

This made two of us.

We rolled down the stairs like a pair of stunt dummies, bouncing every which way. I hit my head at least five times, if not more, landing on a pretty soft cushion that was both comforting and lumpy even if it was cursing and swearing.

My vision cleared long enough to see the front door open, letting in the cool night air as a shadow raced through into the darkness. Beneath me, Bran let out a cough.

"My God, are you okay?" He looked up the stairs and back down again to where we lay in a tangled heap on the landing. "Am I okay?"

I lost valuable minutes untangling myself. It took a few more seconds to stumble over to the open door and look out onto the empty street.

"What the hell was that?" Bran got to his feet and then bent over, wheezing. I tucked my hands into my armpits and pushed the door shut with a hip check, gasping for my own bit of air. Instead of dealing with Bran I leaned against the wall, hoping my claws were retracting as quickly as they had escaped my knuckles. The throbbing told me that they were, but not easily.

People forget cats aren't exactly like the comic interpretations, especially when it comes to claws and how they actually function. Instead of having our nails shoot out like some sort of wacky manicurist's nightmare, we have a more painful experience ending with an inch, maybe two if we're lucky, of claw to attack with. We retract them just a bit to release our prey. I hadn't been good at that, ever, so I had stayed attached to my attacker longer than I should have and suffered for it.

Mine were thankfully rolling back inside my hands, leaving only a trio of little bloody slits to indicate anything had happened. I kept my hands tucked away from Bran's prying eyes as we both slumped on the floor, breathless.

"Are you okay?" He crawled to me, his eyes wide. "Tell me that's not all your blood."

I looked down. My sweatshirt had been shredded in a few places, but the skin had only been scratched here and there. The huge wet scarlet stain on my front startled me.

"I head-butted the asshole." I turned my head to one side and spat out a mouthful of saliva, a light reddish tint to it. It landed in a weak splat on the varnished floor, just shy of the doormat. "And I cut my lip doing it." My eyes went wide. "Did you say you were calling 911?"

"I tried." Bran sheepishly held up a crushed cell phone, the faceplate shattered and cracked. "I don't think it went through. Want me to dial now?"

"No." I got to my feet and winced as the pain started, shooting down my spine and across my shoulder in waves. Damn it, I was too old to be rolling down stairs. "No, don't call anyone."

I limped into the office area, bypassing the sofa and headed for my desk. The top left-hand drawer held an extra-huge container of painkillers. I dry-swallowed a pair of pills and hoped it would be enough to fight off the migraine that was sure to return.

"Are you nuts?" Brandon brushed dirt from his pants. He looked none the worse for wear. His hair was disheveled, giving him a boyish look. "You were just tossed down the stairs and almost killed by some nutcase and you don't want to call the cops?"

I sat down and leaned back, listening to the creaky cries of the old wooden office chair. I had rescued it from one of those second-hand furniture outfits, having no patience with the über-cushioned monstrosities salesmen kept trying to push on me. I didn't want to be comfortable at my desk. I wanted to be uncomfortable because I would do my work and then leave. What's so difficult to understand about that?

The pain started, right between my eyes. Wonderful.

"Are you sure?" Bran sat opposite me, where the

philandering husband had been less than twenty-four hours ago. He pulled out the tail of his T-shirt, previously tucked into the top of his jeans, and wiped his face. "I mean. That guy could have killed you."

Dang, nice abs. I closed my eyes and tried to will the pain away. "You think?" The words came out a bit harsher than I had planned.

He shuffled his chair back an inch before continuing. "Sorry, I just didn't expect you to be so blasé about the entire thing." His eyes went to the office phone. "Are you going to call?"

"No." Pushing both hands against my face for a second helped dull the throbbing behind my eyes. "This was the same guy who killed Janey."

"You know that?"

I resisted the urge to tell him I knew that because his scent was the same as the one I had picked up at the scene and off of the envelope.

"It's a good bet, that's all I'm saying." Pressing against my eyelids with my palms felt good, except for the fear of pushing them so far back into my skull they'd pop out my ears. "This is the only thing I'm working on right now. Who else could it be?" It was a warning to back off, delivered in person by Janey's killer. But he'd only been a kid and I'd scared him when my claws came out. He should have scented me as a fellow Felis the second he came in the room.

He should have known we were family. The fact that he didn't both startled and saddened me.

The pounding stabbed at my logic, shredding it before I could get any further.

"And we're not telling the police because…" He motioned with his fingers, urging me on.

"Because it's none of their business!" I screamed,

slamming my palms on the desk. Jagged bolts of pain bounced around the inside of my skull, erupting out through my eyes and mouth.

I jumped out of the chair and charged for the kitchen, making it to the sink just in time to return not only the beer and coffee I had enjoyed earlier that evening, but also the remains of the delicious Asian dumplings. Bracing myself with my arms on each side of the sink, I gasped and gagged, only making the pain worse.

"Damn it." I spotted the remains of the painkillers floating in the detritus. The faint smell of peppermint drifted up to my overcharged senses, setting off another round of retching.

"I'm calling an ambulance. You need to go to the hospital now." He put one hand on my back, rubbing in circles. If I had been strong enough to enjoy it, I would have.

I turned around and braced myself with both hands on the counter. "Look, I wasn't knocked out. That's not a concussion. What I do need is a hot bath and for you to make me up some tea and toast." The throbbing was beginning to abate just a fraction behind my eyes. "Just let me get cleaned up and then we'll talk about the entire affair, okay?" My head was spinning with the combination of smells filling the air around and between us. "Just let me get out of these clothes and cleaned up."

He peered at me, a suspicious look on his face. "You're not going to jump out the window or anything, right?"

I smiled despite the pain. "Not likely. Help me up the stairs and into the shower. Please." My eyes caught his. "Look, I'm not eager to get brain damage either. But right now I need to get my head cleared and start thinking clearly." The attacker's scent was all over me, which wasn't helping the nausea. It's one thing to have that much contact with a friend, a lover—but not a stranger. It's like being dunked in strange perfume.

"Should call the cops. Get those CSI people over here before you take a shower. But you're going to be stubborn about this." Bran grumbled as he tucked his arm around me, hand tight on my waist, maneuvering me toward the staircase. "And if I hear you fall I'm calling 911 first and then coming up to see you."

"Duly noted." We staggered up the stairs like a pair of old drunks. It was a miracle we didn't fall back down again.

I flinched as we stepped back into my bedroom. The window had been carefully pried open, staying that way thanks to the extremely rusted hinges I had been promising to oil. The bed itself was a bloody mess. The attacker's nose had bled like a fountain, spurting not only over my sweatshirt but across the four pillows, the light sheet and was probably starting to soak through to the mattress below. Wonderful. I hated shopping for stuff.

I released Bran and made my way to the old oaken dresser. A quick search of the bottom drawer found another sweat suit, this one a dark green. It had been a present to myself a few months ago when I had spotted it on sale in one of those fancy shops that I dare not frequent without a clear credit card. My arms ached as I carried the small bundle toward the bathroom, trying to force back another wave of nausea as the smell of the blood threatened my stomach again. Right now the rabbit's foot in the garbage didn't seem so annoying.

"Don't you have anything…more fun?" Bran asked behind me, trying to lighten the mood. "I mean, that's pretty boring nightwear."

I slammed the door, ratcheting the pain behind my

eyes up a notch. I twisted the hot water faucet wide open and waited a few minutes then added a trickle of cold, letting the steam fill the small room. The sweat-shirt went into the corner with the pants. Next stop for both of them would be the garbage pail. There were some things that couldn't ever be cleaned. I grabbed a washcloth and swiped a swath free on the mirror before turning around to see the full extent of the damage.

The full-length mirror on the back of the door revealed a mottled mess of scrapes stretching up one side of my battered body and down the other. My attacker's nails had only scraped across my left ribs, leaving thin lines that were already beginning to heal, courtesy of Felis blood. Wounds would heal but scars remained.

I stepped under the hot water, wincing. I couldn't stop the tears from starting as I ran the sponge over my body, trying to be as gentle as possible but failing miserably. My shoulders were already beginning to stiffen, which meant it was going to be hell to move later on tonight or today, whatever time it was. I added an unholy amount of peppermint-scented body wash to the water pooling around my feet and on the sponge, purging the attacker's scent from my skin.

I started rolling thoughts around to distract me from the pain. My unknown assailant had followed me home from the alley. He'd been the one I'd smelled, hidden somewhere nearby and watching me and Bran go through our search.

He must have thought I was a cop. His nostrils had been clogged with blood, his and a touch of mine, clouding his senses from the start of our fight. He hadn't made me as Felis until my claws had come out, surprising both of us.

At least I didn't have to worry about asking Jess for

descriptions of all the tall men in the Pride. I'd seen his face up close and personal. His Felis face, true, but it was as individual as a human's face when it came to identification.

I sucked up a mouthful of hot water, gargled with it then spat it into the bathtub. The nausea had finally subsided, leaving now only an empty ache in my stomach. I wasn't sure if it was a reaction to the fight, my attempt to Change or just the whole situation.

A burst of cold air shot up from under the shower curtain. I put the sponge back on the small plastic shelf and sighed before putting one hand on the edge of the curtain.

"Bran, I didn't hear a thud. I'm fine and I don't need my back scrubbed." I took a deep breath and balled my free hand into a fist. It was possible the attacker had returned to finish the job. I stared at my hand, pushing myself to get those claws out again. Nothing. I'd have to do this the old-fashioned way.

I yanked the curtain back, one arm drawn back and ready to strike.

Bran stood there, holding a large white fluffy towel he had obviously retrieved from the hall closet. The goofy grin grew wider as he gazed at my naked body, his fingers caressing the towel.

I bounced between fight and flight. I could scream righteous indignation and toss him out of the house or I could grab the lion by the mane and jump on for a ride.

I chose the second.

"Just wanted to check on you." He shook the body-length wrap. "And I see you're looking quite well."

I turned off the water and slowly stepped out of the bathtub, letting him get a full, uninterrupted view of my body. "If your definition of 'well' includes being covered with more scrapes and bruises than I have skin for, then I guess I'm just fine." His eyes widened as I took the towel from him and wrapped it around me. "See something you like?"

He let out something between a whimper and a sigh as his eyes roamed over me. I allowed myself a smug inner grin. Been a while since I'd had an admirer and I was going to make the most of it.

"And before you ask, I like to play in the dark." My eyes went below his belt.

He didn't flinch, instead allowing me to pick up the clean clothing and saunter past him into the bedroom.

The bastard had not only gone and found the best towel in the house but he had made up the bed with a new set of white sheets retrieved from my linen closet. The old ones, neatly folded, lay in the corner. Great. He was housebroken.

I dropped the damp towel on the floor, reveling somewhat in my domination of the situation. It wasn't too often I had the chance to render a loudmouth schnook speechless.

"Your back." The words weren't whispered in awe of my superior form. Closing my eyes, I winced. I had forgotten. Been a long time since I'd been naked in front of anyone other than Jazz.

His eyes had to be locked on the crisscrossing scarlet scars on my back, where it looked as if I had been attacked by a tiger. The scars hadn't faded much thanks to my skin being so fair and I knew he saw them almost as fresh as the day I had received them.

I reached down and grabbed my sweatshirt. It took a second to yank it over my head, my damp ponytail getting in the way.

"Sorry," I mumbled. The sweatpants were next, with

me hopping from one foot to the other as I made my way toward the stairs.

"Accident?"

"Of a sort." I walked down the steps, putting one hand out to balance myself. The bloody smears on both sides of the staircase laid out the trail of our battle to the final crashing halt on the landing. I paused there for a minute, letting the new wave of smells drift across my tongue. "What's that?"

"Tea, toast and I managed to find some jam in the back of the refrigerator that wasn't moldy." The soft laugh reached my ears while he walked down to stand behind me. "Grape, I do believe. And you really need to stock more stuff in there."

"I usually eat out." I made my way to the kitchen and spotted the fat Brown Betty teapot sitting on the table with two cups daintily set out, milk already in the bottom of the mugs. Two slices of toast, neatly buttered and sliced in half, made up the rest of the menu with the aforementioned bottle of jam sitting by my plate with a spoon waiting to do service.

I sat down and picked up the big brown teapot, wincing at the ache in my arm. "Shall I pour?"

"Sure." Bran watched while I filled both mugs and returned the teapot to the tabletop with a resounding thud. "Sore, eh?"

"You think?" I picked up one piece of toast and smeared enough jam onto the bread to make it bend under the weight. "You roll down the stairs and see how you feel."

"Been there, done that." He slid another pair of white pills across the table. "Figured you'd want another set of these since the last ones didn't survive."

"Thanks." I washed them down with a mouthful of hot tea and looked at him over the brim of the mug.

Bran picked up his own mug and cupped it with both hands. "So, want to tell me about this guy? And why we're not having this conversation with some detective down at the police station?"

I chewed the toast slowly, drawing out the experience as long as possible. "There's a lot here I can't tell you about, a lot that the cops don't need to know and can't know."

"I figured that out." Rocking back on the wooden chair, he smiled. "However, if you get killed, it will really, really impact my story in a negative way." A sly wink shot my way. "Aside from making me pretty upset."

The ceramic mug had grown hot to the touch, almost burning my fingers. "I have to call my client first." I took another bite of toast and shrugged, feeling the pull on my shoulders. "You know how this game goes."

"That I do." He got up and disappeared into the other room for a second, returning with my portable phone. "I'll give you a bit of privacy." Another disarming grin. "Let's see how many channels you actually get in this place. I'll be upstairs."

I waited until I heard the reassuring creak of the steps before dialing Jess's number. It rang thirteen times before the line clicked over to live.

"Hello?" Jess's voice struggled through the air. "What?"

"Who in the Pride has a white stripe running down one side of his nose? Male, tall over six feet or so?" My words were clipped. "Bastard just tried to kill me here in my own home and you have no idea of how pissed I am right now."

"What?" Jess's response shot to full awareness. "What the hell..."

"Thanks for your concern," I snapped back, growling into the receiver. "Now tell me who's got that marking."

"What, you think we remember everything about everyone?" Jess snarled, now fully awake, "You know the rules. No computer files, nothing out of the Library unless the Board approves it."

"You know who's got those markings, which family line. If not, find out. I'll be up there by dawn." My eyes moved to the doorway leading to the office. "And I won't be alone." I hit the disconnect button before she could start complaining, then move to whining and then threatening. I wasn't in the mood for it. Jazz wandered in from the other room and wrapped herself around my feet with a comforting purr. She knew exactly what I was going to be dealing with. Another visit to the farm.

Except I wasn't going to the farm alone. I was bringing a stranger into the heart of Pride territory and rubbing it in their faces that I wasn't a part of their world anymore. It would be dangerous for Bran and me but I had to try to get the upper hand in this game before someone got killed.

Like me.

NINE

THE BROWN BETTY had one last cup in it and I drained every drop I could from the battered old ceramic teapot before putting it in the sink. The toast had settled in my stomach nicely with the painkillers, which were probably holding back the headache I should have from calling Jess.

Bran was sitting on the bed, the remote in one hand and in his other a clump of brownish-black fur. My stomach did a flip-flop. He must have collected it from the bedroom while he cleaned up and I was in the shower.

He looked up as I sat on the bed beside him. "CNN's got a good documentary going on the Middle East. That is, unless you really want to watch music videos. About the best thing on at…" He checked his watch. "Four o'clock in the morning."

"What's that?" I rolled the words lightly off my tongue, nodding toward his other hand. "Dog fur?"

"I thought you'd be able to tell me." He dropped the remote on the bed and rolled the fur between both his hands into a small ball. "See, I found this all over your bed. And all the way down the stairs. I'm not seeing a dog around here and your cat's very, very white. So I have to ask myself," his eyes met mine, "what sort of creature attacked you and why aren't you even a little bit surprised?"

I put my fingers on my temples and rubbed hard.

This was not how I envisioned an evening with a hand-some, available man in my bedroom was supposed to go, even in my kinkiest dreams. "I have to get dressed. There's some place we have to go right now."

"Good. I think a drive will do us both good." He stood up and tucked the fur into the front pocket of his jeans. "I'll bag it when I get downstairs. I'm sure you have a Ziploc around somewhere." Before I could respond he had vanished down the stairs into a whole different area of trouble.

I got to my feet and walked over to the window, feeling the cool night air rush in. Looking outside showed no ladder, just the slim drainpipe running from my roof down to the ground. It didn't take a genius to figure out that's how he'd climbed up. In full Change he would have only taken a few seconds to scurry up the thirty feet or so to my bedroom window.

My eyes caught a few more stray hairs fluttering in the light wind, sticking out of various nooks and cran-nies on the pipe itself and the bricks. I could have col-lected them to prove my point that they matched the single strand that I had plucked from the crime scene but I didn't bother. His scent was the same and that was good enough for me.

Now I had to deal not only with a curious reporter but also with an angry Board who was going to be thrilled at having a human on the farm.

A clean T-shirt and jeans replaced the tracksuit and I tossed the still-damp clothing onto the freshly made bed. While I tied up my running shoes, I wondered what sort of reception I was going to receive at the farm. The first time I'd been there it was at the Board's re-quest. This time I was barging in to look at top-secret records and dragging a tabloid reporter with me. This was not going to go over well but I'd be damned if I would let Bran out of my sight at this point. He already knew much more than he should and I didn't want the Board deciding to call a hunt on him just because he happened to be in the wrong place at the wrong time. And it might just temper Jess's reaction to have a witness along. Either way he'd be in danger, but at least if I took him along it'd be on my terms and I might be able to keep him alive.

Bran stood at the bottom of the stairs, tapping his foot. He wasn't going to leave me alone for a second.

I made my way down the steps, wincing as a misstep jarred my shoulder and sent shooting pains across my back and down my spine. This was going to be a great drive. I gritted my teeth and kept walking, aware of Bran scrutinizing my every move.

"So, ready to go? And where are we going?" Bran offered me his arm, beaming as if he were the proverbial cat who swallowed the canary. I took it and wondered why I suddenly felt more avian than feline.

I picked up the house keys off my desk as we headed for the front door. Jazz meowed, weaving her way between our legs and beaming her approval of my company.

"You stay here and keep watch." I wagged a finger at her, ignoring Bran's wide grin. "In other words, keep out of trouble and don't claw the couch." The white cat hopped onto the chair then onto my desk before sprawling across a stack of folders and splaying them over the edge, onto the floor.

"Oh, she's a bright one," Brandon murmured when I sighed.

"She chose me. Keep that in mind." I held back from berating my little sister. She was just doing it for attention. Couldn't blame her, to be fair. In the last few hours I had brought in so many new scents and dangers that if she had disappeared out the window to go back to the streets for a week I wouldn't have been surprised. I was pleased the fuzzaloid was still here.

The deadbolt slid home although it wasn't as reassuring as it had been in the past. I made a mental note to not only get a new lock but also to consider adding a few more, including the windows.

The front yard was bare except for the dying grass I couldn't keep alive for love or money. Bran followed me while I made a sharp turn down the small alleyway to what passed for a parking lot for my car.

Parkdale was full of these small alleys, leftover relics of the days of horse and buggy where you could just squeeze through the lane and pop out someplace else, avoiding the main streets. Some were paved, some covered with cobblestones and all were guaranteed to make you claustrophobic. All were usually inhabited by hookers plying their trade with their latest client or crack-heads getting high. I couldn't tell you the number of times I stepped over used needles or worse, a stack of used condoms.

Bran wrinkled his nose as we approached the Jeep. "Sure it's safe to leave your car out here?"

I turned the car alarm off and unlocked the doors with the remote. "I pay one of the local homeless fellows to watch it. He's usually over there but I expect he's hitting up the dumpsters right now after the bars close down. Lots of good pickings if you're not fussy."

"And you trust him?" He slid into the passenger seat as I fiddled with my seat belt.

"Why not?" I replied as we inched along the alley.

Bran flinched while we skimmed the walls. "I think of it as supporting my local businessman."

We stopped at the same rest area I had visited just yesterday, my mind still spinning with the speed of the events of the past twenty-four hours, not to mention a good hit of painkillers.

Bran jumped out of the car with a wide smile on his face. "Coffee and donuts are on me. Unless you want some sort of healthy breakfast food."

I shook my head, turning the engine off and undoing my seat belt. My shoulders were aching and I needed a good hour or three in a hot tub. I glanced over at Bran's hands and flashed back to that one abbreviated shoulder rub and wondered how a sequel would feel.

"Good. I really don't think I'm ready for the fresh fruit and cottage cheese plate." He got out of the car and opened my door, extending a hand.

I shrugged it off and gritted my teeth, ordering my aching body to move as normally as possible.

The Tim Horton's was filled almost to capacity, the morning commuters rushing to their daily jobs. I envied their enthusiasm and their stamina. I would have gone postal after doing that commute for more than a week. A trio of businessmen swarmed the counter just ahead of us, multitasking by screaming into their Bluetooth headsets and tapping on their Blackberries while ordering some semblance of a breakfast with the largest coffees the franchise sold. Black, of course. Nothing diluted that coffee strength and quality for them.

Hanover tapped his foot as the three customers began to discuss or rather fight over the actual cost of the coffees and how they would distribute the change fairly with whoever would receive the receipt, probably to put on their business account. Finally they left, allowing us to get to the counter before Bran blew a fuse.

A few minutes later we sat at one of the few empty tables in the rest stop chewing on yet more donut holes and sipping coffee. Bran frowned as he rotated a chocolate-glazed globe between his fingers.

"Ever wonder exactly how many calories are in one of these?"

"I don't. Too depressing," I mumbled between a mouthful of coffee and cinnamon. "And don't tell me you're watching your figure."

He preened himself, sliding one of his arms out of the jacket to flex his biceps in a mock muscleman pose. "What, you think I got this by eating junk food?"

Taking the bait, I reached across the table to pinch the steel muscle with two fingers. "Ooh. I'm impressed." Dang it, it felt like iron. I pressed my lips together. "My, you're just one tough reporter, you are. Too bad you're wasting time working for that rag."

His face fell as he pulled away, tucking his bare arm back into the jacket. "The *Inquisitor*'s not a rag."

"It's sure not anything I'd take seriously. How did you end up working for them?"

"You've done your research on me. You tell me." He sipped the coffee with one eye on the businessmen who were now dissecting the bill, item by item.

"I don't know. You graduated with good marks and did all the right things, worked up a good portfolio of interviews and non-fiction articles at small magazines. Award-winning stuff if I remember correctly. Then suddenly you end up on the staff list at the *Inquisitor*."

He dipped a plastic stir stick into his paper cup and began to stir the already murky liquid. "Yep. That was me, bright-eyed, bushy-tailed and eager to get out there and win the Governor General's Literary Award with some hot exposé." Bran nodded, his full attention now on the coffee. "I thought I was pretty hot shit, to be honest. I was going to save the world with some great writing."

The businessmen were now engrossed in their PDAs, each in their own little world tapping out text messages and changing the course of history while sipping good coffee.

"My parents tweaked some noses, got me a free-lance assignment with one of the big Toronto papers." He took a mouthful of cooling coffee and swished it around his mouth before swallowing. "I decided to go native. I ended up hanging out down in Toronto with a group of homeless kids, getting their stories and tracking their progress for an entire year."

I didn't say anything. Beside us the trio began to pack up their Blackberries and Bluetooth gear. They finished their coffees and left a mess on the table despite being only a few feet from a garbage disposal can.

"It was a horrible way to live." He let out a sigh. "Every few weeks I would scamper back to my nice clean condo and get showered and eat a decent meal and then go back to the kids who had probably just washed their hair in the washrooms at the Eaton Centre. They knew I was a reporter but they didn't care. I was the only one listening to them. Not judging, not offering advice, not telling them what I thought, just listening. No cameras, no laptops, nothing but my journals."

I picked up another chocolate donut hole. The three men sauntered out into the parking lot and piled into a huge SUV. They bustled out of the rest stop at high speed, headed toward their next great acquisition.

"Two of the kids overdosed one night while I was at

home, dining on steak. The cops found them in an alleyway with the needles still stuck in their arms. Bad dope. There was a lot of that bad shit on the streets for a few months back then. Lots of deaths." He put one end of the stir stick in his mouth. The black plastic stick bobbed up and down between his lips. "A girl and a boy. They thought they loved each other. She was going to be an artist, used to draw on the sidewalks with that cheap chalk you can buy at the toy stores, a buck for a bucket. They used to pass up on meals to get her chalk."

I nodded again. I knew better than to speak.

"He played guitar. Not great, but he had some talent. Used to busk on the streets every night to get money for the love of his life to get chalk. And heroin, of course."

I stayed silent.

"The rest of the group broke up after that. Did I mention she was six months pregnant?" Bran bit down on the stir stick. "They disappeared and I went to write my story. Turned it in."

"And they didn't print it."

Bran looked at me sideways with a sad smile on his face. "They printed it. Oh, Lord, they printed it. And suddenly every television station, every movie producer was banging on my door to get my side of the story."

I almost coughed up one of the chocolate bites. I remembered seeing some news articles about it, some special reports babbling about a journalist who'd gotten the best story about street life in years. It hadn't registered with me because I'd been elbows-deep in a child custody battle and more worried about the guy fleeing the country than staying current with the news. I'd seen the articles but never realized how important they had been in creating the man sitting across from me.

"But it wasn't about the kids, it was all about me

and my experiences. They didn't really want the story about the kids and what put them there, the social and family problems that pushed them onto the streets and finally to the comfort of a dirty needle. About the agencies that were underfunded and understaffed and how the kids fell through the cracks." Bran shook his head. "It was all about the glamour, all about the reporter and not the story. It became all about me, the rich kid who slept on the streets with the poor kids." He looked at me. "I walked away from it all, turned down all the movie offers and the requests for more stories, more gossip. I already had enough money, I didn't need more. I went back to the streets and tried to find the rest of the group, give them what I could to get them out."

"And?"

"I couldn't find anyone." He turned and looked out in the parking lot. The cars were growing sparse, the morning rush just beginning to abate. "They were all gone. I don't know if they went back to their homes to got some help at a rehab clinic or to another city or just died somewhere in a back alley. I don't know."

"I'm sure they're fine." The words tumbled out of my mouth in a rush. "They're tough, they'd have been fine."

"Maybe. Maybe not." The well-marked stir stick flipped into the empty cup. "But I knew I wasn't going to be able to work like that anymore, doing the serious stuff, putting my heart out there in public. So I decided to do the silly stories, the fun stories, the ones that wouldn't hurt anyone and wouldn't do anything other than supply cotton candy for the mind. Nothing deep, nothing important."

"Except now there's a dead woman." I picked up the second-to-last cinnamon nugget and stared at it. "And suddenly you're not dealing with fun silly cases." My voice took on a more serious tone. "What the hell did you think that picture was?"

"I thought it was a joke." Bran's elbows hit the table as he held his head in his hands. "I mean, it's a dead woman, sure, but we changed it around enough to get away with it and we sure didn't think it was real." His head shot up, one hand landing on my wrist and pinning it to the table. "It's real, isn't it? That wasn't any faked photograph. She was a real cat woman."

At first I tried to pull away then decided to leave my hand there. "Now you're a reporter again. A real one."

"Maybe I've always been." He gave a mournful smile. "Either way I'm going to get the whole story."

"This time it's not going to be about you." I glanced toward the highway. "Time to hit the road."

The traffic had let up a little, allowing us to find a sweet spot in the right-hand lane and putter along at just above the speed limit for most of the way up.

"You're not going to tell me anything, right?" Bran said to the car window.

"Client confidentiality," I mumbled.

"How about I tell you instead?"

The tires caught the edge of the shoulder, bumping us along for a few seconds until I yanked the steering wheel to center us in our lane.

"Ah. Hit home, eh?" Bran leaned back and tucked his hands behind his head. "See, I don't think that was some furry mask on that woman. And I don't think that you were attacked a few hours ago by some psycho wearing a cat outfit." He dug in one pocket of his leather coat and pulled out the small plastic bag filled with fur. "I'm willing to bet that if I had this analyzed and matched up with the hair you found at the crime scene they'd not only be the same but of some weird half-human, half-cat hybrid." He rubbed his hands over the plastic. "I'm just not sure where you fit into all this."

I smiled back, hoping my bluff skill was at full force. "Sorry, not even close. And I'm still sore from that tumble down the stairs, so that's why we just got a bumpy ride." My eyes drilled into the concrete ahead of us. "I think you've been working way too long for that tabloid rag. Next you'll be telling me that there's alien hybrids looking to take over the world and talking via those tin foil hats." The ache behind my eyes started again.

"Hey, I'm just connecting the dots." Bran looked out at the countryside while we spun around the exit ramp.

"Right. File that right next to your Reptilian Overlords story." I ignored the scowl and concentrated on the drive. The throbbing began to lessen behind one eye as I willed my blood pressure to drop and began to mentally compose my pitch to the Board. I glanced beside me a few minutes later to see Bran stretched out as much as he could in the passenger seat, his long legs awkwardly curled up in the small space while he snored fitfully, or at least pretended he did. I didn't trust him one whit, which is why when we pulled onto the dirt road I made sure to hit every pothole and bump to make sure he was awake.

There weren't many cars in the parking lot at the farm. Bran dusted off his jeans as he got out of the car and shaded his eyes from the bright sun.

"Nice place." He beamed at Ruth, who was standing on the porch waiting to receive us. "Hello!"

"Hi there!" She trotted down the steps and extended her hand, not showing a hint of shock. "I'm Ruth. Always glad to meet a friend of Rebecca's."

"Really?" He wasn't overly sarcastic, but I already wanted to thump him in the ribs. "Well, she hasn't said a word about you or this place. So what relationship are you to her?" I could see the mental notebook flip open, blank pages waiting to be filled with personal information.

"Why, one of her aunts, of course! I've just cut up a wonderful apple pie. Let me get you a piece with a good cup of coffee." The elderly woman slipped away from his questions as easily as if she were trying to dodge the old mangy mutt two farms over while raiding the cornfields. Probably did so quite a few times, when she was in her prime. She took hold of Bran's arm and led him into the kitchen, babbling something about putting some meat on his bones and how handsome he could be if he just put on a few pounds, ignoring his slight pro-testations of not wanting to leave me alone.

I took the stairs to the top floor two at a time, winc-ing as my legs protested the exercise. Jess and Den-nis sat in the Board chairs. The third remained empty.

"Where's Davis?" The wheezing noise from my lungs was embarrassing. "I thought I was to present my findings to the entire Board."

"What do you have?" Dennis's voice was low and soft. A small line of sweat formed on his forehead. This didn't look good.

"I know that Janey Winters was killed by a Felis, one with a white streak running down one side of his nose." I drew my finger down my own face just in case they didn't get the picture. "I know that because the asshole attacked me last night in my own house, in my own bed." I was too tired and angry to play nice. "So I want to know which of your bastards have that streak."

Jess stared at me. "You don't come here and make demands, Reb."

I glared at her, ignoring the rules, again. "You told me to find who killed her. I have. So now you know."

"We don't really 'know.'" Dennis cleared his throat. "You're making an assumption on what you've collected so far."

My hand went to the egg-sized lump at the back of my head. "Sure felt like I 'collected' enough when the bastard flipped me down the steps." I took a deep breath and closed my eyes, trying to center myself. The silence between us continued for a whole minute while I worked on not throwing a major tantrum.

I opened my eyes and lowered my voice to a more dignified, calm tone. "What I need now is access to the records to find whoever has the distinguishing mark and either eliminate them as a suspect or continue further investigation."

"And the man downstairs?" Jess demanded. "What does he have to do with this?"

"He's the reporter who received the original picture and wrote the story." The eyes of both Board members went wide. "I believe he didn't do it, but the murderer dropped off the picture with him in order to expose the Pride. Now he's seeking the rest of the story."

"So he must be removed." A note of sadness crept into Dennis's words. He glanced sideways at Jess, who nodded her agreement. "Which is why you brought him here, of course. A wise move on your part."

TEN

I'D FORGOTTEN HOW far the Pride would go to maintain their secrecy. I'd handed them Bran's bare throat on a platter.

"No, you're not going to 'remove' anyone." I stood up and put my palms down on the table. "He's not one of your misfits. He's a human being." Seeing no change in their expressions, I played my trump card. "While the cops might have slid Janey's case into the cold case file, the murder of the reporter who first got the picture would probably provoke them to reopen it. With much, much more curiosity."

The side of Jess's cheek twitched, the waves rolling up the scar and back down again. "This isn't really an area in which you can advise us."

"I beg to differ." I rapped the varnished wood with my knuckles. "If Brandon Hanover 'disappears' then it's going to start a domino reaction that you won't be able to control. As long as I keep him with me I control what he does and what he knows. I won't let him report what would be damaging to the family."

Jess's eyes flashed to my hands, specifically the small scabs between my knuckles. Her eyes went wide for a second.

"So you're prepared to deal with this man, if need be?" She chose each word carefully, jamming them into my face.

"If need be." A sudden snowball of nausea lodged in my belly.

Jess sat back in the chair, dismissing me with a wave of her hand. "Keep in touch and give us updates as your investigation progresses."

"And the files?" I remained standing.

Dennis frowned. "We're going to allow you limited access. An envelope has been filled with the information you requested. It'll be available downstairs for you to read before you leave."

"I can't take it with me." I rolled my eyes. "Because, you know, that would make my job easier."

"Don't get all worked up." Jess got to her feet, signaling the end of the discussion. "There's only a handful of Felis who meet your description. I think you'll be surprised." Her eyes flashed again to my hands. "As are we, I think."

I opened my mouth to respond then closed it. There wasn't anything I could do right now that wouldn't make things worse, and probably get Bran killed. I spun on one heel and made my way to the stairs.

I could hear Ruth's voice through the entire house as she led Bran on a rambling tour of the huge first floor, detailing every nook and cranny. Considering the house had been in her family for more than two hundred years I wasn't surprised at all. Maybe Bran could get an article out of it, something nice and mild and not dangerous in any way. On my way through to the kitchen I noted that the nursery had been discreetly removed, the cribs tucked away in a closet somewhere and the children cared for elsewhere.

I sat down at the small dinette table in the kitchen and opened the small postal envelope with a single piece of paper inside. Three names typed in capital letters, double-spaced.

Frank Langley. Jonathan Magee. Sven Hammerhold. Nothing else. No locations, no ages, nothing.

I tore the page into small pieces, resisting the urge to shred it with my teeth. This was about as helpful as the Board was willing to get but at least I had a place to start. Now I'd have to rely on my investigative skills to fill in the blanks and determine which one of these three had charged in my window a few hours earlier and tried to kill me.

I tossed the envelope and the shredded paper into the garbage before walking outside onto the porch. The sun had just hit the high point in the sky and it was a clear, beautiful day in Northern Ontario. A breeze came in from the west across the fields, carrying the scent of the fresh corn and more than a few Felis wandering around.

"How did you do it?" Jess appeared beside me. I didn't jump but shuffled my feet back and forth, scuffing the runners against the rough wood in my contained shock.

"You're still too quiet." I teased the older woman, hoping to change the subject.

"You tried to Change. Did it work?" Her voice was low.

I shook my head. "Not really. Claws, that's all. Enough to keep me alive. Which is more than you're giving me now."

Jess leaned on the wooden railing and stared out at the dirt road leading to the house. Her denim work shirt had a few rips and tears in it, with her faded jeans. A light breeze ruffled her near-white hair.

"I'm glad it wasn't Dennis." She picked at a loose splinter in the railing with thick fingers. "That would have been hard to deal with." She glanced sideways at me. "Just remember that your loyalty is to us, first and foremost."

The pain behind my eyes flared up as I spun on her. "Loyalty? To the system that tossed me out when I was fifteen?" I slammed my hand down on the railing. "I'm loyal to the truth, wherever it leads me. And if that conflicts with your version of reality, well I'll just have to live with the consequences."

She turned toward me, her face calm. "You've done pretty well so far, Reb."

We stared at each other in silence for a minute before Ruth and Bran walked out of the house. Bran had a piece of apple pie in his hand, partially wrapped in a napkin with a few bites already missing.

"This is the best pie I've ever tasted." He mumbled through the crumbs, a childishly wide smile on his face. Ruth smiled and handed me a small cake box.

"I put the rest in here for you to take home. If it makes it there, of course." She beamed as Bran's eyes went wide. He stared at the box as if it contained hidden treasure. "We'll see you again, I hope."

"We'll have to see." I looked over at Jess. "Depends on where the trail takes me."

"Best. Pie. Ever." Bran called back as he made his way down the steps toward the Jeep. "Oh, we'll be back."

I hugged Ruth goodbye and nodded to Jess before walking off the porch. The box was warm and the odor of apple and cinnamon filled my senses as I loaded it into the back seat.

"Your aunt's a pretty nice woman. If that's really what she is." Bran locked his seat belt in place as I turned the key in the ignition. He waved at her, receiving a gentle smile and wave back. Jess was still watching us, her stare firmly focused on Bran.

The wheels kicked up a cloud of dust that followed us back out to the main road and back to the highway. I kept a sharp eye on the rear-view mirror.

"So, what did you find out? Was that chick your contact? Another 'aunt'?" Bran wiped his mouth with the empty napkin and tucked it into his pocket. "Damned fine pie."

"Ruth makes fantastic pie." I turned my head to the left, looking for an opening in the traffic. "As far back as I remember she's always been baking. Cookies, pies, soup and stews. Anything you can think of she can make." A tractor-trailer roared by, leaving enough of an opening for me to slip the Jeep in. I pushed the gas pedal down and watched the speedometer race up the dial.

Bran sat quietly for most of the way back, probably in a sugar coma. Suddenly he turned to me. "Which of them is the client?"

"I can't tell you that." I kept looking straight ahead. The traffic was beginning to get a bit thicker and the last thing I needed was to crack up the Jeep because I was getting into an argument.

"You can tell me." I caught his bright smile out of the corner of my right eye. "It's not Ruth. That much is obvious. Jess? Someone else?"

"None of your business." It took a bit of restraint not to point out that my "client" had been willing to kill him and dispose of the body. There were plenty of places on the farm to hide a corpse and lots of machinery to make sure you never found a trace, despite what television would have you believe. Jimmy Hoffa may not have had Felis in the family, but the Family had some Felis in it.

"Rebecca!" The shout brought me back out of my

reverie into the reality that I was about to rear-end the SUV ahead of me.

I stomped on the brake pedal, standing up with my head hitting the ceiling of my own car. Beside me Bran grabbed the dashboard with both hands. I wanted to scream that he would end up with broken arms if he did that and the airbag deployed, but my mind was racing and my body tensed up for the inevitable crash.

Somehow, someway, the truck ahead of me leaped ahead, accelerating away from us even as the brakes screamed and the wheels dragged on the asphalt. I yanked the wheel to the right and pulled onto the shoulder as we screeched to a stop. My right hand yanked the transmission into "park", gears grinding in opposition to my rough treatment. Cars continued to speed by us, oblivious to the near-disaster I had almost caused.

Bran let out a low whistle and peeled his hands from the dashboard. "God, are you okay?"

"I'm not sure." I lowered myself into the seat, tension shooting up and down my spine. A roaring filled my ears as I leaned forward and rested my forehead on the steering wheel. "I think you should drive."

"You think?" He slumped back against the cushions. "I think I just lost the pie." Bran gave a low laugh and unbuckled his belt. "Move over and I'll walk around."

I slipped across the seat and took up residence on the passenger side, watching Bran maneuver his way around the front of the car into the driver's seat.

"Your place or mine?" The engine roared as he put it back into gear and pulled out into traffic.

"Mine. I still have work to do." I closed my eyes and let my head fall back on the small cushion. "I think I'm just tired."

"I can believe that." Bran's voice came to me down

a long dark tunnel. "I'll buy that you don't have a concussion, but I'm not buying that you're okay. You're running on very little sleep, a heck of a fall down those stairs and I don't think that meeting went as well as you planned."

I wanted to point out that I had just saved his miserable life, but decided it would be better to just take it easy, rest and ignore the traffic with its blaring horns. The smell of freshly cooked pie was so darned good and it better not be smeared all over the inside of that box and...

The car's stopping jarred me out of my light sleep. I jolted upright and stared out the windshield at a gray wall that was definitely not my house's narrow alleyway.

Bran turned toward me. "My underground garage. You're going to sleep someplace safe."

I opened my mouth, a plethora of excuses, arguments and curses about to surge out but instead a loud yawn broke loose, forcing me to cover my mouth.

Bran laughed when he opened my door, balancing the pie box in one hand and extending his other hand to me. "My point. At least get a few hours rest where we know no one's going to break in and come after you. Or me." He sniffed the box. "And we have pie."

I let him lead me through the cement structure to the elevator, slumping against the wall as we rose through the condominium complex to his floor and to his residence. Between the headache and the stress of the past few hours I was shutting down physically and it was only a number of minutes before my mind would close shop.

He opened the front door and led me to the kitchen

first, keeping one hand around my waist while he slid
the pie box onto the marble counter.

"Now, to bed with you," Bran said, walking me
across the open floor to the bedroom. We stepped
around the divider to a huge double bed, covered with
a dark green fluffy comforter that called to me.

I fell face-first onto the bed, letting out a rather raun-
chy moan as I curled up into the softness, wrapping it
around me. Part of me noted Bran pulling off my running shoes and placing them at the foot of the bed, but
I didn't care. I was in a soft, dark place where the pillows were cool and the quilt was warm and that was all
I wanted right now.

The delicious smell of Ruth's apple pie woke me,
the deep rich scent of cinnamon almost overpowering
my senses when I sat up quickly. I was still in the bed,
bundled up in the comforter, but a fast glance to the
windows showed darkness outside and the city lights
sending crazy jagged silhouettes across the floor.

I moved around the bookshelf wall to see Bran sitting
on a stool at a marble island in the kitchen, crouched
over a large piece of pie.

"About time you got up. I was going to come get you
in a few minutes anyway." He grinned. "And this pie
reheats beautifully."

Muscles stretched and joints popped as I padded
across the floor in my socks to join him. He slid a piece,
possibly half of the original pie, across to me on a fresh
plate. "Need to build up your strength."

I took the offered fork and dug in, trying to clear the
cobwebs from my mind. The nap had done me a world
of good, least of which allowing the information to mar-
inate in my mind. The brown sugary mess I shoveled
into my mouth was really helping me think.

"Tea? Coffee? Soda?" Bran grinned as he watched me devour the slice. "I was thinking about ordering Chinese, since we've already had dessert."

"Soda. Whatever you have that's diet," I mumbled between mouthfuls, "and General Tso's Chicken. And sesame noodles. And wonton soup." A piece of crust got stuck on my lip. "And plenty of rice."

"Good to hear you've got an appetite. I'm tired of women chewing on a single lettuce leaf and telling me that they're full." He pulled out his cell phone and hit one of the buttons. "Local place is on speed-dial and they know me pretty well."

I watched him chatter off an order, half in English and half in Chinese. Wonderful. He could be ordering us a whole roasted suckling pig and I wouldn't know it.

"Be less than an hour." He spun around and picked up the cake box on the counter. "And I think Ruth makes great pie, but her garnishes are good too." The lid flipped open as he pushed the box toward me.

A series of folders sat under the empty aluminum pie plate, bent and folded to fit the box. I snatched them up and flipped them open, one at a time. Three files, each displaying one of the names I had been handed.

"Yep, she makes good pie." Bran leaned in, way inside my personal space again. "You've got a bit of apple just here." His index finger touched the right side of my mouth, scooping it up. He retreated to his seat and popped the morsel into his mouth, giving me a wide grin.

I tamped down the heat rising in my cheeks and tried to ignore him, staring down at the pictures, at three men, none of whom looked like the one who had attacked me less than twenty-four hours ago. I spread the files out across the marble top island.

"So, why did she have to smuggle these files out to you in a pie box?" Bran picked up both plates and put them into the sink. He walked around to stand behind me, peering at the papers. "I mean, if you're working for them…"

Ignoring the pointed question, I studied the three pictures again, grateful that the Pride's identification photos hadn't been taken during a member's Change. That would have made things even more complicated than they were now. And it seemed that it was getting more so with each hour, thanks to having Bran around.

The papers included didn't have much more than the addresses and basic information about each man, which wasn't very helpful. Two of them were in British Columbia, which was on the other side of the country and the last lived in North Bay, hardly within commuting distance for a murderer. Still, they had the same visual marking my attacker had and that was a starting point.

"So, again, what's the big secret here?" Bran reached around me to tap on one of the photographs, putting his lips close to my ear. "You go to talk to your client and he gives you nothing. Your aunt sends you these files secretly because…" He rolled the last word into a question.

I closed my eyes. "Can I get that soda, please?"

His deep musk threatened to block anything other than the mental image of him, naked, back in that warm comfortable bed I had just left. Then he moved away and I regained a bit more control.

"So, I guess these are your suspects?" The can of soda made an annoying hiss as he opened it and poured the contents into a tall glass. Bran took up his position across from me again, placing the drink within easy reach.

"In a way. None of these men could have been the one who attacked me last night." My finger tapped the photographs, one by one. "Wrong areas, wrong ages. Unless they've managed to perfect a transportation ray and time travel it's very unlikely that they were responsible for last night's events."

"What's the link?" He stared at the three photographs, pulling them free of the paper clips then spreading them out side by side. "They don't look alike."

I bit down on my lower lip, hunting for a good lie. I couldn't find one. The silence hung between us like the old Berlin Wall.

Bran looked up at me. "Right. So when are you going to let me in on the big secret?"

I took a long, refreshing drink of the caffeine-laced soda. My eyes widened. "This is not diet."

"Nope." He grinned unapologetically. "Figured you'd need the sugar rush." Bran looked down at his watch before walking to one of the cupboards. "Shouldn't be too much longer for the food. I assume you know how to use chopsticks. Or should I get forks?" He pulled down a pair of plates that looked and screamed good china.

"I'll use my hands if I have to." I reattached the photographs to the proper files. A double-check confirmed that none of these Felis had been my attacker. You didn't change that much when you Changed.

My eyes widened when I flipped the last page. At the back of the file, taped to the folder, was a small sample of fur securely sealed in a plastic see-through bag. Wow. The bastards did keep records, and obviously fine ones at that. Probably did have our DNA on file somewhere, in a deep dark bunker.

Bran still faced the counter, busy placing a set of knives and forks on the plates. I glanced at him. He hadn't seen the fur. I closed the files quickly and shoved them into a stack. As if on cue the phone rang, diverting his attention even further.

"Right. Come on up." He smiled at me as he hung up. "Chinese food has arrived!" His gaze moved toward the folders. "How about we call a truce until after we eat? Then we can get a-brawling on a full stomach?"

I nodded. "Just don't get in the way of my chicken. I'll kill for that."

Bran walked toward the front door. "Okay, but don't even think of looking at my curried shrimp."

We attacked the food as if we hadn't eaten for days, scooping mouthfuls of hot soup down our throats at a speed that would have guaranteed indigestion in most mortals. Bran signaled his enjoyment of the meal with a huge burp between forkfuls of rice and shrimp. "Excuse me. It's good food."

"That it is," I mumbled with a mouthful of rice. "What were you telling them in Chinese?"

"Extra meat in the dishes." He pointed at the chicken with one fork, then to the shrimp and finally to a beef and broccoli dish. "They give me a bit better service and larger portions because I give good tips."

"On who's going to be the target of your next exposé?"

"No, usually ten to twenty bucks." He rapped his fork on the edge of the plate. "I like to think of it as boosting the local economy." Bran patted his stomach, pushing it out to exaggerate the bloating. "Wow. Haven't felt this good in a long time."

"It is good food." I speared another piece of chicken. "I'm a bit tired of donut holes, to be honest. Good, but hardly nutritious."

"You think?" Bran laughed as he stood up and went to put his plate in the sink. "Coffee or another drink?"

"Coffee, please." I pushed the near-empty plate away from me, ignoring the last spoonful of white rice. "At least I can claim I left something behind. Makes me feel less of a pig."

"Bah." He scraped the handful of grains into a trash bag under the sink. "I like my women with a bit of meat on their bones."

I didn't react to the sly wink, choosing instead to rest my elbows on the table while stifling a yawn in my hands. My eyes went to the folders, now discreetly tucked under a stack of napkins.

"Just so you know—I don't do dishes." Bran reseated himself on the stool, facing me. "I toss them out and buy new ones."

"You do not."

"Maybe." He reached out and snagged the folders, pulling them back into plain sight. "So, are you going to tell me what's going on here or do I have to keep playing the idiot?"

My fingers returned to my temples, rubbing lightly while I closed my eyes. I wasn't sure if the penalties would be as high for him as they would be for me, but with a killer out there it wasn't like it was going to get any less dangerous.

"Do you still have that handful of fur from my house?" I asked.

"Sure do." He reached into his pocket and pulled out the bagful of black and brown colored fur, still neatly rolled into a ball. "What, you going to get DNA analysis done?"

"Not enough time." I took the bag from him and set it on the table. "Not to mention I'm not sure if I can charge my client for the lab costs." I took each folder and opened it to display the small tuft of hair neatly attached to the file. "What I can do is see if they match."

"How?" His eyes were focused on the three samples as I spread the folders out, ripping each small bag free. "I was kind of curious as to why you were getting hair samples in those files."

I paused and considered my options. I had to find Janey's killer and this would be the fastest method. It could have deadly consequences depending on how Bran handled the information.

Janey Winters was dead. Brandon Hanover wasn't. I could save him.

I closed my eyes and tried to put myself into a neutral state, allowing my natural abilities to come forward. It was one of the first tricks they taught us as kits, essential to maintain that inner control keeping us from Changing every time we got pissed off. Without learning inner control you ended up on an emotional rollercoaster, rocking and rolling with every flash of feeling. Mike had called on that control when he had started to Change involuntarily.

As Felis we learned how to push out a lot of the smells and scents around us—it was a case of prioritizing what you needed and what you didn't. Right now I had to close off everything and call up that individual scent from the alley and from the attacker, then compare it to the samples.

I could sense Bran's confusion and fear, a heady mix calling to me. It took an effort to push his scent to one side and focus on the task at hand.

I reached for the bag from my house and opened it close to my nose. A deep inhalation brought the rogue's scent home, reminding me of the initial attack. My heartbeat jumped into the danger zone.

"Okay, now I have a control to work with." I exhaled the words in a whisper. The bag went back on the table, closed up to preserve the purity of the scent.

I picked up the first small sample and sniffed it, then the second and the third. It was like a kaleidoscope of colors rotating—all the same basic colors but I knew which patterns belonged to whom. There was something wrong though, something missing.

"None of them match." I frowned and shook my head. "But there's a sort of trace with this one." I looked at the source of the fur sample.

The file belonged to the Felis from North Bay, Frank Langley.

"But it's not him, not directly." I cleared my mind and my lungs of the odors with a harsh cough, replacing the spinning circles of color with the comforting familiar scents of the present. "Maybe a relative or a child. It's something, at least. I've got to call Jess and see what's up. There's more to this than what they have in the file." I reached for my cell phone and sent a short text message to Jess. It was too much to hope to be able to get a direct connection at this time of the night and there was more of a chance she'd pick up a text.

Bran stared at me, then at the hair samples, then back at me. "How did you…what did you do?" He hopped off the stool, wide-eyed. "What did you do?"

Bran picked up each small bag and stared at them, studying the colored strands as intently as I had. "You just sniffed them. Just smelled them." His voice was a low whisper as if he had to convince himself of what he had just seen.

My heart began to race. I was totally busted.

Part of me wondered why I hadn't thrown him out of the room, faked being sick, anything to keep him from seeing that part of me. Another part, a soft whisper, asked if I'd done it on purpose to get to this turning point in our relationship. The third part threw up her hands and wanted more pie.

His eyes locked with mine. "What the hell is going on?"

I shook my head. "I can't tell you."

"You can't tell me?" He replied with a smile. "What, will you have to kill me then?"

My face said it all. He moved closer, way into my personal space.

"Really?" Bran repeated, sliding so close I could swear we shared the same breath. "You're going to have to kill me?"

"Not me," I whispered, closing my eyes.

"Well, that's good, 'cause I'd hate to have to get into a fight with you." The heated air caressed my cheek. "Unless it's in bed and then I don't mind losing."

I opened my eyes to stare at him, feeling the blush on my skin. "You don't get how dangerous this is, do you?"

Bran nodded. "I get it. What you don't get is that I think finding her killer is important enough to risk it." The left edge of his mouth twitched up. "It's what I should be doing for a living, Reb. So tell me what's going on and let me in."

"I am a member of a family of people, different from what you're used to. Homo sapiens, I mean. I guess it'd be sort of Felidae sapiens. I think." I was rambling. "We're not that different. Well, I'm not, but I'm different from them. The family, I mean. The Pride. The killer, the guy who attacked me, he's one of us. Well, them technically." I covered my face with my hands, afraid to breathe. "I'm shutting up now. I'm shutting up." A ball of nausea started forming in my stomach, threatening to rid me of all that good food.

ELEVEN

I OPENED MY eyes to see Bran leaping around the apartment like a kid on Christmas Day who just got the keys to the toy store. He beamed at me as he continued his frantic dancing. "I knew there was something strange about that place, about you. About Ruth..." He stopped, his hands in mid-wave. "The pie, that is apple, right? Not cat chow or something like that?" His fingers clutched his belly. "I'm not going to cough up a hairball, am I?"

The laugh rolled up from my stomach, replacing the nausea. "Oh, it's apple all right. And you should taste her pumpkin pie. Or her *tourtiere*." I swallowed, pushing back the last of the panic. "What do you mean, you knew. About me?"

He advanced on me, wagging his finger in the air. "You were too..." He waved his hands in the air, making shapes. "There was something about you, something feline. It was like you were hunting something, the way you grabbed on to every clue. I've seen investigators work before and you were nothing like them. One tough chick."

"A what?" My face went redder as I slid off the stool and placed my hands on my hips. "Did you just call me a 'chick'?"

Bran stopped, a worried look on his face. "Well, I guess it'd be more of a 'kitten,' then. Or 'lion cub.'

Or..." He frowned. "What do you call yourself, anyway?"

"The proper name is Felis, for your information. And I haven't been a kit for a long, long time." I walked over to the sitting area and plopped myself down on the leather sofa. "And if you want to talk more about this you had better start calming down. I didn't expect this sort of reaction."

"What do you expect me to do?" Bran bounced over to where I sat. "You've just revealed a whole new line of man. A whole new group of people living in society, but not really—with their own rules and regulations." He paused, frowning. "You're not married or something like that, right? It's not some sort of harem thing where you and ten other women belong to some alpha male?"

I rolled my eyes. "Please. As if." The nervousness in my stomach was beginning to turn into annoyance.

"Okay, wait." He sat down opposite me and leaned forward with his hands outstretched. "Can you change? Can you go all furry? Like Janey Winters?"

"I cannot." I felt a bit of uneasiness at the way the conversation was going. "The fellow who attacked me last night, for example, was fully Changed. That's how he got up the side of the house and in the window."

"But you beat him down." Bran's forehead furrowed. "And you said you can't change."

"I can't." I rubbed my eyes with the palms of both hands, trying to figure out how to explain things. "When I was ten my parents died in a car accident. I was raised on the farm, home-schooled by Ruth. I wasn't lonely. There're lots of kids around on the farm. It's sort of a nursery and vacation spot for Felis who want to get away from the city and relax." I couldn't stop myself from shivering. "Then my life got turned upside-down."

An image flashed up from my memory.

Stumbling alone down the dirt road toward the highway with nothing more than the clothes on my back. The bloody bandages sticking to my skin from a "farm accident."

The pain began in my chest, threatening to cut off my words. "I…Something went wrong with me. I stopped being able to Change when I was about twelve. The Board gave me a few more years to see what was wrong, whether it was just a case of hormones screwing things up. But it didn't come back." I flexed my fingers, feeling the phantom pain of the claws return. "So they had a meeting, a Gathering. It happens every year when the kits are declared full members of the Pride, nothing more than ceremony."

A deep breath pushed back the anxiety attack. "It's usually a party. But for me, it was a test. If I couldn't Change under stress, under attack by another member, then I'd be outcast." I looked down at my fingers. "I failed."

"The scars on your back," Bran whispered.

Tears began to well in my eyes, threatening to blind me. "So I left and got shunted into foster care and I went to college, got a job and then qualified for my PI license."

He shook his head, his forehead furrowed. "That's horrible." His hands balled up into angry fists, the knuckles white. "That's just…inhuman."

I laughed, choking back the tears. "We're not human, silly." Wiping my face with the back of my hands I continued, "It's no big deal. I wasn't going to fit in anyway. Better off out here, says I."

Bran pressed his lips together. "Doesn't make it right."

"Well, I'm not going to disagree with you there." I sniffled, taking deep breaths to force myself to calm down. Right now an emotional drive down memory lane wasn't one I could handle.

"And Janey Winters was one of the...Felis, you said?" Bran kicked over into reporter mode, his tone changing. I could imagine him reaching for a pen and pencil in a minute.

"Affirmative." I smiled. "And who you gonna call when one of your family has been killed?"

"Another cat woman. One who knows the system but isn't hooked into the cops and doesn't have any moral problems about hunting down the killer outside of the law." He slumped back in the chair and let out a huff of air. "My head is spinning here."

"Glad I could help." I chuckled. "And now we're tracking down a killer who seems to have targeted Janey for no other reason than the fact that she's a member of the Pride."

"Family. Pride. Felis." Bran put the palm of his hand to his forehead. "I'm going to go nuts trying to remember all this."

"I wish you wouldn't, to be honest." I bit my bottom lip. "As you can guess, it's not usually permitted for us to tell humans about our existence."

"Well, you have to admit that it's one hell of a story." His eyes went bright as he spoke. "Story of the century, actually."

"If you could get anyone to believe you." The brightness dimmed just a fraction.

"Which is why you got involved." He nodded as he

popped one finger in his mouth and began chewing on the nail.

I resisted the urge to slap his hand away.

"Better to keep it in the family, so to speak."

"So to speak."

His eyebrows rose. "And I'm willing to bet that I'm not the first one to find this out, right?"

"Ah." I blinked wildly, trying to gather my thoughts and buy myself some time to phrase it properly.

"Ah." Bran pointed at his chest. "So I'm now about to get whacked by the head Lion or Cat or whatever?"

"You were a target before I told you." I felt my face grow warmer. "Jess wanted to whack you today at the farm."

"What?" He jumped to his feet and began to stride back and forth across the hardwood floor. "Kill me? Does she know who I am? Who I know?" He stopped and glanced over at me. "That's why, isn't it? Because I'm a reporter?"

"Well, duh." I tilted my head to one side. "We usually don't like to make headlines." A shiver ran down my spine at the memory of the Winters image. "It's pretty easy to discredit the odd photo here and there, make it out to be some sort of faked shot or some silly kid in a Halloween costume."

"Except I'm the one who started all this." He collapsed into his seat, the dismay evident on his face. "I'm the one who published that photograph."

"Which was sent to you by the killer." I omitted the part where he had been a viable suspect. "Who wanted you to publish it to show that we're not invulnerable. And to try and bring attention to our kind. 'What is she?' was your cue to find out who we are and expose us to the world." I walked back to the marble island and picked up one of the folders. "And these were the three men who, in their Felis form, had a white streak down one side of their nose."

"Which explains why they look nothing like each other in those photos," Bran murmured. "Not likely you'd keep that on file, eh?"

"I don't know," I confessed. "All I know is that the family has files on everyone but doesn't give it out to anyone who's not either on the Board or who's got a darned good reason. All I had coming out of the farm was three names. Ruth was the one who broke the rules and gave us the rest."

"They're that tough?" Bran shook his head. "And here I thought getting info out of the government was bad."

"Worse." I clipped the three bags of fur back into their respective folders. "And all hell's going to break loose when they find out that I got hold of these."

"Even if it helps you catch the killer?" He crossed over to stand across from me again and picked up the small furry ball he had originally collected from my house. "I don't mean to be judgmental here, but you're talking about a murderer within your own community."

"I know." I drew a deep breath, trying to put my thoughts into coherent words. "You have to understand that we really don't have to deal with this sort of thing. Murder is just…" A hand waved in the air. "We fight. Oh Lord, we fight. But Felis don't just kill Felis. Not outside of our justice system. Secrecy is our first rule and our most important. It's good to a degree but it's hell on an investigation."

"So you're fighting the system." A weak smile crept across Bran's face.

"Basically." I nodded. "The system works to protect

us and keep us secret from the outside world. Except now the outside world isn't the enemy."

"The enemy is us."

"Yep. Now you see the problem. Which is why Ruth broke the rules by giving me those files. It would have taken days or weeks for me to track down those three names without the files, and longer for me to actually determine who was and wasn't a viable suspect." I tapped the small fur sample with my finger.

"Sounds to me like someone wanted to make your job as hard as possible. Go by the rules line by line, word by word. Considering it's an inside job, I'm not surprised."

"Whoa." I held up one hand. "But they hired me to find the killer. It may be someone inside the family but we're not talking anyone on the Board." At least not now that I had cleared Dennis.

Brandon leaned in, his scent washing over me and threatening to derail my train of thought.

"I guess they wanted you to have to work for it." He laughed. "So you were able to determine which batch of fur matched the one in the house by just smelling them?"

"Well, it's a whole series of sensory inputs," I babbled, glad for the chance to maneuver the conversation away from internal politics. "When I was in the alleyway I could tell that it was one of the family by the scent, but not who specifically. Then when he was attacking me I got a full whiff of him, allowing me to make a match." My fingers moved over the table to the thick ball of black and brown colored fur. "I expect if we went back to my place and grabbed that sample from the alley it'd match this one."

"Amazing. Just amazing." He gazed at me, the gentleness in his eyes breaking down all my defenses.

"What?"

"You. Them. This." He swept his hand over the files. "I knew there was something different about you, something I liked."

I swallowed, feeling the butterflies in my stomach flap like a tissue in a twister. It'd been a long time since I'd considered going to bed with anyone, much less someone who knew my secrets. I didn't want to screw this up but I couldn't see any way around the tough questions. "You're not...uncomfortable with me? Knowing who I am?"

"I knew who you were when I met you in the bar." He moved in, his voice low and soft.

"You knew one part of me." I closed my eyes.

"I knew enough." His lips grazed my earlobe, stopping to tug lightly on the delicate skin. "What you were before, what I was before, that doesn't matter in the long run. It shouldn't matter. It's what we are now, where we go from here that defines us."

"I don't Change anymore." I gasped as he bit down just a bit, catching the skin between his teeth. The sharp pain drummed down my veins, sending a rush of heat below my waist. "I may have manifested the claws during the fight, but that's all."

"You sure?" he whispered. "Not that I mind. I've been scratched before."

"Not like this." I couldn't help smirking. "I could mark you for life."

One hand crept around my waist while the other pulled my shirt free of my jeans. "I hope so." The fingers paused. "I shouldn't be looking for a tail or something, should I?"

I chuckled. "No, no tail. Not now, anyway."

"Good." The hand on my waist slid lower. "Not that I'd be offended…"

The breath caught in my throat. "You don't find me… disgusting?"

He pulled back and moved around to stare at me, nose-to-nose. "Why would I?"

"Well," I swallowed, his scent whirling around me like a F5 twister, "I'm not exactly your normal human."

Bran nodded. "No, you're not." A soft smile appeared on his face. "Doesn't matter if you got fur in strange spots or not, I'm still liking you a lot."

"A lot?"

"A whole lot." His head dipped down to snatch a quick kiss. "And, frankly, I don't feel like talking right now."

"An investigative reporter who doesn't want to talk?" A moan escaped as his lips began to work along the side of my neck, nipping and tugging at my exposed skin. I rolled back in his arms, letting him nibble wherever he wanted.

"If I recall my Animal Planet shows accurately, offering yourself up in such a vulnerable position shows that you trust me." The whisper threatened to shatter what little reserve I had left as he pulled my shirt over my head and tossed it out of sight.

I fumbled with his shirt, fingers numb with anticipation. "Maybe. Okay, yes." I ran my hands over his chest, pleasantly surprised at the light fur covering his skin. "Maybe you've got a little Felis in you after all."

"Maybe. Does that mean I get to be on top?" A tingle ran down my spine as he drew his fingers leisurely down my back, stroking the scarred skin before expertly snapping my bra open. "Or do I have to wrestle you for it?"

"Maybe. Yes. I don't know." I let out a sigh, surrendering to the mixture of emotions, exhaustion and plain old lust drowning me. "Shut up and keep touching me."

BRAN ROLLED ONTO his back an hour later, wheezing slightly. "Dang. I'm exhausted."

"Liar." I put my hand on his bare chest and ran it slowly down his skin, slipping under the comforter to my ultimate goal. "Looks like you're not totally done."

"You bring out the best in me." He leaned in to capture my mouth in a deep kiss.

"And you bring out the worst in me." I groaned as I twisted to one side, feeling my muscles protest. "I'm not sure but I think I've just broken one of the Pride rules."

"Rules?" Bran frowned.

"Sleeping with a human after telling him all our secrets."

"Ah." He grabbed my hand and placed it back on his chest. "I'm sure there's an exception there under 'interrogation' or something like that. Always a loophole somewhere to exploit."

"And yet," I replied, "will you call me in the morning?" A tremble crept into my voice, unbidden. It was one thing to have a one-night stand, another to have a lover who knew all about me. And if it was the first option then there would be repercussions that would extend far beyond this encounter.

"Sure. And in the afternoon and in the evening." Bran leaned forward and placed a kiss on my forehead. "I'm not a casual-sex type of guy." He locked eyes with me. "I'm not going to tell you I'm ready for a commitment beyond what we've got right now but I can promise you that I'll keep your secret right here." He pulled my hand further up his chest, over his heart. "Forever."

"Thank you." Tears came to my eyes.

Bran kissed the tips of my fingers before curling his hand around mine. "However, and I do hate to say it, we should get back to work. All play and no work… whatever."

I let out a deep sigh and withdrew my hand. "Spoil-sport. And here I thought you men were made of stronger stuff."

"Oh." He sat up and grabbed at his chest in a mock heart attack. "You wound me."

When I spied a few deep scratches on his arms and exposed skin, I winced. "Not quite, but I'll be gentler next time." I threw the blanket off and padded naked toward the kitchen, picking up various pieces of my clothing as I went along. "Coffee or tea?" It was quite a relief to not have to hide my back from him. Still, my shirt was the first and only piece of clothing that went back on.

"Any Chinese food left?" Bran yelled after me. "I seem to have worked up quite an appetite."

"Don't know why. I was doing most of the work." I peeked inside the near-empty containers. "Probably enough for a plate or two, if we're not greedy."

He appeared at the marble island, pulling his T-shirt back on and hopping from one foot to the other as he stepped into a fresh pair of underwear. "Wait a minute. I'm not, like, sworn to you now or something strange like that, am I?"

I grinned at him, my head cocked to one side. "Oh, now you ask. What, you afraid that now you're part of a secret male sex slave harem?"

"Ooh!" He rubbed his hands together, a wide childish grin on his face. "Promise?"

"Only in your dreams." I dumped the contents of the containers out onto two fresh plates, mixing the assorted remains into a heap. "You reheat. I always burn this sort of stuff."

"Right." He stepped around the counter and gave me a quick peck on the cheek before retreating to the microwave with the two plates.

Suddenly my ears caught the low trilling ring of my cell phone. My eyes went to the three folders sitting on the table where we had left them.

Playtime was officially over.

I strode across the room and dug my cell phone out of my leather jacket's pocket.

"Reb, we need to talk." Jess's voice was harsh and low.

"Langley. I need to know what relatives he has, what kids are out there."

The silence on the line hung between us for a few minutes. "Not now."

"What you mean, not now?" My voice rose.

"Ruth's dead."

The cell phone fell from my numb fingers and bounced along the hardwood floor for a few feet before skidding to a stop. Bran raced over, dropping to his knees and catching me as I collapsed. He snatched up the phone with one hand and barked into the receiver. "What happened?"

"Who is this?" Jess roared, so loudly that I could hear her. "Where's Reb?"

"She's right here. What did you say to her?" He ignored the question, hugging me close. "What did you say?"

"Let me talk to her," She demanded again, louder this time.

I plucked the phone out of Bran's tight grip.

"What happened? Who did it?" I ground my teeth, my anger growing with every second.

"No one killed her. She fell and broke her neck in the barn." A crack in Jess's armor showed, a sob breaking loose. "Damn it, Reb…She didn't deserve this."

"Who does?" I leaned into Brandon's warmth and closed my eyes. "What happened?"

"It was an accident." The words came through clenched teeth. "She fell off the ladder and broke her neck while trying to get to some of the barn cats. She always had a soft spot for the kittens."

"Where's Ruth now?" Bran's eyes went wide when he realized who I was talking about.

"She's already at the funeral home. She had no living family, so gonna be buried out back, where she wanted to be." Her voice cracked again. "Damn it, girl…I'm gonna miss her. She was one fine woman."

My gaze went to the folders sitting in the kitchen, just out of sight. "She was. We'll be there tomorrow for the funeral."

"The reporter?" The ice crept back into her tone. "You can't bring him here again. Things are going to be tense enough, you don't want to bring a firebrand to a pool of gasoline."

"No one will do anything to him. Not unless you call for it and if you do, the whole deal's off." My jaw tightened, the low growl escaping with unfamiliar strength. "One hair on his head gets out of place, I rip some throats out."

"Hardly a threat you can carry out." The retort was sharp and fast.

"I have as much right to be there as anyone else." I let my breath out slowly. "Jess, she would have wanted me to be there, no matter what. You know that."

"Granted," she grumbled.

"Are you sure it was an accident?" I winced inwardly, dreading the explosion about to erupt. "Ruth...Ruth gave me some files I think she wasn't supposed to give me."

"What?" Instead of yelling, her voice went calm. This scared me even more.

"She gave me a pie on the way out. In the box were the Pride files on the three names you gave me." I waited a second before continuing. "It's possible that the killer found out."

"Hmm." I could almost see her nodding, her expression thoughtful. Jess loved to solve logic problems. She could work her way through one of those cheap volumes from the corner store within a day when she put her mind to it. "We assumed it was an accident since she's never had an issue with anyone. You know everyone loved the old gal."

"Well, I think someone did have an issue." I glanced at Bran. "But I wouldn't tell the rest of the Board yet."

"Why?"

"Because this might involve them." I plunged ahead, not caring about how it might sound. "Jess, Davis wasn't at the meeting. You told me that he wasn't keen on me having any access to the files, not even for you to give me names. You cut a deal to give me just the names, I'm guessing."

"Davis wasn't there because he had a business meeting to attend in Midland. He approved of our decision. He suggested we just give you the names."

"Maybe he found out that Ruth gave me the files."

"Hell of an accusation to make, kit. Got something to back it up?"

"Nothing but a suggestion you take another look." I shook my head. "I'm coming tomorrow and I'm bringing Brandon Hanover. Period."

"I'll alert them that due to…extenuating circumstances we're allowing an outsider there. Just make sure he doesn't do anything stupid." She growled, sounding more like the Jess I knew and feared years ago. "Like fall in love with you."

I cut the connection.

Bran looked at me. "Guess I'm not the most popular person out there today, eh?"

I let him cradle me in his arms. "Right now I've probably got that spot. Let's just say that it's not all that acceptable for us to mingle with the common folk."

He chuckled and dropped kisses into my disheveled hair. "They don't know what they're missing."

"Yeah. Missing." I let out a sob, the reality sinking in that one of my oldest friends was gone and that I could possibly have contributed to her death. I buried my face in Bran's chest, letting the tears flow.

"Tell me about her," he whispered, running his fingers through my hair. "Tell me something you remember."

It was my first solo hunt, the brisk morning air burning my lungs as I leaped over the low fence and dashed through the tall grass. The rabbit's scent was hot in my nostrils as I tried to remember all the tips and tricks the others had told me.

Suddenly the ground fell out under me, my left foot disappearing into a deep hole while I continued forward. I fell to the ground with a scream, hands flailing ad trying to grab something, anything to break my fall.

But it was useless, my ankle was broken and now I had more to worry about than just failing in the Hunt. So I did what I did best and what Ruth had encouraged me to do—improvise and adapt.

It took two hours of waiting in pain and silence, not moving an inch, before the rabbit hopped close enough for me to reach out and grab it. I snapped the neck with a growl and tore into the hot meat. At least I wouldn't starve before someone found me.

"So this is how you repay me. Late for dinner." Ruth appeared out of the brush. Downright beautiful in her Change with red highlights in her tawny fur, she crouched by me and clucked her tongue as she examined my ankle. "Broken, that's sure. Let's get you back to the house and I'll set it up." She grinned and took the rabbit corpse out of my hands. "And I've got fresh apple pie for dessert."

"So she carried you back." Bran wiped away a tear, drawing his fingers across my face. "And you passed?"

"With flying colors." I sniffled. "The Board was impressed that I could work 'outside the box.' At least, then they were." My words hardened as I remembered the circumstances that had brought me to this place and to Ruth's death.

"How about a bit of a rest?" Bran rocked me back and forth. "Let's grab a fast meal and head back to bed."

"We'll eat then I'll need your computer for a bit." I wriggled free. "I want to do some research on Langley before we go up there tomorrow. Besides…" I tapped him on the tip of his nose. "I believe you need some time to regain your stamina."

Bran huffed, mock anger on his face. "Why, I never!"

"Probably. But you can be taught." I crawled to the computer desk and hit the buttons to activate the system. "And don't forget the diet soda." My jeans were draped over the back of the office chair and I shuffled my way into them. "Actually, forget the diet part. Sugar is what I need right now." I settled into the chair, trying to tune out the man hovering nearby. "And put more clothes on, please. No distractions."

"Only if you do the same." A pair of jeans flew by me. I grinned and began getting dressed.

I closed my eyes and I took a series of deep breaths, trying to reach that quiet place again. Ruth had been in my life for as long as I could remember, helping me through the difficult years after my parents died.

She had been the one to dress my wounds after that last, horrible Challenge, none of the other Pride members daring or wanting to come near an outcast.

"You stay in touch with me, no matter where you go," she had murmured, pressing cool moist strips against my burning skin. I had flinched under her touch, tears running down my face.

"But the rules say—" I had bitten down on my lip, stifling another yelp as the bandages shifted. The social workers had been called, the front story arranged to say I'd been injured in a farm accident and just couldn't stay out of foster care any longer. We were to meet on the dirt road as far from the farm as I could walk, making the exile and my banishment as public as possible.

"I don't 'do' rules. You stay in touch with me. Send me one of those April Fool's cards every year. I'll know who it's from."

And I had. Every year on the first of April I had sent out a generic card with no return address. I never received any cards but she knew I was alive and that would have to be enough.

Closing my eyes, I forced the memories back. Ruth's

death would be meaningless if I couldn't find a way to connect it to Davis, Davis to Langley, and Langley to Janey's killer and my attacker. I stared at the computer screen, fingers resting on the keyboard. Time to get my head into the game.

An hour later I had little more than I had started out with. Bran frowned when I banged the dark oak desk with one hand.

"Hey, don't blame the messenger." He sprawled on the couch with his phone up to one ear. At least he had read my mood enough to keep his distance, choosing to hog the lines and work his own angles. "I'm still trying to get through to my contacts in the RCMP. They might have a file on Langley." Bran hopped back up and began to pace around the floor as if we were on a hunt together. I could almost imagine him creeping with me through the woods, tracking our prey.

"Except our attacker isn't really him." I stared at the screen as if my scowling would bring up the information I wanted. "It's not quite him, it's some sort of relative. I can't exactly explain it or put it better than that."

"I don't really get it, but okay." He came up behind me, pushing the ponytail out of the way to kiss my neck. "By the way, where'd your tail go?"

"My what?" I was still distracted by the lack of progress.

"Your tail." He trapped the phone between his chin and shoulder and wiggled his butt at me. "That long thing that keeps getting trapped under rocking chairs and all. You said you didn't have one now, so what happens to it?"

I cut him off with a wave of my hand, middle finger extended. "Surprised you remember that bit of the conversation. Actually, that disappears after the first year. We stop changing into full feline form, we end up a sort of hybrid human-Felidae as you saw in the photo. The tail ends up being absorbed into the body. We don't have them as adults at all."

"Dang. Make a nice little fashion accessory." He wriggled his behind as he strode on by, encouraging me to reach out and slap him on that sweet little ass.

My cell phone began to ring. I put it to my ear. "Yes?"

"I'm looking for Ms. Desjardin. This is the Toronto Police Service." It wasn't Hank or anyone I had worked with.

"You've got her. What's up?" I steeled myself for yet more bad news. The cops never called to just say hello.

"Do you still reside at 333 Triller Avenue?"

"Yes." My pulse began to increase exponentially with each word. "I'm at a friend's right now. What's wrong?"

"I'm sorry to inform you that someone broke into your house last night. Neighborhood Watch reported the incident and a patrol car arrived soon after. We were unable to find an intruder but we did secure the scene. How soon can you come home?"

"I'm on the way." I hung up on him and pushed the chair back from the computer desk with such fury I think it left skid marks.

"*Merde!*" I grabbed my jacket, startling Bran who was still waiting on his own connection. "I have to go." I wheezed as I struggled to get my shoes on.

"What happened?" Bran bounced to his feet and walked over to me. "What's wrong?"

"My place was trashed last night." I dug in my back pocket and found my wallet. My fingers trembled as I checked the contents. All my credit cards were there. I knew my house and car keys were in my jacket pocket. At least I didn't have to worry about identity theft, not right now. "I have to go see what's left. Five bucks says that Attersley's there as well, wanting to know what's going on and if it's got anything to do with the Winters case."

TWELVE

"YOU SHOULDN'T DRIVE." Bran plucked the car keys from my numb fingers. "It'll be fine." He stroked my cheek with one finger. "It'll be fine."

"No, no it won't." I shook my head, looking back toward the folders on the table. "I'm not sure if it's ever going to be fine again."

Bran pulled me into a bear hug. "It'll all be okay. I won't let anything happen to you."

I chuckled into the shirt, smelling both of our scents on the fabric. "Don't try to play the tough guy. It doesn't work for you."

"Oh, sure. Mock my inherent manliness." The exaggerated sigh tickled my ear. "At least let me pretend to be your protector."

I nodded. "Just don't get in the way if it starts going physical. You have no idea how rough Felis can be."

Hanover grinned, reaching back and patting his back with one hand. "Oh, I think I have some idea."

I jerked a thumb toward the door, feeling my face get warm. "Let's get going before something else happens."

We made our way to the elevator and down to the parking garage, my heart rate rising with each step. I slid in on the passenger side and wondered about insurance, repairs.

Jazz.

We drove in silence, Bran allowing me to be alone with my thoughts while he maneuvered the Jeep along

King Street. We got stuck behind a streetcar that was obviously not the real Red Rocket, the driver spending an inordinate amount of time at each light and stop. Bran glanced over at me and yanked the wheel to one side, racing up a side street and pulling us back onto Queen Street.

We slowed down to a crawl when we turned onto Triller and pulled into a rare parking spot not far from my house. There were two police cars in the narrow street, one of the uniformed officers leaning on his car's hood and scowling as a prostitute walked by, waving at the man with a wide grin. I didn't have the heart to tell him that "she" was a "he" who had better legs than most women I knew, including myself. Cosmic injustice.

The plainclothes detective met me at the space previously occupied by my front door, a young pup who stared at me with a bland, textbook-home-invasion-file-report-and-leave look. "Yeah?" He scowled.

I wasn't in any mood to play with a kid. "I know Attersley's here. Get him." I scowled back, knowing mine was much better.

The young man stared at me for a second. He turned and cupped his hands around his mouth before bellowing up my stairs, "Hank? Some woman here to see you!" He returned to his previous position of leaning against the wall while studying his notes.

"Hey." Attersley let out a sigh as he trotted down the stairs, the standard brown suit stretched to its limits on his oversized frame. "Sorry you had to come home to this." The balding overweight detective glared at Bran. "You gotta be Hanover."

"Good to know my rep's still going 'round the station." Bran said as he caught up with me.

The front door, well…wasn't. It had been kicked in,

the wooden door blasted off the hinges and lying in my hallway, heavy shoeprints all over it. The forensic peeps were still all over it. Hank nodded at me.

He glanced at the reporter for a second, then back to me. "Any reason why someone would want to break into your place?"

I shook my head. "Between thee and me, Hank, nothing I was working on would create this sort of reaction. Nothing." I hated to lie to him but I had no choice. As it was, staying at Brandon's for the night may well have saved my life.

A white blur sped by one of the CSI men, startling the dark blue coveralls enough to have him jump back a foot and scramble for his pistol. The ghost resolved at my feet—Jazz, wide-eyed and bushytailed.

I reached down and waited, allowing her to climb into my arms at her own speed. She wasn't a young kitten anymore and just a bit arthritic, so it took her a little bit longer to do anything. The burst of energy we had just witnessed might have just burnt her out for the day.

She snuggled into my chest and began to purr, a rumbling torrent of happiness at finding me again and of relative safety. I stroked her long Persian fur and mumbled to her while I waited for the investigators to finish. Her body began to go slack, getting heavier as the old girl began to relax.

"No idea what they took, if anything. Looks more like they just trashed the place from top to bottom." The senior officer talked to Hank, within earshot of the two of us. "No prints on the door. Guy was smart enough to use gloves for that. Got a good set of footprints, but without something or someone to match them with, well…" He shrugged and closed up his metal chipboard.

"Right." Resting his thumbs on his bulging waistline

and belt, Attersley turned to the two of us. "They'll be out in a few minutes. I'd call up the insurance adjuster and then see what you can salvage."

He handed me an unfamiliar business card, a fat construction worker grinning off the glossy cardboard at me. "They'll come and help board up the doors and windows. Tell them you know me. Get you a good rate." He scowled at Bran. "Be careful about the company you keep, Reb."

The stout detective turned to walk away and stumbled over a loose piece of stone, recovering in time to strut toward his unmarked bronze sedan. The two police cars eased their way out of the narrow street with enough three-point turns to make a puzzle expert green with envy.

I looked at the gaping maw of the front door while the remaining investigators packed up their tackle boxes and headed for their van.

Jazz purred loudly from her position in my arms, her claws digging into my jacket.

"I have to go in now," I whispered to the white cat. "You just behave yourself, okay? I'm glad you weren't hurt." She let out an angry meow, as if to challenge my assessment of her attack abilities.

I entered the front door with a slow shuffling step, trying not to squeeze the life out of the cat. My night-vision kicked in just in time to be confronted with the devastation.

It looked like I had been hosting a frat party for the boys from hell. My couch torn open and the stuffing scattered everywhere, my office desk's drawers smashed into kindling and anything resembling a piece of paper torn and shredded.

"Wonder what they were looking for." Bran appeared

beside me. He reached out for Jazz, pausing as she surveyed the outstretched hand with her nose twitching for a few seconds. Her purr skipped a beat and then continued when he stroked her head. "Hey, sweetie. Glad you're okay."

Jazz let out a growl, her claws digging into the leather just enough to let me know that she knew and agreed with my assessment.

It hadn't been a random break and enter, no mob of crack-heads looking for something to sell for a few rocks of happiness.

Someone had been looking for something.

I took a deep breath, filling my lungs with the smells and scents of the house. The different odors mixed and matched around me, jumbled up with the policemen and the different outdoors smells they were carrying along with aftershave, other women and men and one definite cough-drop-hiding-the-booze flavor. I couldn't tell if it was any of the men from the files or my original attacker. It was all just a jumbled blur threatening to make me throw up.

Brandon looked at me. "Let's get out of here." He stepped over a piece of wood once belonging to the bottom of my couch, now jutting into the air like a flagpole. "Do you need anything from here? I mean, right now."

I shook my head. I was numb from the inside out, my brain freezing up like I'd swallowed a gallon of ice cream.

"Let's go back to my place. You can deal with this later."

"He was here looking for me. For any information I had that could lead to him."

"Davis looking for the files?"

I shrugged. "Maybe. Maybe not. Could have been Langley, could have been the kid looking for a rematch."

Bran stroked Jazz under her chin, encouraging her to loosen her grip on me. "Whoever it is, he arrives and you're not here. If he's looking for the files he's tearing up the house to search for them and comes up empty. If not he's just trashing the house 'cause he's pissed you're gone." He glanced toward the kitchen.

I spotted the remains of the Brown Betty on the floor.

"Damn. That was my favorite."

Jazz trilled for attention, drawing my eyes to hers. She pawed at my arm once before pushing her way under my jacket, snuggling next to my warm body.

She had the right idea. "Let's go." I looked down at the white bundle nestled in the crook of my arm. "Does your corner store deliver?"

"If they don't, now they will." Bran pulled his cell phone out. "Name it."

"First let's call these guys." I handed him the card, still cradling the fuzzaloid. "Just dial it and hand it to me. I don't think I want to let her go right now."

The workmen assured me they would have the house sealed up within the hour, instantly snapping to virtual attention when I mentioned my police reference.

"Just secure it. I'll worry about getting back in later." I shifted the dead weight in my arms. She had fallen asleep. "All I'm looking for right now is making sure that no one wanders in before I get a chance to get the insurance people out here." The supervisor responded by saying the workmen would put a padlock on the front door then drop the key off with Dan, my favorite doorman, within the hour. I handed the phone back to Bran.

"We're good." I drew in a sharp breath and looked around me. A bowl filled with dried flowers had rolled across the hardwood floor, dumping out the cheap pot-pourri inside. My stomach lurched at the image of some man searching through my bedroom, my bathroom. Tearing my life apart.

"Let's go." Bran's arm went around me and started to pull me out of the debris. "We can wait in the car if you want until the guys arrive."

"No, let's go." My voice was an octave higher than normal. "I don't want to be here right now."

Bran helped me into the passenger seat of my car yet again, stopping to stroking Jazz's head where she lay on my lap sound asleep.

She remained that way the entire drive back to the condo, probably in part because I couldn't stop petting her. The old street cat had moved in years ago and it was difficult imagining my life without her.

Dan nodded with a tip of his hat when we stopped at the front desk on our way up, not even raising an eyebrow at the sight of the white bundle in my arms, listening to the details and stating he would be waiting for the workmen. Bran unlocked his door and stepped aside, letting me walk in first.

"What do you need?" He picked up the receiver while we settled onto the couch.

"Litter box, litter and food." I looked down at the sleeping cat with a smile. "And just so you know—she snores."

"Just like her owner." Bran chuckled.

Less than an hour later Jazz let out a loud meow and climbed down from my lap as Bran filled a huge soup bowl with dried cat food. She dropped her face into it as if she hadn't eaten for days. I rolled my eyes from where I sat on the leather couch.

"Drama queen." I turned my attention back to the

Langley file, now spread out in front of me on the coffee table. The other two had been tucked away out of sight in what Bran called his "safe place"—a wall safe that probably could be broken into by an experienced safecracker, but I didn't want to discourage the man.

Frank Langley had a pretty boring life. He had left the local Pride and gone to North Bay to marry Kelly Purvis, a member of another Pride from out West. They had no children and nothing of note in the file. Even if he had access to a private jet, he couldn't have travelled down to Toronto and back out again multiple times to accomplish the killing and now the various attacks on me. Not to mention his wife being sworn to expose him if he dared to put the Pride at risk. And no motive to speak of—I doubted he had ever even heard of Janey. She was too young to have been with him in the same group of kits and he was too old to have much to do with a kit like her.

I ran my finger over the printout, looking for anything that would explain how his scent, slightly warped and diluted, ended up in my house and on Janey Winters's body. There were no children in the marriage, no previous marriages on either side.

"We should get going." Bran's voice jolted me out of my reverie, low and sad as his hands landed on my shoulders, squeezing lightly. "I'll drive, if you want."

My mouth opened and closed. I had totally forgotten about Ruth's funeral. Covering my face with both hands, I shook my head. "I didn't even look at the clock."

"It's okay." He leaned down to stroke Jazz's back as the white cat hopped up and settled beside me on the black leather couch. "Been a rough few hours."

"You said it." I got up and gave a low laugh as the feline moved over, curling up in the warm spot in a satisfied ball of fur. "I'll drive." I nodded in response to his concerned glance. "I need to do something right now."

We didn't stop for coffee and donuts on the way up.

Bran cleared his throat every few minutes, fidgeting with the tie he had fastened over the dress shirt. He had kept the jeans on, giving in to my request to not make it too fancy. Myself, I was still wearing the shirt and pants from the previous day. Or two. I wasn't sure, but I hadn't wanted to go shopping and actually deal with anything other than the case at hand. Besides, hopefully the smell would keep other members at bay.

Bran's hand rested on my knee for most of the way up, squeezing lightly whenever he saw how tightly my jaw was clenched. It wasn't a good day to start anything, much less continue an investigation.

The parking lot was full when we arrived at the farm, every square foot of gravel taken up by cars in a thousand shapes and sizes, from huge Hummers threatening to dominate the skyline to small Austin Coopers looking like little clown cars. I slipped the Jeep into a space at the back, as close to the road as possible.

I wanted a quick escape route.

Bran looked at me, the question written on his face. I undid the seatbelt and laid my head back, closing my eyes. It was hard to find the words, much less force them into a coherent sentence through the exhaustion.

"This is going to be...difficult. Outsiders aren't usually allowed anywhere near the farm, much less to a funeral."

"I'm sure there's a nice little cemetery out back to hide the bodies." His grin disappeared as he saw my serious expression. "Right. And you're bringing me here."

"And I'm bringing you." I stared at a particularly menacing pickup truck across from us, the red-and-orange flames flaring out from the jet-black paint. "But, as I've been reminded many times, I was outcast and thus create a rather interesting predicament as far as the rules go. I'm sworn to the Pride's laws as much as I want to be."

"Sorta like being Catholic." Bran laughed.

"Exactly. Think of yourself as one of those heathen Protestants walking into a group of rabid Catholics." I opened my eyes and reached into my jacket pocket and handed him my Taser. "If anything happens, anything—use this, get back here to the car and run." I took the keys out of the ignition and put them into his hand. "Don't worry about me. They won't kill me."

"You think." He tilted his head to one side. "Like you said, you're a bit of a special case."

"True. They may beat me up but they won't kill me." I kissed him lightly on the lips. "And if anything happens, please take care of Jazz. She's old and grumpy, but she's like a little sister to me."

Before he could respond, I opened the car door and hopped out. My feet began crunching on the gravel as I walked toward the main house. To one side stood the barn, once a pleasant childhood memory but now a crime scene. I'd never be able to think of it in any other way now. A stiff wind brought a thousand scents washing over me, filling my mind's eye with images of people I hadn't thought about for decades.

Jess was the first to appear, wearing a dark-blue dress that had gone out of style twenty years ago and was now back in style. She trotted down the steps from the porch and approached us at a goodly speed, intercepting us before we got close enough for our scent to be carried too far.

"Reb." She hugged me, pointedly ignoring Brandon.

"What's the word?" I pushed my emotions down again, fighting the urge to cry like a lost child.

"The service was held down the lane, at the chapel. Just finished not long ago." She pointed back the way we had come. "She's due here anytime to be placed in the graveyard." Her nose wrinkled. "You're pushing your luck, you know."

"Nothing new there." I stuck my hands in my pockets to keep them from trembling. "Have you done any more investigating since we spoke?"

"Yes. And you'll find out soon enough." She glared at Bran. "You realize that if you speak of any of this, even the slightest whisper, that you will be hunted down and killed?"

"I got that impression." He rocked back and forth on his heels. "But thanks for the warning. And the wonderful welcome."

"Don't be. You're still not out of here alive."

"Someone trashed my place last night." The words brought Jess's attention back to me, where I wanted it. "Someone was looking for those files."

"It wasn't Davis. He hasn't left the farm for days."

"Are you sure?" Bran asked.

The steely gaze had broken lesser kits. He didn't wilt but he didn't challenge her.

"I'll check on it." She spun on her heel and walked away from us, back toward the house.

"Where should we go?" I hated asking but she'd know where we'd be best placed.

Jess stopped on the steps and looked back over her shoulder. "You should go to the graveyard and wait. We'll be there soon enough."

"Not even invited into the house? Rough crowd," Bran said to me in a loud whisper as I led him to a small path leading between the main house and the barn. "Not even a cup of coffee? More pie?"

I took his hand. "No offense, but I'd cut back on the sarcasm for today. In fact, it'd probably be a good idea for you to stay as silent as possible." My mind was racing through probable scenarios while we made our way along the stone walkway. "And, for God's sake, don't challenge anyone. Stay behind me and look as small and insignificant as you can. Slump your shoulders. Don't stare directly at anyone. Don't let yourself be goaded into a fight."

"Because it'd be unsightly at a funeral?"

"Because you'd lose."

Bran frowned as we approached the graveyard. "Don't have a lot of faith in me, do you?"

"Not when it comes to these men. I've seen them take out twelve-point deer with their bare hands on a hunt."

A small crowd was already beginning to gather at the far corner of the graveyard. The wrought-iron gates connected to the fence running around the five acres of land were open for one of the few times that I had recalled—more often than not Felis chose to be cremated and their ashes spread across the Farm fields to nurture future crops.

I walked Bran between rows of stone crosses that had been there for generations, some so old the rain had washed the names off, leaving anonymous white-stained lines no one remembered. When we approached the newer rows, I led him off to one side.

The slate-gray monument held two names. A stone angel perched atop with his trumpet pointed at the heavens.

Bran looked at the engraved names. "Your parents."

I knelt down and pulled a handful of weeds out from one side.

He looked around. "Are these all your…relatives?"

"In a way." I stood up and gestured to one side. "Plenty of history here." The crowd was beginning to grow, people walking past us on the path. One man turned and glaring at us, his mouth falling open as if to protest. A woman yanked on his sleeve and silenced him with a look. She scowled at me before pushing her mate onward with a hard shove between his shoulders.

"Let's go." I took Bran's hand and returned to the main trail leading to the freshly dug grave, slipping into an empty spot in the slow parade.

The polished wood coffin lay across the open space, suspended by a pair of strong canvas straps. Custom dictated that the Board members lower the body, with family assisting. With no one else alive on Ruth's behalf it would only be the two men and Jess, all of whom stood before the grave.

Dennis fumbled with his tie, Jess scowled at the clouds and Davis nibbled at his fingernails. Around them the rest of the Pride began to gather, men and women dressed in everything from black suits to track suits and casual wear.

Jess cleared her throat, being the First. "Ruth Huckleton was a good woman. She cared for our young with the compassion and patience of a saint—which I'm sure was sorely tested by many of the kits she helped raise."

A soft ripple of laughter ran through the crowd. I stayed at the back, downwind, with Bran behind me. I could just see the edge of the coffin. Nothing fancy, just a plain box. Felis rarely put money into fancy memorials and the like. The angel on my parents' grave was an exception. Ruth had been the one to show me the small sculpture, paying for it out of her own pocket. "Your parents deserve something better than just that." She had perched the angel on the top of the grave marker. "I'll make sure they glue it good."

"She was truly one of a kind. And she will be sorely missed." Jess's eyes sought me out through the crowd, somehow locking right onto me like a guided missile. "We will not see her type come this way again."

She took hold of one of the straps. The two Board members moved around the open grave to pick up their own, wrapping the loose ends around their forearms. Two men stepped forward to pull out the wooden planks holding the coffin up, the Board men shifting forward in the upturned dirt as they took control of the weight. I sucked in my breath, hoping Jess would be strong enough to lower the coffin without dropping it. With only three of them it was a concern, the box wobbling from side to side.

The coffin began to descend slowly but evenly into the grave. A collective sigh went up from the gathered members as it disappeared from view. I stared straight ahead between the bodies, trying to see my old friend for one last time.

The three released the straps and tossed them into the grave after the coffin. Dennis pulled out a handkerchief from one pocket of his suit and dabbed at his eyes. Jess looked down into the open hole. Davis shuffled his feet and scratched his nose.

Jess suddenly spun around and grabbed Davis by the lapels of his jacket. "Why did you do it? Why?" she roared into the startled man's face.

The dark-haired man tried to stumble backward, out of Jess's grip but was unable to. "What? What are you talking about?" He glanced around the crowd. "I don't know what she's talking about!"

I moved forward, pushing my way through the crowd. "Jess! Jess!"

One senior spun around, gripping the hand of his elderly mate. "What—" His eyes went wide when he recognized me. "Rebecca." He spat the words out like a curse.

"Jess, what are you doing?" I stood on the edge of the grave and watched as she picked Davis up with one hand, wrapping it around his throat and swinging the hapless man out over the gaping hole. No one moved. All eyes were on Jess.

She turned her head just far enough to one side to let me know she had me in her sights before returning her full attention to the terrified man in her grasp. "I went and checked the barn. I found the break in the ladder. I know you put it there—I smelled your foul stench on the wood." The words came out in angry puffs, her Change already beginning. "Why did you kill her?"

Davis's face went scarlet as he went limp, his feet dangling in the air. "What did you expect me to do? She shouldn't have broken the rules!" One arm flailed out toward me. "Ruth did it for her. A misfit. She ignored the rules for her."

"And you killed her for that?" Jess roared and tossed Davis to one side. The man bounced once, twice in the damp soil before he skidded to a stop. People moved away as if he were contagious.

"Jess, this isn't anyone's business but ours." He got to his feet and stabbed a finger at me. "We should have kept it in the Pride. We had no need to call in a misfit!"

"That decision was debated and decided on by the Board." The words were said in a calm, deliberate way as she rubbed her hands together. "And you disrespected that along with murdering one of our own."

"No." Davis shook his head. "No. She broke the rules and had to be punished." His eyes raced through the murmuring crowd, seeking out someone. "She needed to be taught a lesson. I did what had to be done to keep the family secure."

"You could have challenged her," Jess snarled. "You could have brought it to the Board. What made you think you could do this by yourself?" She shook her head. "You knew there was a chance she'd be seriously hurt, that she wouldn't be able to catch herself like a younger woman might. But you went ahead and did it anyway."

"I had to," Davis babbled. "It was for the best. We have to keep our business to ourselves." Again he looked into the mob, a furtive desperate glance.

I spun around, looking for whomever he was talking to, but it was hopeless with the crushing mass now surging forward, a low growl beginning to emerge from the group.

Bran put his hand on my shoulder. "What's happening?" he whispered, moving closer.

"The worst thing in the world." I swallowed, trying to dampen the emotional rush flowing over me. The anger was building in the Pride, the realization that Ruth's death was preventable, and worse, the result of one of our own taking the law into his own hands.

Jess tugged at her dress, pulling the fabric apart with ease. Light brown fur now obscured her front. The face was reshaping itself, the nose retreating inward as the teeth grew and extended past her lips. Her pupils became small feline slits as a tongue flicked out over super-sharp incisors. The scar on her face became more highlighted, the marred skin bereft of fur. Her ears became furred and pointed at the tip.

The thin dress fell to the ground with a slender pair of panties, leaving her naked. I heard Bran's sudden intake of breath behind me even as the rage rumbled across the group around us, reacting to Jess's actions.

"I Challenge you," she rumbled at Davis. "Change, and defend yourself."

He shook his head. "Jess, it wasn't like that. I didn't want to do it, it's just that—" Again he swept the crowd, seeking someone. "She laughed at me, told me there were things bigger than the family, than our Pride. Me, a Board member." He kept looking around. "I couldn't Challenge her and bring it out into the open so I cut into the ladder, just a bit. It wasn't supposed to kill her, just make her fall, give her a warning to behave herself. It was an accident. An accident." He pulled at his tie.

"That doesn't matter." Jess flexed her hands, the claws now fully extended between her fingers. "You are charged with murdering Ruth Huckleton through your intentional actions. As Senior Board member I declare you guilty." She gazed over the assembled crowd. "I will deliver the penalty."

"What's she talking about?" Bran whispered in my ear, his body now pressed up against mine, one hand wrapped around my waist as he stared at them. My head was spinning with both the rush of information and the growing wave of anger about to break loose.

"This is the Law. Pride law." I forced the words out as Davis scrambled backward in an effort to escape. He found the exit blocked by a wall of waiting Felis, their arms crossed in front of them to form a living barrier. I closed my eyes, scenting the Change happening around us.

Clothing dropped to the ground, shirts tossed to one side as they all Changed. Most remained partially clothed since this wasn't a full hunt and was more of a symbolic gesture than anything else—but the claws were real and so was the hatred running through the men and women around me.

Jess lifted Davis's face to heaven with one claw under his chin and roared again. "Will you offer no resistance?"

The middle-aged man sat on the ground, not meeting her gaze. He hadn't even tried to Change. "I call on the mercy of the Pride." The words were whispered, but we all heard it. "I throw myself on your mercy."

Jess stood over him and looked around the assembled Felis, almost all of whom had Changed. "Will anyone speak to try and save this man's life?"

I was torn between two worlds.

The man who'd taken the life of my oldest and closest friend was in front of me begging for his life, his belief in protecting the Felis so strong he'd kill to keep the secret secure.

Letting Jess kill him would be Pride justice.

But it wouldn't bring Ruth back and it wouldn't give me what I needed to find out who killed Janey Winters. What Davis knew would die with him. Jess couldn't or wouldn't care right now, deep in her blood lust.

Pride justice had turned me out onto the streets decades ago.

Now I had to use it to find Janey's killer.

"I will." I moved forward into the clearing, leaving Bran's warmth and support behind.

THIRTEEN

JESS LOOKED AT me. "Rebecca, this is not the place for your childish prattle." A trace of sadness crept into her words. "You are here as a visitor, not even as a full member."

A murmur began to rise and fall as others recognized me, the discussion of my exile being brought up again. The Pride had been divided in deciding what to do. In the end it had fallen to the Board and no one had objected to their decision.

"I beg the Board's indulgence to present the argument." My mind raced to form the words and present them in as formal language as I could. I pointed at the man on the ground. "This man did what he thought was necessary to protect the Pride. That, in and of itself, is no crime. In fact it is expected and demanded of each and every one of us." I spotted a few furred heads bobbing in agreement. "The death of one of our most beloved members was, by his own words, an accident. He only intended to scare her into returning to the trail of complete secrecy, one of our most sacred rules." A few more members began to mumble.

I raised my voice. "If a cub injures another one while playing, we do not strip him of his hide. We allow him to atone and make restitution as best as he can. If we believe in this, then how can you take the life of a member who has declared his actions to be an accident— a horrible, unfortunate accident involving one of our

most beloved members, but still…an accident." I spread
my arms, hoping the submissive pose would win more
over to my side. "Put aside the name of Ruth, adored
as she was by all of us, and see this as it was—an accident—and punish him for that crime. Punish him but
do not kill him." I took a deep breath. "Mercy is not a
weakness."

Jess looked over and around me, her nose twitching as she tried to take an accounting of the Felis surrounding us.

Bran stepped up behind me, his pulse racing and fear
radiating off of his body along with a certain amount
of arousal. His hand landed on the small of my back,
pressing into the damp fabric with a sudden tenderness
that brought tears to my eyes.

Dennis approached us, still unchanged. He put one
hand on Davis's shoulder and looked up at Jess. "We
have lost too much already, Jess. Let's not add another
body to the count."

Jess arched back and roared again into the sky, her
hands outstretched and claws at the ready. She grabbed
Davis by the throat and lifted him off the ground, shrug-
ging Dennis's grip off.

"You have been judged and found guilty of a crime,
of causing malicious injury to another member of the
Pride." Her free hand lashed out, claws finding vulnerable skin. "You are thereby stripped of your mem-
bership and banished from this Pride. Seek your home
elsewhere. Maybe there is another group that would
take in your wretched, pitiful soul."

Davis dropped to the ground, his face a bloody mess.
Jess spun around and advanced on me. She stopped
when our noses touched, one furry and one not. I could
smell the morning's bacon and eggs on her breath.

"Do not push your luck anymore. Leave." It wasn't a request.

I backed away. Bran walked beside me as we made our way through the crowd. A young male snarled at me, his lips rolling back to expose bare teeth. A mother snatched her curious young out of our way.

"You have his scent on you." One senior jumped out in our wake and spat on the ground as she pointed at me. "You whore."

"Get the Taser out," I whispered to Bran as we continued our retreat out of the crowd. "Be ready to use it."

He didn't say anything.

We were on clear ground, the entire group now behind us. I could hear bare feet pawing at the grass, digging up clumps in their eagerness for a kill. The blood lust had started and Davis wasn't the only possible target.

"Keep moving. And don't turn around." I kept pushing Bran backwards along the trail until the wrought-iron gates passed in front of us. No one looked toward us, no one attempted to follow.

Another mighty roar came from the crowd, probably Jess trying to regain control.

"That. Was. Intense." Bran wiped his forehead with the back of his hand as I finally spun and faced forward.

"We're not out of here yet." I grabbed his hand and broke into a jog, glancing over my shoulder every few seconds. "You're driving."

It was only after the car doors slammed behind us that I dared to breathe, watching Brandon start up the engine and back us out of the small space. I could catch the eagerness on the air, the hunting instinct rising and falling with every breeze.

Maybe I hadn't saved Davis after all.

"Just gun it." I pointed down the gravel road. "Don't even think about the speed limit until we hit the highway." He followed my instructions without question, spitting gravel over the other cars as we raced down the lane and away from the farm.

"So...is every party like that one?" Bran joked as he slid the Jeep into traffic. A tractor-trailer zoomed by, honking angrily at our invasion of his space. "Idiot." Bran flipped him the bird. "Don't piss me off, not today," he yelled through the closed window.

"Smooth move." I puffed out short breaths through my mouth, inhaling through my nose. It was the best way of cleansing my senses of the overflow. "Just get us back to your place in one piece, please." I closed my eyes and forced my fear back into the darkness in my mind's eye, the nightmarish images of being torn apart by my own family no longer front and center.

"Roger that." He paused for a minute before speaking. "Think they killed him anyway?"

"I...I don't know." I looked out the window at the passing farmland. "Davis thought he was doing the right thing, disciplining Ruth for making the decision to give me Pride files on her own."

"Except that if she hadn't, you'd be further away from grabbing this killer than ever." He drummed his fingers on the steering wheel. "So is Davis related to the murder? And if so, how?"

"I'm not sure. He was looking at someone in the crowd. I didn't see who, but it's enough for me to wonder how much he really knows." The traffic was slowing now as we approached Toronto, the Gardiner Expressway a tangle of trucks, commuting cars and lost tourists who had picked the wrong time to visit the city.

"Is there any way for you to find out who was in the group?"

"Not a chance. People would have come from all over to pay homage to Ruth, maybe even from other Prides. Even if I dared to ask for a list I don't think anyone would have taken an accounting of who was there."

"Damn." Bran expertly wove from lane to lane, squeezing the Jeep between monster trucks spewing diesel fumes.

"Jess'll probably let him live because I gave her a chance to catch her breath and realize we need what Davis knows." I rubbed the edge of my nose, banishing the last of the overlapping scents. "Gave her a chance to save face and put the responsibility for her reversing the decision on me." I shrugged. "They'll be angry, but more at me than Jess. I'm a better target than a Board member."

The Jeep moved into the right-hand lane, preparing to take the exit that would bring us back to Bran's condo. "I might not have your heightened senses but I was getting a whole lot of hostility from those men and women. And not just because you're the cutest one there."

"It's pretty complicated. I'm not really sure if I get it myself." The cars around us slowed to a crawl. "I'm a bit of an anomaly in the system. So they don't really know how to deal with me."

Bran turned the wheel, maneuvering us into the underground parking lot. "But that still doesn't solve the problem of who killed Janey."

"Exactly." I unbuckled the belt as we came to a stop. "Langley isn't the killer—he's too old and he couldn't have traveled down here in time for all the events. He also doesn't have a motive, as far as we know."

The car door opened. Bran took my hand and pulled me out, snapping my reverie. "Well, let's take a short break and catch our breath. If what you're saying is true, then we're getting closer to the actual killer." He gave me a sad smile. "Otherwise he wouldn't have trashed your place. He must have really thought you had the files there and that they were important to revealing his identity."

We waited only a minute for the elevator and got in, turning to face the finely polished doors. I winced at our distorted reflections. The warped images echoed the confusion in my mind.

The doorman touched the brim of his cap. "Mr. Hanover." He smiled at me, his eyes sparkling over the thick moustache. "Good day." He held out a small envelope. "Your key, miss. They said that it's all sealed up just fine."

Bran nodded. "No one comes up to see me without you calling for permission. No one." His stern voice snapped the veteran to attention. "Let's just say that it's a precarious situation right now."

Dan nodded, his bushy moustache bobbing. "Affirmative, sir. No one gets through."

"You realize that's not exactly reassuring to me," I murmured to Bran as the doors shut again and the elevator began to ascend to his floor. "The guy who dropped off your photograph got up here, no problem."

"Gotta do something. I don't like all this danger getting closer and closer to you."

Jazz looked up from her position on the leather couch as we walked in. The white cat mewed her annoyance when I sat down beside her. She moved to curl up on my lap.

Brandon picked up the Langley file. "Let me try again to get hold of my Mountie contact."

"He won't have anything on this guy." I shook my head. "It's unlikely Langley has done anything illegal other than maybe a parking ticket or two. We tend to try and keep a low profile." A pounding began behind my eyes as I let out a deep sigh. "Them, me, we…I keep getting confused. I thought I had left all of this crap behind me."

He dropped the folder on the table and sat down beside me. Jazz took the opportunity to stretch out across both laps, getting a two-for-one deal on petting. Bran began to stroke my hair with one hand, the other running through Jazz's white fur.

"Look, how about we hit the showers and then grab a nap. I'll set my dogs on Langley and see what they can turn up. You've got to be exhausted."

"I'm pretty wiped," I admitted. My head was still spinning from my sudden show of bravery in facing down Jess and a whole pack of angry Felis.

He got up, curled Jazz into a ball and placed her in the warm spot he had just vacated. "You stand watch while I take your mistress away for a bit."

The white cat looked up at him with disdain. I got up on my own, chuckling.

Bran glanced from me to the cat and back, a sudden look of concern on his face. "You're not related or anything, right? This isn't some freaky mutation thing, is it?"

I laughed, feeling a bit of tension lift from my shoulders. "Not a chance. She's an ugly street cat that wandered into the house one day and decided to stay." I leaned down and scratched her behind the ears. She responded by closing her eyes and purring in that ragged, disjointed way I had come to love. "We're about as related as you humans are to spider monkeys. Or something like that."

"Okay. Just checking." Bran grinned. "Didn't want to offend your great-grandmother or something like that." He put one hand around my waist and pointed toward the bathroom. "Let me put the tracers out and I'll join you in a few minutes."

I hesitated. "Bran, I'm not sure I'll feel like...I mean..." The burning in my face revealed my embarrassment.

"Hey," the tall man put up his hands and laughed softly, "believe it or not, not all men are wild sex machines." He looked at me, his eyes deep and soft. "You've had one helluva day. The last thing on my mind is making love to you." A naughty sparkle appeared. "At least right now." He strutted toward the computer desk, picking up the portable phone en route. "I'll see you in there. And don't laugh when you see the peppermint body wash. It's one of those aromatherapy things I read about once."

Jazz meowed after me as I stepped into the bathroom and stripped off the smelly clothing that had covered me for way too long. The shirt went into the far corner of the room atop the jeans and underwear, the sports bra dangling over the heap. "Gonna have to burn those." My nose wrinkled up at the intensity of the odors. At times I didn't relish having such a wonderful sense of smell.

The hot water was exactly that—hot and plentiful. I stepped under it and started to scrub every inch of my skin with the washcloth plucked from the small inset shelf. It's bad enough when you have to wear a shirt for more than one day, but mix in the rush of aromas from a pack of angry Felis, and I ended up with a creation that almost made me nauseous again.

The shampoo was a standard bland generic blue liquid, almost fluorescent. As I rubbed it into my long hair I began the dissection of the morning's events. Too much didn't match.

Davis had been a Board member for decades, chosen after a long and arduous process that had every eligible member of the Pride chomping at the bit to prove him or herself worthy. Openings didn't come too often and it was a job that held such a high level of responsibility that Board members didn't work—they had too much to do. But Davis threw it all away…For what? What would make him risk everything he had to threaten Ruth?

"Who what?" Bran began to rub my back, spreading out a new layer of soapy bubbles. The smell of peppermint rose up to cover our bodies. "You were thinking out loud."

I shifted my muscles, wincing as they protested. It had been a rough few days. "Davis. I don't know why he went after Ruth."

He moved to massage my shoulders and neck, rubbing the heated skin. "He was pissed that she gave you the files. He's somehow involved with the killer."

"Somehow. It'd take a helluva lot to pull Davis into this mess." I closed my eyes as the steam drifted up and over us. "But it's not Davis. The scent, it's not the same. Not even close."

"So what's the connection between Langley, Davis and your mysterious killer?" Bran said in my right ear.

"I don't know. But it's there." I put my hands on the tiled walls and let out a sigh as the rubbing continued down my back. Bran's fingers paused for a second at the scars and then proceeded to lightly brush across the puckered and injured skin. "This okay?"

"Yes. Feels great." I sighed my appreciation as he continued his gentle touching. "It's a relative of Langley's, somehow. Imagine one of those shows where they show the DNA readings and say that it's a brother or son or something."

"But there aren't any children. None that we know of, to be fair." Bran moved his hands off. "Pass the shampoo, please? I'm pretty rancid myself."

"Right." I handed the bottle back over my right shoulder.

Bran huffed and spat as the hot water splashed over my head. "Dang, you're short."

"Didn't seem to matter to you before." I tilted my head back to catch some of the water while he reached over and adjusted the showerhead.

"Horizontally is a whole different matter," he murmured into my ear.

I sighed, pushing my mind back to work. "His wife is sworn to report any birth, even a miscarriage, to the Board. That way they can track the bloodlines and make sure that no one marries too close to each other."

"Ah, the second cousin story." He coughed. "Excuse me. So if you don't report it, what happens?"

"You get found out eventually." I pulled my hair around to my front and started squeezing some of the water out. "It's something you can't really keep secret. Imagine your family, a huge family of hundreds of people, and trying to keep your pregnancy a secret. Just doesn't happen."

"And what about half-breeds?" A stream of water shot over my left shoulder. "Sorry."

"No prob." I tilted my face upward, letting the hot water run over my face and neck. "It doesn't happen."

"How does it not happen?" Bran reached past me, turning the hot water dial. "From what I've seen you Felis enjoy sex. A lot."

I chuckled as I rotated my shoulders, feeling the tension begin to lift. "It's impossible. A Felis doesn't have the ability to impregnate or be impregnated by a regular human."

"Oh." There was a slight trace of either disappointment or relief in his voice. I couldn't tell which.

I chewed on my bottom lip, not wanting to open up that area of discussion right now. "It's just that it's never happened before, ever—no one knows if it's a genetic thing or what. We haven't been able to access the science to find out the exact reason behind it but there hasn't ever been one to date. That's why we allow family members to marry outside of the Pride. They can't bring their mates to the farm, can't ever have kits or really participate in the Pride's daily life. It's too tough for most of us." I lifted up one foot then the other to flex my leg muscles. "That's why most Felis stay in the circle, find our mates either within the Pride or visit other Prides to look for possibilities."

"Talk about keeping it in the family." He chuckled. "So how is Davis connected to Langley and through him to the killer?" Bran reached around me and started turning the large silver knobs. "You done?"

"Done and ready for a nap." I yawned as the water disappeared, swirling down around our feet. "Let me sleep on it."

"No problem." He stepped out of the shower stall and grabbed a white fluffy towel. Gesturing me forward, he wrapped it around me and rubbed my arms. "Feeling better?"

"Totally." I stood up on my tiptoes and kissed him. "It's been a bad few days."

"Well, I'd like to think not totally." Bran grinned and picked up a second towel. "I won't bother setting the alarm, it'd be too annoying." His arms went around me again. "And, for the record I find your snoring very attractive."

"I'll remind you of that when you're poking me in the ribs trying to make me stop."

FOURTEEN

I woke up to see Jazz nose-to-nose with me, a line of drool running from her lower lip to the comforter tucked under my chin.

"Thanks." I extracted a hand from under the blanket and poked the slim feline. "Now if you don't mind…"

She stood, stretched her lanky frame in every direction possible and then strutted off over the bed—making sure to hit every sore spot on my body as well as tromping over Bran's back and legs.

"Ugh," he moaned into the pillow.

"Be thankful you weren't sleeping on your back." I rolled out of bed and checked the clock. "Almost four o'clock."

"Morning or evening?" The mumbled response came.

"Evening. Afternoon. Whatever." I opened one of the three old oaken wardrobes. "I might have to steal some of your clothing today."

"Please do so." He rolled onto his back and yawned, stretching his arms out to their full length. "We can go shopping later on or if you want, we can just buy online and have it delivered."

I nodded, inspecting his clothing. Finally I settled on a pair of jeans. They rode low on my hips, and I rolled the legs up a few times. The white dress shirt was snug, but not too tight.

"I like you in my clothes—" Bran leered as he swung

his feet around and sat up, "—even more when you go commando."

My face scrunched up. "I'm not happy about it. Trust me, it's more of an annoyance for us women than you guys."

"I doubt that." He stood up and arched back, letting out a loud yawn. "Especially those of us who have a lot to lose in that zipper, if you catch my drift."

I turned, pursing my lips as I drew my eyes down his naked body. "Oh, I think you've got nothing to worry about."

"Ooh..." Bran mimicked being stabbed in the chest. "You know how to hurt a guy."

"You have no idea." I rolled up the sleeves of the shirt and padded barefoot around the corner toward the kitchen. "Tea and toast sound good?"

"No Chinese left?"

"Not even a grain of rice." I opened the refrigerator and glanced around the shelves. "Stocked nicely, I must admit."

"Thanks. Have a full list delivered every two weeks." Bran appeared at the marble island, tugging at a dark blue T-shirt with some obscure logo on it.

The phone rang. Bran scrambled for it, hopping over Jazz who instinctively lay down directly in his path.

"Hello?" His face went from playful to serious in a second. "Yes, she's here."

He passed me the phone and mouthed "Jess" with a scowl.

I put the phone to my ear. "Reb here."

"Davis wants to talk to you," Jess rumbled. "He's down at St. Joseph's Hospital."

"He's alive?" I couldn't hide the surprise in my voice.

"You argued on his side, didn't you? Now he wants to see you. Probably going to thank you."

"You know it's not that." I returned the sarcasm, word for word. "It's got something to do with Langley."

"Langley?" Jess failed to hide the surprise in her voice. Or she didn't care. "Is that who this is all about?"

"Yes and no." I looked at my watch. "Where are you?"

"I'm at the hospital with Davis. We brought him here after the accident. You know how that farm machinery is."

I rolled my eyes. "Good cover story. I'll be there as soon as I can."

Bran slid a plate of buttered toast across the island toward me, one eyebrow raised.

"And don't bring the human," Jess snarled. "You're in enough trouble as it is."

"What?" My blood pressure rose. "What the hell business is it of yours if I'm sleeping with a human? You practically disowned me years ago and only called me in to make sure no one else found out about your precious secret. Now you're trying to run my life again? I don't think so!" I slammed the phone down then picked it up again and tossed it across the room. It bounced three times, startling Jazz into turning around and finding a more comfortable spot on the leather couch.

"Why do I just feel like I've started dating the top cheerleader and I'm the geek working in the computer lab?" Bran placed a huge teapot on the table and slipped a tea towel under it. I stared at the monstrosity, the vibrant violets clashing with yellow pansies and something swirling off the handle that had to qualify it for Best of Show in some Antique Showcase somewhere. Bran laughed at my response. "My grandmother's, before you say anything. Don't bring it out too often. Don't usually need more than a single cup." He placed two mugs down beside it and nodded toward the phone, still lying on the other side of the room. "So…"

"Davis is alive and wanting to talk to me." I picked up one of the pieces of toast and munched on it, my appetite returning with a rush. "Got any jam?"

"Grape. In a squeeze bottle." Bran set the purple plastic container before me. He sat on a stool and faced me as he poured out the tea. "So…"

"And Jess doesn't like me being with you. Go figure." I spread the jam across the bread with a finger and then popped the jelly-covered digit into my mouth despite Bran's raised eyebrow.

"I do have knives, you know. Butter knives. Made for spreading such things as jam. And peanut butter." He didn't move. "She can't call you out or kill you or anything like that, right?"

I paused, seeing my confusion mirrored in his face. "Technically…I'm not sure." I added a dash of milk to the tea from the small carton sitting on the table. "See, it's not really *verboten* to be involved with a regular human. Like I said, you can marry them but it's a strain on the Felis."

"So…better to date them and keep a secret than go the whole way and let the secret out?"

"More or less." There was a spot of jam on my knuckle, prompting me to lick it off. "Let's just say that you've got to be darned serious before you get hauled to the farm and introduced to the family."

"So how serious are we, then?" He stared at me, putting his mug to his mouth.

The blunt question caught me with my tongue half

out of my mouth. Pulling it back into a suddenly dry crevasse I glanced down. "I'm not sure."

It was the honest truth. I'd had my share of one-night stands but there had been only one man who had ever been worth telling my secret to and he was standing in front of me.

Bran held up his hands. "I'm sorry. This isn't the right time to start this conversation." He rolled the white ceramic mug around on its edge. "I tend to jump ahead of myself."

"Yeah. Me too." I scrambled for something to defuse the situation before I screwed it up even more. "We better get to the hospital." I swallowed the rest of the toast, drinking my hot tea at breakneck speed with my eyes closed. I didn't want to see Bran's face.

"You feel up to driving?" I opened my eyes to see him smiling at me. "Or do you want me to take it?"

"I'll be fine." The relief in my voice was probably screaming out between the words. "Let's just go and see what he wants." I wagged a finger at Jazz. "You stay here and guard the place. You didn't do such a good job on the last one, you know."

She yawned, displaying her yellowed teeth. I took that as an affirmative.

There was an accident on Queen Street, forcing us down to King Street for the trip to St. Joseph's. It actually wasn't that far from my original house, no more than a half-hour or so, but considering my current address happened to be nowhere, it was far enough.

I smelled Jess before I saw her, the tall woman standing at the vending machines in the lobby. She turned toward me, her scarlet scar getting louder as she spotted Brandon beside me. Her jaw tensed when I approached.

I might have saved Davis's life but I had tweaked her honor.

"Where's Davis?" I moved inside her personal space, letting her know I wasn't going to be intimidated.

"He's just recovering from some surgery." The silver-haired woman reached down to pluck a paper cup of coffee from the small plastic holder. "Seems his face is pretty scratched up. Going to need a few more operations before he gets handsome again." She sipped the hot coffee, her expression stoic.

"Strange how that happens, eh?" Brandon moved to stand beside me, a wry smile on his face. "Don't think we've been properly introduced yet." He offered his right hand. "Brandon Hanover."

The challenge was evident. Alpha against alpha—the game never changed. Part of me wanted to relish Jess's discomfort at being challenged by a stranger and part of me cringed at the thought of what Jess could do to Brandon. The hormones rolled out from both in impressive waves as Jess gripped the offered hand, her eyes locked with Bran's.

I stood back and let them have at it. Better now in a public place than on the farm or worse, a back alley somewhere. If Bran could hold his own, it'd make things a whole lot easier. At least medical help was on hand.

A full two minutes later the lock was broken, both of them releasing their death hold at the same time. Jess nodded. "Good enough. Now let's go see Davis."

I glanced at Bran who beamed as if he'd won the lottery. I wasn't sure if he'd learned this on the streets or in some book somewhere, but he had managed to maneuver that minefield better than some kits. He fell back exactly a full step behind Jess, acknowledging her authority as if the damned human had been fully briefed on how to deal with alphas.

There was another man outside the room, obviously one of the family. Whether he was there to make sure Davis stayed put or to make sure no one else attacked him, I wasn't sure. The blond nodded at Jess as we walked by him, only raising an eyebrow at Bran and me. Good training.

The hospital room was the typical antiseptic haven with a single bed set by the window, the bars on the windows strategically placed to not make it look as if the staff was afraid of the patient jumping out. There were no flowers, nothing to show that anyone occupied this room other than the man lying in the bed.

Davis looked like the classic Claude Raines version of the Invisible Man, bandages wrapped around his head so tightly I wondered if he could even hear.

"Rebecca." The muffled voice came out from between lips hidden under layers. "Thanks for coming."

My first instinct was to put my hand out toward his. He raised his right hand and gripped mine, a weak, limp effort. I sat on the edge of the bed. "No problem." My gaze stayed fixed on his, not willing to show my fear at his appearance. He could probably scent it on me but I wasn't going to give it away.

"I'll be outside." Jess looked from me to Brandon to Davis. "We'll talk later." She strode outside without looking back.

Bran swallowed loudly, leaning against the wall with arms crossed. I tried to ignore him and focused on the man in front of me.

"I'm glad you're alive." It was true, even if I despised him for what he had done. I had never been so mad to want someone dead.

"Thanks to you." His eyes were sad and dark. "I'm an idiot."

"That's for sure," Bran mumbled. He put his hands up before I could respond. "Sorry, sorry. I'm just going to stand here and look pretty."

Davis looked at Bran then back at me. "He's right. I put my own wishes ahead of the good of the Pride and that was wrong."

"You killed Ruth." I tried to keep the hatred out of my voice. I probably failed. "You killed her when all she was trying to do is help me solve a case you asked me to work on."

Davis reached up with one covered finger and scratched the tip of his nose or where it would be under the bandages. "You know how many surgeries I'm going to have to undergo before I can even show my face in public?"

"More than ten?" I couldn't help sounding cheerful. "You know how long it's going to take to put my place back together after you ripped it apart?" It was a shot in the dark.

His head dipped. "Don't make this harder than it is, please. You may have saved my life, but it's not really going to be worth living at this rate."

I shifted my legs. "Why did you get so upset about Ruth sending me the files? What do you have to do with Langley?"

His eyes registered surprise, enough to bring Bran off the wall. "Frank? What do you know about Frank?" Davis grabbed my wrist. "What do you know?"

"I know that somehow he's related to the Felis who killed Janey. And who trashed my house." I didn't pull away despite Bran's nervous eyebrow twitches. "Tell me what you know." I pulled my fingers into fists. "You owe me a life-debt."

"That I do." He released my wrist and sighed as he fell back onto the pile of hospital-issue pillows at his back. "First, I have to tell you that I never thought it would come to this. I thought you'd just check into things, give us a fat bill and be done with it." His eyes flashed to Brandon. "I thought you were…less than capable in this area."

"You thought I was more of a misfit." I leaned forward. "That's it, isn't it? While Jess had confidence in me you figured that I was too degraded as a Felis and too crappy as an investigator to hunt this guy down." My face grew hot. "Yet here I am, here you are and one of us isn't going to be worried about dressing up for Halloween. Two kids are without their mother and a husband is mourning his wife and wondering what she did to deserve being attacked in a dark alley." My tone went low and dark. "And don't think that I'm that helpless." I lifted my hands and shoved my knuckles toward him, displaying the new scars. "Think I could undo all that hard work?" I flexed my fingers. "Think anyone would mind?" My tongue flicked out to wet my lips, my heart pounding faster. "Think they'd be able to stop me? Think they'd try?"

Bran's hand was on my shoulder. "Reb." The single word brought me back from the edge of my rage. I slid off the bed, standing at the foot.

"Tell me what connection you have to Frank Langley and Frank Langley to the killer." I jerked my thumb at the door. "Or I'll let Jess get it out of you."

A shudder ran through him at the mention of Jess's name. Obviously the beating had been worse than I had thought. "Okay, okay." He put up both hands. "Just put in a good word for me with Jess."

"I'm not going to promise anything. I saved your life. Don't make me regret it." After a few minutes of silence, I rapped the footboard, rattling the bed. "The clock is ticking."

He took a deep breath, glancing at the door. "Frank and I were crib brothers." Davis looked at Bran. "You probably don't understand that, but it's like being raised with a lot of brothers and sisters. You feel a sort of bloodship with them, something you just don't grow out of." A sharp cough burst out of the bandages. "On our first hunt we tracked a buck. Damned thing turned out to be a twelve-pointer, charged at us. I froze, Frank pushed me to one side and saved my life." His fingers rose and fell on the crisp white sheet. "We took it down but I owed him." He shook his head. "You never forget friends and family."

I nodded. "I had that. *Had* being the operative word. Keep talking."

"When Jess told me about your request I knew that Frank had the streak down his face—it's been there as long as I've known him. But he's too old to have been the guy who attacked you. I called him and asked what was going on. I mean, there's only so many Felis out there with that particular marking scheme."

"No kidding." I caught Bran's questioning look. "It's not a common trait. We all have different markings. It's like fingerprints."

"Exactly. There were three men on that list but I just felt that Frank had something to do with it. Call it a hunch or something."

"Animal instinct?" Bran flinched as we both glared at him. At least I did, I wasn't sure if Davis did.

"I knew it wasn't Frank." The bandaged man let out a sigh. "When Jess told me that we were giving you the list I was pissed."

"Enough to kill Ruth?" I said.

"No." He shook his head. "I never wanted to kill her. I just wanted to remind her of her loyalty to the family first."

"You called Frank. Told him about the investigation, about Ruth giving me the files."

Davis nodded. "He thanked me and said he'd appreciate anything I could do to keep it quiet. Said he didn't need anyone butting in on his business."

I covered my eyes with the palms of both hands and couldn't respond for a minute. "His 'business'? We're talking about the death of a woman."

"He didn't know about the barn. I didn't tell him anything about that. You can't hold that against him." A whine crept into his voice.

"Okay. Let's leave that for a second." I took a deep breath, quelling my rage. "What business?"

Davis picked at a loose thread on the blanket. "I'm not sure."

"Look, you bastard." I leaned in with both hands on each side of his bandaged head and grabbed where I thought his ears would be. The squeal told me I was right. "You spill what you have or I start taking those bandages off." I showed him my hands again. "Thread by thread."

He lowered his voice to a whisper, so low that I could barely catch it. "He said that it was his son. I don't know more than that."

"But he doesn't have any children with his current wife." I glanced at Bran, then back. "He's got a mistress? Someone in the Pride he's been nailing on the side?"

Davis dropped his head. "You'll have to ask him, I didn't get all the details."

"But you got enough to risk your standing for him." I moved away from the bed. "I hope he appreciates it."

"Reb," Davis called me back as I opened the door, "it's family. You know how that works."

I swallowed back the foul taste in my throat. "Yes, I know how that works."

Bran followed me out into the hallway. I waved Jess over with a nod of my head, the blond guard moving farther down the corridor, almost out of earshot.

"I don't get it." I shook my head, crossing my arms in front of me. "Davis is saying that Frank's got some sort of son, someone's who's off the radar. That's who we're looking for."

"It can't be." Jess's jaw clenched, sending a ripple along the scar. "There's no children that are unaccounted for. Not one."

"Are you sure?" Bran asked.

Jess stared at him.

Bran continued. "Listen, I get the idea that you control all the information about the group and all that. But what if someone gets knocked up and doesn't tell you who the father is?"

"Never happen." Jess shook her head. "You don't know anything about us. Keeping a secret like that would be impossible." She glanced at the floor for a second as if working to find the right words. "We don't get upset about unmarried women having children. All we ask is that they register them so we keep the bloodlines straight. There's no shame—just an obligation to do right by the kit by keeping the records straight, which means putting down a father."

She looked at me. "I've never see Frank Langley registered as a father for any kits. Ever. And every record comes across my desk at some point."

It felt like I had sand behind my eyes, grinding my thoughts to bits. "You'll have to contact the other Prides, see if he's in their records."

"Gone you one better." Jess smiled, a predatory grin. "I've sent someone to retrieve Frank and Kelly Langley from the farm. They came down for Ruth's funeral. They should be here in a matter of hours." Her eyes went to Brandon's, locking steel on steel. "We'll figure this out."

I rubbed my forehead with my right hand. "This still isn't making sense. Who would want to kill Janey Winters? Why? What does she have to do with Frank Langley?" A low throbbing began behind my left eye. "This isn't connecting."

The youngster down the hall shuffled his feet, tucking both hands behind his back. I looked at the closed door. "He seems sorry enough."

"Don't make what he did right," Jess said.

"I didn't say that." I tapped the tip of my nose with one finger. "But I can tell you that it had to be something pretty close to Davis's heart to have him threaten and assault Ruth. You don't just go tossing your weight around that woman." I caught myself thinking and speaking in the present tense, as if she were still alive. My chest ached with the truth.

"True." Jess nodded.

"Why did you wait until the funeral to call him out?" I kept talking before my nerve gave out. "You could have done this upstairs, kept it internal."

Jess looked at the closed door. "I wanted him to have to answer in front of the whole Pride, not just in a private meeting."

"Public humiliation." I felt the tension twist down my spine. "I know how important that is to you."

Jess didn't flinch. "You were tougher than he was."

I pushed the flash of anger away before it could consume me. "What made him think he could pull this off?"

"Hubris. Humans don't have a monopoly on pride," Jess snapped. "Damned fool figured being on the Board means you can fix everything. It don't."

The older woman opened her mouth to say something else and then stopped. Her eyes went wide. I caught the smell a microsecond after she did. So did the guard down the hall, who barreled through us as we stood there, stupid, and barged into the room. Jess followed with the two of us bringing up the rear.

The smell was of fear, feces and of death.

FIFTEEN

"Damn," Jess swore under her breath, jumping over the bed toward the window.

Davis had undone some of the bandages and tied them to the top of the metal bars covering the window before climbing up on the small chair provided for all guests. His face, half covered with bandages, was emotionless as he hung from the makeshift gallows. Crisscrossing stitches ran across his exposed skin like a railway switching yard.

"Call the doctors," Jess barked at the kid as she grabbed the lifeless legs and leaped on the stool. "Reb, get him loose."

I fished in my pocket for my penknife, my hands shaking too much to get a grip.

Jess snarled and reached up, extending her claws.

Bran caught the unconscious body as the nails slid through the used bandages with ease and lowered him to the bed just as the nurses burst into the room.

Jess spun around, retracting her claws before anyone could see. The corridor filled with yelled commands and pounding feet.

The door flew open and a half-dozen medical personnel rushed in. One man grabbed Davis's body away from Bran. The others moved between us and the unconscious man, forming a barrier.

"Out, everyone!" The doctor waved his arms as

they ripped open Davis's shirt, piling on like a football scrimmage. "Out!"

I shepherded the kid out, giving Jess a few more seconds before she followed with Bran. The blond kid fell to his knees in the hallway, retching and coughing on an empty stomach. I patted him on the back. "It's okay. You didn't do anything wrong."

Jess towered over the two of us, her face scarlet. "Want to explain to me what just happened here?"

I lifted myself up to all five-foot-four inches. "Looks to me like he just tried to kill himself. What do you think?"

"I think it has something to do with the investigation. What did he tell you?" Her eyes narrowed. "What did he say?"

"I've told you everything." Out of the corner of my eye I saw another nurse push a cartful of equipment into the room. "Guess he didn't want to face you or the Pride again. Get smacked up for hiding his connection to Frank Langley."

"Don't start to presume that you know what the Pride would or wouldn't do!" There was a flash of anger in her face, the eyes threatening to go Felis. She clenched her fists, shaking where she stood.

"Don't go there." Brandon stepped between us, so much inside Jess's personal space I took a step back. He stared directly into the older woman's eyes. "Don't blame Rebecca for your own mistakes." He pointed to one side, to the kid still slouched against the wall. "Don't blame him and don't blame her. And you can't blame Davis for keeping with your stupid traditions and then feeling torn between family and your damned secrets!"

Jess's right hand snapped up and grabbed Bran by

the throat. "Don't presume to talk to me as an equal, human!" The claws began to come out again, far too close to Brandon's neck for safety. At that range they could easily pierce the jugular.

The blond kid jumped up beside me, ready to charge in.

I swung my arm up and blocked him. "No." A strong shake of my head brought the situation home to the kit. I bit down hard on my lower lip. If the kid got into it I'd have to follow and we'd all lose in the end.

This wasn't something I could fix.

It was all on Bran's shoulders.

"I don't think you want to do that." Bran spoke calmly as if we were placing another order for Chinese. He looked down. "Your decision."

I spotted his right hand pressed up against Jess's chest. I had assumed it was to fend her off, but upon closer inspection I saw my Taser—pressed right up against the shirt right at her heart.

Jess grunted.

Bran smiled, his neck flexing against the claws. They weren't razor-sharp but she could easily swipe across his throat and rip him open like a fish.

I had no idea if the small electrical charge generated by the Taser would just shock Jess or stop her heart.

Jess stared at Bran for a long minute, one edge of her mouth twitching. Finally she smiled, letting loose with a deep laugh I hadn't heard for years.

She lowered the reporter and released her grip, pulling the claws in quickly. No one around us was paying attention, everyone dealing with the health crisis in the room beside us.

"Well played." She looked at the kid. "You could learn something from this human, Rick." Jess took a step back and turned to me. "I'll bring Frank and Kelly to you."

"Bring them to my place." Brandon glanced around us. "I'm tired of driving out to that farm and I think it's good for us to get into a neutral spot, put Langley off his game, so to speak."

Jess nodded. "Agreed." A pointed look directed at Bran. "I already have the address, thank you very much." She looked at the closed hospital room door. "We have to sort this out before anyone else gets hurt or killed."

A doctor opened the door and slipped out, closing it behind him before we could see anything. "Mr. Konnerburg's family?"

Jess drew herself up to her full height. "Davis has no family. I'm the designated next of kin in the paperwork."

The young blond man looked around the small circle at the rest of us before continuing. "He's alive. He might have cut off his airway long enough to cause brain damage but we don't know right now, not until we do some tests." He looked to the floor before continuing. "Do you have any idea why he would have tried to kill himself?"

Jess silenced us all with a look before speaking. "No idea. He didn't say anything other than how stupid he felt falling into that hay baler."

"Well, he'll be moved to a more secure ward to make sure this doesn't happen again. We're not sure if he'll ever regain full consciousness at this point, but we have to do everything we can to protect him from himself." The doctor scribbled some notes on the clipboard he held in one hand. "We'll be in touch as soon as we have anything else to report."

"Thank you, doctor." Jess shook his hand, crushing the delicate fingers. As the doctor moved off, shaking the numbness from his hand, Jess turned back to us. "I'll have them there soon enough." With a brusque nod to Bran and me, she hustled the kid down the corridor and out of sight.

"That was pretty interesting." Bran leaned against the wall, taking a deep breath.

"You think?" I reached over and plucked the Taser from his fingers. "I'm taking this back."

"But I like it." He chuckled. "It's such a cool toy."

I glared at him, putting my hands on my hips. "Do you know how close you were to dying there?"

"Pretty much." He kissed me lightly on the lips. "I'm not totally oblivious to what's going on around here. Jess is pissed off 'cause you've got me involved and I've got to play big man to keep her from swatting me around like a flea. And she's even more pissed because you've also got me in bed and I'm such a hot commodity that she can't stand it."

I smiled, stepping back and crossing my arms. "Not too sure about the last point. But you might actually be catching on to all this…" My hands waved in the air. "Politics. I was never all that into them."

"Well, now might be a good time to start." He nodded toward the hospital room. "Because this is becoming a bigger and stranger jigsaw puzzle by the minute."

The nurse at the counter watched us warily when we walked past her station toward the elevator. Obviously she hadn't been impressed by our family reunion.

"Frank isn't going to be happy, I can tell you that." I sat in the passenger seat of my own car once again, leaning my elbow on the window while I tried to clear my mind. Driving wasn't the best way to do that and Brandon seemed to like taking over the wheel. "We have anything to eat at the apartment?"

"Plenty of munchies." He arched one eyebrow, a half-smirk on his face. "Any special kitty treats I should order up?"

I smacked him in the arm, hard. "Don't push it. You may have been able to face Jess down once or twice, but this sort of power game doesn't stop." I looked out the window and watched businessmen walk briskly up and down the streets, racing into one building and out of another in a hunt that never ended. "With Davis becoming...incapacitated, there's now an opening on the board. The last time that happened there was a hell of a lot of challengers, a lot of fights and more than a little blood spilled." I shook my head. "Right now there's probably a near-riot on the farm while they start jockeying for position."

"You could run. Take a spot on the Board." The Jeep slipped into the underground parking lot with the attendant waving at Bran again.

"Like they'd accept me." I rolled my eyes.

He pulled into the parking spot. "Don't be so hard on yourself. You're a pretty tough broad. They could do a lot worse than put you in charge of this crew." Bran moved around the car to open my door. "You've got a chance here to bridge the old and the new. That's the sort of crap that got you into this trouble in the first place, right?"

The elevator was empty when we stepped inside. I clenched my teeth, forcing down the sudden rage threatening to overwhelm me. "There's a lot about this society that you don't know and that you'll never know. So please don't go thinking that because you stared down an alpha and got all snuggly with me that suddenly you're an expert on me, my family and the Felis." Unbidden a growl broke loose from my throat, a warning I hadn't meant to send out.

His jaw dropped. He looked away and studied the elevator buttons, the leather sleeves of his duster flapping loose as the numbers flashed by on the screen.

The anger disappeared, replaced by an overwhelming sense of guilt. I reached out and touched his elbow. "Bran, I didn't mean…" I didn't know what to say. There was no way I could explain it to him, the devotion I still had to the Felis, despite their treatment of me. Even if I couldn't Change I was still family.

Now I had gone and screwed up a perfectly decent relationship because I was an idiot. Never let it be said that I was the brightest of the litter.

The elevator doors slid open. Brandon walked out without a word and stepped toward his front door without glancing back.

"Brandon!" A quick jog brought me beside him as he fumbled with the keys. "I'm not trying to be insulting. I'm just telling you that you can't use me as a window into Felis society." I slammed my hand onto the door, just above the handle. "I'm not part of it. I stopped being a part of it when they threw me out."

The key slid into the lock. He pushed the door open but remained standing outside with me.

"They threw me out when I was fifteen." I stood behind him. "They threw me out into a world I had only read about. I knew nothing about what was out here. All I knew was that I was a misfit, a genetic throwback and I wasn't good enough for them."

The words caught in my throat. "I've spent twenty years trying to forget that, all of it. So don't think that I'm holding anything back or that I just don't want to tell you. I'm caught in the middle here and I don't know anything other than that right now I would rather be anyplace else doing anything else. But I can't."

He didn't look at me. "Are you trying to convince me or convince yourself?"

"I don't know." My shoulders sagged with the sudden weight that had somehow dropped onto them. "All I know is that you're here and I'm here and I'd rather be anyplace else dealing with anything else with you." A weak smile appeared on my lips. "Sort of schizo, I guess."

"No." Bran turned around to face me. His eyes flashed caramel for a second then warmed to dark chocolate brown. "I know a bit of what you're experiencing. Been there done that. But you can't let them define who and what you are." He pointed at himself. "And you can't let me do that either, otherwise it's not going to work between us. You have to form your own family within the Felis, even if it's just you and me." His head tilted to one side. "Is any of this making sense?"

"Yes. And no." I let out a heavy sigh. "I'll do my best, but just understand that some of this isn't easy and it's not going to be, ever." I stretched my fingers to their full length then curled back into a fist. "Nothing is ever what it seems with the Felis. Nothing."

Jazz appeared, weaving her way in and out between our legs with her usual loud and ugly purr. Bran reached down and picked her up, cradling her in his arms. "As long as you don't tell me that I have to call her 'Auntie.' That'd be just a wee bit too much for me to handle."

I chuckled and scratched Jazz behind the ears. "Not as far as I know. However, she does act like an old lady with attitude."

The white cat let out an annoying meow as if to admonish the two of us and then arched back out of Bran's grip, making him lower her to the ground carefully.

"I'm going to go back online and see what I can get about Langley again." I walked to the computer and began the start-up sequence. "There might be some sort of link somewhere that the family hasn't documented or something they haven't been able to keep under wraps."

"Can't hurt to try." Bran said from behind me. "I'll work the phone lines again. I've got some connections at the cop shop—let's see if Langley rings a bell with anyone."

"He doesn't have anything on his record."

"Nothing that's documented." He touched his index finger to the side of his nose. "But who knows, maybe he's been caught and warned away from some place or someone or something." A lewd grin and wink accompanied his statement. "Never know when a cop's gonna give a man a break 'cause he's sympathetic to the perp. Especially when a woman's involved."

I rolled my eyes and spun around in the chair. "Spare me."

"Not a chance." The low laugh came from behind me. "Not a chance, Reb."

An hour later the phone rang, a short two ring sequence. Bran picked it up and waved to me where I sat at the computer desk. "Thanks, Dave. Please send them up." He tossed the phone onto the table. "Jess's here along with Frank and Kelly."

I walked into the kitchen and stared at the complex machinery. "Can you start up a pot of coffee and a pot of tea? I think we'll all need at least that much."

"No problem. I don't have any scones, however." Bran grinned as I scowled a response. "Don't get all kitty-PMS with me."

"Oh, you have no idea." I walked to the front door. "Just behave yourself. Frank's not going to be happy being here and out of familiar territory and I don't think Jess's exactly nominating you for blood brother status any time soon."

At the first knock Bran slid across the varnished hardwood floor in his socks, reaching the door before me. He opened it with a wide smile and gestured for Jess to enter.

Her eyes locked with mine across the room. "Rebecca—Frank Langley. Kelly Langley." Ignoring Brandon completely she waved in the two adults behind her, immediately taking control of the situation, the room and our lives. "We'll sit over there."

Jazz sat up from her position on the soft leather chair and yawned loudly when Jess approached. Picking up on the cues, she hopped off with a disgruntled meow and disappeared around the divider into the bedroom portion of the apartment.

Frank Langley was, to all intents and purposes, nothing more than a huge bear. When he sat down on the sofa he reminded me more of one of those Chinese pandas displayed in the papers every few years when they managed to procreate and continue the survival of their species. The balding, plump man sank into the cushions with a terrified look in his eyes. His wife sat next to him, grabbing his hand with an intensity screaming both fear and anger. She was blond and blue-eyed, a tastefully thin woman whose face was a mask waiting to be painted.

Jess didn't sit.

She went to the kitchen area and picked up one of the fresh mugs of coffee Bran had set out. She took a deep sniff of the fresh brew, her eyebrows rising in shock and approval.

Bran retaliated by offering her milk from a small creamer plucked from the refrigerator. I tried to ignore the power play going on but I couldn't help feeling a little pride in the way Bran was handling himself.

"Hello." I offered my hand to the Langleys. "My name's Rebecca. Has Jess spoken to you about why you're here?"

"I'm…not sure." Frank reached into one pocket of his oversized pants and pulled out a handkerchief that would have doubled as a tablecloth. "She said something 'bout Davis and some problems."

Kelly sat up, her back ram-rod straight with her hands now folded in her lap. "We were at the Gathering earlier. It's awful what happened to Ruth." Her eyes flashed to one side, toward her husband. "Awful."

I didn't have to be a psychic to feel the restrained fury in her words. She knew something was wrong and she knew it was her husband's fault.

"Right." I didn't have time to mince words. "I'm investigating the death of Janey Winters, a teacher here in town. She was killed by a Felis."

The couple rocked back in their seats as if I had bitch-slapped them both at the same time. "What?" Frank stammered while Kelly just stared at me, her mouth hanging open.

"You heard what I said." I reached down and flipped open the folder on the table. Frank's face stared up at the two of them, his blank look in the photograph mimicking real life. "This is your file. I requested it because during the investigation I was attacked by a Felis with a white streak down one side of his nose." I dragged my index finger down my face. "According to family records there aren't a whole lot of men with that particular marking. You're one of them."

"That p-p-p-proves nothing," Frank said. He waved his hands in the air as if he were trying to fend off a mosquito attack. "There's got to be a lot of Felis like that. A lot of fellows." He looked at his wife. "A lot of fellows."

She glared at him and then crossed her arms. I cleared my throat, bringing their full attention back to yours truly.

"That particular scent, not to mention a hair sample, was also found at the scene of the murder." I watched Frank wipe his brow again and pat his eyes dry. "I know it's not you because it's not your scent."

He slumped down into the cushions. It wasn't relief at being found innocent. There was something else there, a sense of foreboding.

He knew the truth.

I reached into my pocket and withdrew the plastic bag filled with the loose fur from my room.

"This is what we found at my house." I offered it to Kelly first. "It has the scent of your husband but only partially. That would indicate that there's some sort of genetic connection between my attacker and your husband."

She opened the bag and pressed it to her face, inhaling deeply with eyes closed.

Her face went scarlet a second later.

Kelly Langley slammed the bag down on the table and turned and slapped her husband, hard. I flinched as her fingerprints began to form an angry rash on his pale skin. For his part, Frank sat there in silence, his hands in his lap. He hadn't tried to fend off the attack.

"I knew it. You told me I was seeing things that

weren't there, that all those business trips were legit, all the overnight hotel stays." She burst into tears, hiding her face in her hands.

Jess appeared with a box of tissues plucked off one of the bookshelves. She knelt down at Kelly's side and offered her the box. "It'll be okay." She said in a low, comforting tone and began to rub her back. "It'll be okay." She didn't look at Frank.

Frank sat there, his face growing redder by the second. His eyes went to Jess, then to his sobbing wife, to Bran standing behind me, to the kitchen counter and finally to me. His mouth opened and closed again in a long sequence of empty stutters. Finally he stopped, shook himself and spoke.

"It was…she was…" He glanced at Jess, the fear shooting out in frantic pulses. Jess put her hand on Kelly's shoulder, snubbing Frank.

"Who was it?" I walked around the table and sat on it, facing Frank. The wood creaked under my weight. I leaned forward, almost butting noses with the terrified man. "Who was it?" I growled, putting as much alpha into it as I could.

SIXTEEN

"HER NAME WAS Kathy." The sweat poured off his face. "She said she was on birth control. She said that it would be fine."

"Was she the only one?" Kelly barked, lifting her tear-stained face to face him. "Was she?"

He flinched at every syllable as if it was a strike with Jess's claws, his hands twitching and ready to fly up to protect himself.

"Hey." I snapped my fingers to get Frank's full attention. "She asked you a question. And we need the answer. When, where and who is she? And is she the only one?"

"There was no one else, I swear. It...I mean, it's not possible. That's why I didn't say anything, I thought she was lying." The panda was rambling almost incoherently now, the words running out of his mouth in a brilliant display of verbal diarrhea.

"Wait a minute," Bran said from behind me, his voice so low I almost failed to catch it. "You're saying that you impregnated a woman—a regular human?"

Jess glanced at me and raised an eyebrow as if to ask that I rein my man in.

"It..." Again the handkerchief came up in a vain attempt to dry his face. I could smell the fear, the anxiety...the relief? "It...Her name was Kathy Wright. She worked at the hotel front desk." He shivered. "It was only a few months before I broke it off. When she called and told me she was pregnant I didn't know what to say. I knew she'd been faithful to me, or at least I'd thought up until then I was the only one."

Kathy let out a deep sigh, a painful moan.

Frank didn't look at her. "I knew it couldn't be mine but I told her I wasn't leaving my wife. She told me that it was fine, that she'd get an abortion and no one would know." His enormous shoulders rose and sank in a shrug. "I didn't even think about it until she sent me a letter, years later."

"She had the baby." I motioned with my hands for him to continue.

"She had the baby." He wrestled with the damp cloth. "Told me that she wouldn't bother me again, but she wanted me to know." The handkerchief fell out of his hands. "A boy."

Suddenly Kelly lashed out again, this time with claws showing.

The only thing that saved Frank's throat was Jess's speed. Her hand shot out, grabbing Kelly's forearm and yanking her back. It wasn't enough to save Frank's face, not totally—but it was enough to keep her from ripping his throat out.

The plump man fell to the right, one hand pressed to the deep gouges on his face while he stared at his wife in disbelief.

"Kelly!" Jess grabbed both hands and spun the angry woman around to face her, the Change starting on both their faces. "Stop it!" She roared with full authority. "Stop it!"

Kelly took a deep breath. The claws on her hands, one set already bloody, began to retract.

Jess remained in Changed shape, her furred face now aimed at the unfortunate man only a few feet away.

"You have a child?" The words reverberated through the apartment with such impact it felt like a yell even though she had whispered the words. "You have an undocumented child?"

Frank nodded, a bloody handkerchief pressed to his face. "She told me that she'd leave me alone, never ask for money." The words came out in a sad whine. "I never thought it was mine. You know we can't do that, but I didn't want to insult her by saying so…" The words trailed off when he saw no relief from Jess's anger.

"There's an easy solution." I picked up the bag of loose fur and handed it to him. "Scent this. Tell me if it's your son."

He took the bag from me. Frank pressed his nose to the opening. The deep cuts across his cheek still oozed blood. He needed stitches.

Frank's eyes opened, bloodshot and teary. "It's her. I can smell her. Kathy, I mean. She's here, she's right here with me. It's my son."

Jess reached over and snatched the bagged handful of fur away from him, her teeth bared. The elder Felis stood up and grabbed Frank by his shirt, dragging him to his feet.

I went to stand up, to try and move between them. Jess shoved me away with her free hand, sending me crashing to the bare floor.

Kelly curled up at the far end of the couch into a fetal position, crying uncontrollably into her hands. Brandon sprang out from behind the marble island and helped me to my feet, keeping a firm grip on my arm as he glared at the angry woman.

"Jess," I gasped. "You can't kill him. We have to know more." I wasn't sure if there actually was anything more Frank could offer but I was very sure Brandon would have trouble disposing of a body.

Jess snarled into Langley's face, the saliva dripping from her fangs. "You...you have broken so many rules that I don't even know where to begin." Her eyes narrowed. "And you had the nerve, the gall to try and get Davis to help cover for you."

Frank squirmed in her grip, not daring to even try to Change. "Davis called me when he heard that my name was being bandied about for your investigation." He swallowed once, the sound bouncing around the silent room. "I didn't know there was a murder, I just didn't want my affair to come out. The rumors, the gossip." His eyes drifted to the woman on the sofa, still sobbing into her arms. "I didn't want to hurt her more than I already had." The overweight man sighed, his eyes downcast. "I accept the decision of the Board."

"The decision? The decision? Now you want us to make a decision when you made yours without any consultation?" She bellowed, her spittle landing on the terrified man's face.

Jess spun around and tossed the hapless Langley across the room. The overweight man bounced across the hardwood floor, landing against a set of bookshelves. A handful of paperbacks fluttered down onto his unconscious body. A page stuck to his face and absorbed some of the blood.

Jess spun around to face Bran and me, still fully Changed. I stepped out in front, fighting the urge to cower in front of a stronger foe. In the back of my mind a young girl curled up in a fetal position, terrified at having to face Jess again.

"I'll be able to track her down, given time." I forced the fear back down, my voice as steady as I could make it. "A last name, my police contacts—I'll have a name and an address of this woman soon enough."

"And then?" Jess whirled around and pointed at the hysterical woman on the couch. "What do we do? You know that kits have to be helped, tutored, trained. There's a rogue out there, a rogue male..." She shook her head, letting me fill in the blanks.

"Wait a minute." Bran's steady voice snapped the tension in the room. "You said that a human can't breed with a Felis, right?"

Jess stared at him as if he had materialized out of thin air. "Yes."

"Right." He pointed at Frank. "So how did he get her pregnant?"

"The obvious way." Jess's tongue flicked out over her teeth. "Reb, did you have to get a stupid one too?"

Brandon put up one hand, at just the right level to not challenge her authority. "If that's true then this Kathy has to be a Felis, as well. Or you're dealing with a genetic mutation that hasn't happened before. Or..." His eyes narrowed. "Exactly where did you hear that our kind can't breed with yours?"

Wrinkles appeared on Jess's forehead. "We've just always known."

Bran moved closer, his head down slightly. The bastard knew just how to work in front of Jess so not to push her buttons. "Have you done genetic testing?" His gaze flashed to one side to meet mine. "Exactly how many Felis have married outside the family?"

"Ah..." I glanced at Jess. "Two? Three? I don't know."

She snorted. "A handful, if that."

"In how many years? How many generations?" Bran shook his head. "You don't even want to date outside the Pride, it's not surprising that so few of you consider marrying humans." His stare went past Jess and me and focused on the far wall. "How can you pull any sort of data from that sampling that can be reliable? When it's all based on legends and sayings?"

"Hrmph." Jess didn't encourage him but she didn't stop him.

"Right." Bran continued, "You can't make that sort of decision based on a handful of people. It's likely that we are alike on some biological level but maybe there hasn't been a lot of half-breeds because of the stigma you place on breeding outside the family." He waved at the weeping woman. "This is all because you Felis are so close-minded, so afraid to step outside your safety zone. If it scares you you hunt it, you kill it and you throw it out without thinking about the consequences." He nodded in my direction. "I've already seen how great the family is when they come up against something strange or different they can't control."

His tone had crept up into the danger/challenge zone.

Jess took a few steps toward Bran. Her lips curled back, showing way more teeth than I was comfortable with.

I moved closer to Bran, reaching inside me to see if I could call my claws up again. I knew even if I could it'd be an uneven fight.

Bran stood his ground, lifting his head to stare straight into Jess's eyes. "You could have others out there, lost boys and girls without a family because you decided that they can't exist." His voice rose again. "This was a long time in coming but it's here and now you have to figure out what to do with it. You can't ignore them or banish them from your precious secret society." He gave me a sad smile before returning to face Jess. "Time to man up, as the saying goes."

Jess's right cheek twitched, the scarlet mark dancing up and down on her thin fur. "We always assumed that it was impossible because it hadn't ever happened." She shot a glance at me. "We may have...misjudged the depth of that belief."

To his credit Bran moved back into submissive pose, letting his knees buckle just enough to avoid staring at her eye-to-eye. "A mistake is one thing. Not correcting that mistake when you have the chance is another."

Her lips twitched upwards as she nodded. "Point taken." Another look my way. "This one's smarter than he looks." She paused, her expression shifting from Board member to woman. "And if there's more of them out there..." A pained look crossed her face. "Oh, Reb... if there's more..." Her voice cracked, showing a side of the old broad I hadn't known existed.

"Let's take this one step at a time." I nodded toward Kelly who had curled up with her eyes closed. "First, you take care of her."

Bran walked behind me, retreating from Jess. He placed his hand on my shoulder and squeezed lightly in a show of support.

I patted his hand. "Bran and I will track down the woman and the son and take it from there."

"If you can." Jess exhaled, her teeth beginning to retract ever so slowly. "I'm not sure if this shouldn't return to the Board's control."

Brandon frowned. "Wait a minute. You're going to take the case away from Rebecca?"

"This is beyond what we first thought," Jess said as she began to return to human form. "Now we're dealing with a much more dangerous situation."

I crossed my arms and stared at Jess. "You hired me to find out who killed Janey Winters and I'm going to do that. With or without the Board's approval." I rose on my tiptoes. "With. Or. Without."

Jess stared at me for a minute. Her tongue flicked out to wet her lips, fangs still drawing back. "If he's a rogue male you're dealing with an unknown quality. And he's already tasted blood." A sudden softness appeared on her face. "There's a chance he'll have to be killed, and I don't think you've got the spirit to do it." Jess put up her hand before I could answer. "Don't start. At least, not right now."

"Not right now." I looked around the apartment. "Because right now you've got two people to take care of. And don't even think about sweeping this all under the carpet. If Frank meets with a sudden 'accident'…" I drew in a sharp breath, choosing my words carefully. "I'll make sure that all the major media outlets find out more about the Felis and our Pride than you ever thought." I tilted my head toward Brandon. "I can make a lot more noise than you can make quiet. There's been enough blood shed over this."

Jess looked at me. "You've developed quite an attitude in the past few years." A smile twitched the edges of her mouth. "Your parents would be proud of you."

I smiled back, resisting the urge to stomp on her foot in a childish rage. "Get them out of here and let me do my job, and tell Dennis that I'll have a full report for him as soon as I can. Including a bill."

The tall woman chuckled. "Understood." She nodded to Brandon. "Thanks for the coffee."

Bran answered her with a brusque nod then looked over to where Frank was slowly regaining consciousness. "If I get complaints from the neighbors…"

Jess shrugged and walked to the precariously leaning bookcase and the man at the bottom of it. A single
shove pushed the shelves back into place and another
brought the portly man to his feet. "Send me the bill
if you need to."

"I..." Frank stammered as Jess pushed him toward
the front door. "I'm sorry. It was just a fling, so many
years ago...I had no idea..."

"We're going back to the farm." Jess helped Kelly
to her feet. "The Board will have to decide how to deal
with this, and I think everyone needs a bit of a time out."

A few minutes later there was only the two of us and
Jazz, who hopped up on the couch and curled up at one
end to begin the lengthy routine of cleaning her snow-
white fur, tail-tip to ear-tip. The feline let out a loud
and lengthy yawn before returning to the task at hand.

"Dang." Bran shook his head. "That girl knows how
to relax."

"Ain't that the truth." I poured myself a fresh cup of
coffee and added a healthy spoonful of sugar and a dash
of milk. "But at least we have a suspect now."

"A hybrid." Bran rolled his tongue around his mouth,
pushing out his cheeks. "Never thought I'd be dealing
with a story like that." A wild look came into his eye.
"Wonder what sort of *bling* I could get for this..." The
sentence trailed off when he caught my vicious glare.

"Do. Not. Even. Go. There." I took a sip, trying to
force my pulse down to a decent level. "You're lucky
we didn't have a bloodbath here."

"Right." He poured himself the last of the coffee.
"Kelly was pretty pissed, that's true."

I cradled the mug in both hands. The marble island
was a cool oasis compared to the heated discussions
that had just occurred. "But not surprising. Married

for all those years and now she finds out there's a bastard son out there."

"In slight defense of Frank," he grimaced as he spoke, "very slight defense—he thought it was impossible for a human female to get pregnant." Bran picked at his shirt and removed a single white cat hair from his right arm. "You'd think that more Felis men would be out there getting it on the side. Instant birth control."

I chuckled into my coffee. "You just saw how his wife reacted. Think of that happening without Jess around to save you."

Bran sucked in his breath over clenched teeth and sent out a whistle that startled the white cat on the couch. She paused then returned to her cleaning routine after assessing for danger.

"That...would be scary," he mumbled into the coffee, almost too low for me to hear. "Not that you'd ever have to worry 'bout that."

"Problem is, how do we find Kathy Wright?" I walked to one of the windows and looked down.

A streetcar ran by, clanging the bell as it trundled along the steel tracks. The long cables ran down to the back of the metal bullet, providing power for the lumbering mammoth. Around it smaller cars zipped and dodged, looking for a way to sneak around and in front of the monster as it dumped commuters and picked up new ammunition.

"All we have is a name and even that might not be real. She could have changed her name or gotten married or just disappeared." A trail of young children toddled down the sidewalk, hanging onto a piece of rope with a teacher at the lead. A small caravan of clothing racks rumbled behind them, blouses and scarves waving in the wind and threatening to break away and smother the streetcar in a revolution of color. The gears began to grind, albeit slowly, in my addled brain.

I dialed Mike Winters. He picked it up on the third ring.

"Hello?"

"Mike, it's Rebecca Desjardin. I'm sorry to bother you but I have a quick question—did Janey mention anything about her students? Any problems, any kids who were a handful for her?"

"No." The confusion was evident in his voice. "She had just transferred to that school, actually. It was an emergency assignment. The old teacher was hospitalized with a stroke. She took over his class, a last-minute thing."

I waved my hands in the air, mimicking writing. Bran scrambled around the apartment as I kept talking. "What school was this? And what course?"

"David Thomson High School. She took over his history classes not too long before she died." He stumbled over the words for a minute. "Do you think it was one of her students?" The words became frantic, tumbling out one after the other. "One of those kids? She wasn't even there long enough to find the teachers' lounge, never mind start a fight with a student or give one a reason to have a grudge against her."

"I'm exploring all possibilities." I put on my soothing tone. "Just following up on some leads."

"It was just a temp assignment. It wasn't planned. You think it was a kid?" Disbelief and dismay came out in every word.

"It's just routine." My fingers itched to have something to do. "I'll let you know when I have something concrete to report."

"The kids went out to the farm." His words were

clipped and terse. "They went a bit wild. A lot of crying and yelling."

I nodded. "Can't blame them."

"I wanted to, you know. I wanted to." Mike wheezed into the receiver. "We didn't go to Ruth's funeral because it would have been too much. They can't handle it, not all at once."

"I understand." I closed my eyes. "I'll be in touch." A few more mumbled sympathies and I hung up the phone.

Bran shoved a pen and notepad at me. "Write." While I scribbled the information, he peered over the countertop at me. "A student, hmm?"

"Roll with me here." My writing moved across the empty pad in huge, looping spirals. "One of the first things every kit learns about is how to control ourselves, how to not Change when it's not a good time. When it's not safe. How to deal with the overwhelming amount of odors in the air around us and how not to react to them."

"Like what?" He stared down at the wild lines. My notes looked like wild balloon herds migrating across the page.

"For example, when a woman's…Well, at that time of the month when she's most fertile." I felt the heat rise on my cheeks. "Maybe you've noticed or maybe not— we smell pretty good. Well, multiply that by a thousand and you get what an average Felis male has to deal with. The rush and emotions…" I closed my eyes. "It's not as bad for the women, but we get pretty horny at times. To put it bluntly."

"And when you hit puberty…"

"You learn how to control yourself, what to do and what not to do to stay in command of your urges. It's the same as with humans, but a whole lot harder. And that's with the help of other Felis and family around."

I jabbed the pen down at the words scribbled on the paper. "If this kid's grown up with little or no training in self-control he's a ticking time bomb ready to go off."

"And when he walked into that classroom and spotted Janey Winters, smelled her..." Bran nodded, a thoughtful look on his face. "It must have been pretty overwhelming."

"Exactly." I picked up the phone and dialed Information. "But I don't think he attacked Janey to rape her. I think he was looking for a kindred spirit. He knew she was different, like him."

"He might have just wanted someone to talk to." Brandon picked up the empty coffee cups and put them in the sink. "Raging hormones and all."

"Even as adults we have trouble keeping our hormones in check." I scribbled down a number. "How many horny teenage boys chase after girls daily and vice versa? Compound that with a Felis bloodline..." I shook my head. "Odds stacked against him double."

"So why send me the photograph?" Bran asked. "Whether he killed her intentionally or by accident he didn't have to do that."

"A cry for help, maybe." I fumbled with the phone. "His mom can't tell him what he is and he can't find any information on his 'condition' because the Felis keep that sort of thing under wraps. You can't Google us and find anything other than myth and rumors. He can't go to the cops after killing Janey and ask them what he is. He can't ask Janey 'cause she's dead. Maybe he figured you'd investigate and tell him what he is." I couldn't help smirking. "No better way to find out what sort of freak you are than to go to a reporter who loves freaks."

"Only you." Bran shook his head. "A shrink would have a field day with that."

"There's a reason why most Felis avoid working in the psychiatric field."

Bran grinned, watching while I spoke briefly to the operator then to the school secretary. He flinched when I turned the air blue with my swearing and hung up.

"They won't give me any information. Seems they're concerned about privacy issues."

"Well, can't blame them." Bran shrugged when I glared at him. "Hey, they're worried about psychos and stalkers these days. Not the same atmosphere as we grew up in."

"Speak for yourself. I spent more time playing in the long grass stalking imaginary monsters than you did, I bet." I rapped the end of the pen on the table. "Mind you, it might be all for naught. Without a name we're dealing with dozens of kids, maybe hundreds."

Brandon turned the water on briefly and splashed liquid into the cups. "She might have changed her last name from Wright. Or gotten married. Remember, it's not the sin it used to be to have a child out of wedlock or whatever it's called these days. Lots of men out there who don't mind being stepfathers." He let out an exaggerated sigh. "Oh, those wacky kids these days."

"Shut up and grab your jacket." I strode across the room, eyes darting about as I looked for my own.

He didn't move, leaning on the counter. "It's almost six o'clock, girl. Ain't no schooling going on right now."

My eyes went to the window again. True enough, the shadows were beginning to creep across the street. The streetcars continued to grumble and groan their way across the intersection but with more and more weary people just wanting to get home.

"Damn." I shook my head. "No wonder the secretary sounded so pissy. Must have caught her on the way out the door."

"Probably." Bran opened the refrigerator door. "How about steaks for dinner? Get you geared up for hitting the school in the morning." I opened my mouth to protest but he overran me. "Look, there's no good going to the school right now—aside from showing your cards too soon. Take it from a gambler, you don't flash your hand before you know what the other guy's got." He gestured toward the computer table. "Go work on that while I get these on the grill."

"Might as well research the area," I grumbled, sitting down with a thump in the chair. The keyboard beckoned with the well-worn keys urging me to just take a breather from the marathon I'd been running for the past few hours.

"Tell me about Ruth." His words drifted over to me from the kitchen area along with the enticing sizzle of a good hot grill. I took a deep breath, inhaling various spices and the delicious scent of raw meat.

"One minute." My fingers ran over the keyboard as I accessed various databases and started up the search engines. Anyone who's got a whit of paranoia in their soul will tell you that thanks to the internet your entire life is an open book—and they're not far from wrong. Depending on who you are and what you do and who's looking, you can pretty well dig up a lot of dirt on anyone. Add in a few little back door secrets into databases I collected over the years through my investigative work and I usually was able to find something, anything on a person.

"Ruth was an amazing woman. Takes someone with a lot of patience to keep the kits in line." I frowned as the data flashed across the screen. "Kathy Wright seems to not exist currently, at least not in any format I can find."

"Go figure." The moist slap of meat hitting the grill started my mouth watering. Some instincts you can't fight or don't even want to. "Raising the kits?"

"Well, you have to understand that from birth, we're a pretty rowdy bunch. Takes a strong hand to handle a baby to start with, never mind one who can change into a kitten at any time. More like a baby bobcat, to be honest. A lot of Felis parents liked to come and drop the kids off for a break, catch their breath." The screen flickered and changed, coughing up new information. "There's been no unexplained rise in crime in the area around the school. That's good."

"So he's not just indiscriminately killing and attacking. That's something positive." The scent of melted butter and sliced onions hit my nostrils. "So Ruth kept you kids in line?"

"So to speak. More of corralling us to make sure we didn't kill ourselves." My stomach gave an answering growl to the aromas floating around us. "She had the patience of a saint."

"To deal with you, probably." The snicker was accompanied by a resurgence of sizzling as the steaks were flipped over. "What do you think will happen to Davis?"

"If he lives? Probably retired to a nice house somewhere with a caretaker." I wished my stomach would stop rumbling and distracting me. "Jess won't want anyone else to know what's going on until she can put the information out there in bits and pieces under Board control. Put him someplace safe, make up a story and everyone's happy."

"Really? You think anyone outside of the family

would buy that?" The sound of a cork popping. "Got me a good bottle of red wine here. I think we both need a drink after today."

"True but I'd rather have a beer, if you have any. Don't really feel in a wine mood." The screen flashed again and burped more results. "People will believe anything if they want to. You buy what the media tells you, what's the difference?"

"Point." The clink of silverware. "Food is ready. I assume you're comfortable with medium rare."

I spun around in the chair and grinned at him across the apartment. "You know me way too well."

Jazz let out a plaintive cry from her perch on the couch when I pushed the chair back, glancing toward her full food dish. I wagged a finger at her. "Not going to happen." She cocked her head to one side, rolling her front paw outward. "Okay, maybe after dinner."

Outside a streetcar's brakes wailed and screamed, but there was no answering crash of steel on steel. Jazz responded by twisting onto her back and ignoring us.

We ate dinner in silence, two bottles of cold beer sitting between us. Brandon looked over at where I dissected the bloody slab of meat into small bite-sized portions before eating.

"You want to talk about it?"

"What?" I ripped a mouthful of steak free with my fork.

"You're not upset." He waved the knife toward my plate. "You just lost your home, your surrogate mother and witnessed a whole lot of gore within a day or two. Not to mention that entire scene at the farm." He daintily put a small piece of steak into his mouth. "That might just be a bit much for some people to deal with."

"I guess." I pushed one of the roasted red pepper

slices through a small puddle of blood. "I suppose I'm not that flustered because I knew eventually it'd pull me back in. It's part of the Felis lifestyle, the fighting and the consequences. It's in our blood." The small line of fat running along the edge of the steak fought hard when I pressed the knife down. "I guess I never really got used to it not being there. If that makes any sense."

He nodded. "I can see that. It's a strange, strange world."

I peered over the dark brown bottle.

"No, just different. Different rules, different lifestyle. Just different," I snapped.

He didn't say anything. His knife poked down between a sliver of bone and meat, wedging the two apart.

"I'm sorry." I dragged the last piece of meat to the edge of the plate, leaving it alone. "I guess I am upset. I just don't know what to do about it. You, me, Jess…"

Brandon's eyebrows rose. "That threesome is not appealing to me at all."

I smirked. "Duly noted." A small onion slice danced in the blood, tempting me. "I just don't know what to make of her. She was the one who…who…" I couldn't get the words out. Instead I rolled my shoulders. "She's the one who recommended me for this because of who I am, what I am."

"How well did you know her, you know, before?"

"Hardly at all." I speared the lonely piece of steak. "Ruth said Jess knew my parents but I never asked about it. Never seemed to be the right time." I added the last bit of onion. "Still isn't."

"If not now, when?"

I chewed slowly, putting my energy into shredding the meat. "How about after we find this kid?" I couldn't help letting my annoyance slip through.

Bran nodded. "Okay. I get that." He pointed at the couch with his knife. "Am I there or in my own bed tonight?"

"Are we fighting?" I smiled, tipping the bottle toward my mouth.

"I don't know." He chuckled. "Are we?"

"Only if it's foreplay." I waved my fork. "And before you even go there, no—Felis are not more prone to S&M than anyone else."

"I wasn't thinking that." His right eyebrow arched upward. "But, now that you mention it," he said, "as you know, I am open to new experiences." His eyes caught mine. "And I like exploring all angles." He drew his eyes down and over my body, his tongue flicking out to wet his lips.

I pushed the near-empty plate away from me, feeling a delicious tingle begin to surge through my veins. A good slab of meat in my belly and a handsome man across the table. Yeah, I could make this work.

I glanced at Jazz. "You're on guard duty tonight. Don't mess up." She answered with a long, leisurely stretch of each toe to its full extent, reaching out with one leg then the other. I turned back to Bran. "We're good."

He tipped back his own bottle of beer, finishing it off. "Bet I can make you purr."

"Felis don't purr."

"Bet I can make you." He leered at me, sending a thrill up my spine.

"Just don't forget to set the alarm clock."

SEVENTEEN

THE NEXT MORNING we were standing in front of David Thomson High School at seven o'clock, both of us bleary-eyed and less than bushy-tailed. Brandon handed me a Starbucks cup of coffee, shuffling his feet from side to side.

"Your own fault." I shook myself awake again.

"Well, I think it was worth it." He grinned at me. "Now I know what makes you purr." His attention returned to the scene in front of us, ignoring my blush. "Are you sure this is a good idea?" he mumbled, taking a sip of his own brew.

"No. But it's a good place to start." I gestured toward the empty school parking lot. "As long as I stay upwind of this kid, I'll be fine. He won't be able to tell that I'm anyone other than just another adult."

"Except that we're technically trespassing," Bran said. "Sooner or later someone's going to tell the office that there are two people hanging out near the parking lot and we're going to be chatting to the police about how we're not predators."

"Except by then we should know who the kid is. Besides, we've got identification and a good reason to be here. Cops won't mind. Much."

"When we know who the kid is…" Bran took another sip and shrugged, adjusting the light jacket lying across his shoulders. "What do we do? Can't just walk to the cops and tell them that he's the killer 'cause he smells bad."

I looked at Bran. "He doesn't smell 'bad.' Each Felis has their own individual scent." I turned my attention back to the parking lot. "You've got one. You just don't know it."

He sniffed his armpits, making a scene of it. "Oh, I can tell." His hand reached over and down to pinch my bottom. "And you smell pretty darned good yourself at times."

I slapped his hand away despite the wanton thoughts intruding into my mind. "Work, Bran. Work. I'm hoping we can just talk to this kid and reason him into custody."

"How do you figure that? He's killed one woman and attacked you, as far as we know. Not exactly a poster child for hug therapy."

"He's a lost, confused kid." The school buses had begun to arrive, accompanied by a fleet of minivans as parents dropped off their precious cargoes—that couldn't or wouldn't ride the buses. "It's likely he's got no self-control to start with, no idea of what's going on in his mind and body. Like I said—puberty's tough enough without being a Felis."

"Yeah. I remember those days. Except I wasn't running amok and killing my teacher." Bran nodded when a gaggle of giggling schoolgirls strutted by, ignoring us with a toss of their collective heads. "Just as I remember."

"Huh." The yellow buses began to discharge their cargo. I looked up and sniffed the air. "Still good. As long as the wind doesn't change, we're good."

Bran nodded, scanning the growing crowd of students. "I hope you're right. Otherwise this could be a very bad scene."

A light breeze drifted over us and I caught the familiar odor.

"There." I pointed toward a cluster of young men, jocks by the looks of them. Varsity jackets with the usual stream of lettered patches down one arm, a bunch of surly faced, pimply annoying little men, and one of them was my boy.

The wind shifted, sweeping my breath away as the different scents dragged over my senses and reversed, taking them to the crowd. None of which would notice unless they were Felis.

A tall young man peeled out of the crew and stood to one side. He dropped his backpack to the ground and raised his face to the sky.

He was just a little taller than Brandon, jet-black hair cut into a shaggy mass and long, lanky arms pushing the limits of his team jacket. He began to spin around, his dark brown eyes searching for the source. His nose was twitching, pulling in the scent of the woman he'd attacked.

He saw me.

I saw him.

He broke into a run, sprinting away from the student crowd. I threw down my coffee and followed, ignoring Brandon who had no chance to catch up.

A herd of clucking seniors appeared in my path when I charged down the sidewalk, nattering about some reality show. I pushed my way through despite their cursing and gestures, knocking more than one expensive electronic gadget to the ground.

He was picking up speed. I dashed out onto the road, hoping the pavement would help me make up the distance. I ignored the shards of pain shooting up my right hamstring, focusing on keeping him in sight.

My pulse began to sound in my ears, my running shoes hitting the pavement in a perfect rhythm. The boy's scent was strong in my nostrils and I was on a hunt, slipping back into old routines as if I had just been on the farm yesterday tracking my first hare. The slap-slap of my leather jacket on my shoulders rang true as I dodged around a car door, carelessly flung open by a woman who hadn't checked her rear-view mirror.

The young man ducked down an alleyway, picking up speed and then losing it again as he leaped over scattered boxes and debris. His steps were becoming slower and labored with his staggered wheezing flying back to my ears. He hadn't trained for a long distance chase and certainly not for being the hunted, not the hunter.

The alley wasn't too far from where he had killed Janey. It stank of urine and feces—and not just the animal type. Stacks of cardboard boxes lined the walls, soaked and disintegrating sodden masses, threatening to catch my toes and send me flying. I was gaining on the kit.

The dark-haired kid slammed into a wire mesh fence so hard I wondered if he had knocked himself out. It sure would help. I was beginning to reach the end of my adrenaline-fueled rage and needed a break.

The boy spun around and roared, Changing so fast I nearly impaled myself on his claws as I skidded to a full stop.

He had the light stripe down one side of his face, identical to Frank's, but he wasn't an old man on the downside of life. He was young, eager and untrained, and had already tasted blood. Not the rabbit blood or deer blood from my youth. Human blood.

Facing him was a crippled Felis who couldn't Change. A woman with fifteen-plus years on him—

most of which had been spent without the ability to Change.

I knew who I'd put my money on, and it wasn't the old broad.

He ripped off his jacket and snarled at me, revealing a set of gouges on his forearms from our previous meeting. His face contorted and finished Changing as he yelled again, fangs now fully visible.

"Look…" I put out one hand and tried to look and sound as comforting as I could—Ruth trying to console an upset kit. In my mind's eye I flashed back to her trying to tell me my parents had died and that I was on my own but not really alone. There was always family.

"Look, I'm like you. You know that." I spread my hands out, palms exposed. "I know we got off on the wrong foot before, but we've got this in common. Let me take you to someone who can help you learn about what you are, who you are. I can do that." I forced myself to smile. "You're not alone. You don't have to be."

"You're a cop." The low growled response came. "You want to put me in a cage."

"No." I studied the kid. "I'm like you."

"You say you are. You smell like you are. Show me." He motioned me forward with one furred hand, his claws catching the dim light in the alley. "Show me your claws again. Show me some fur, cop. Or are you just trying to trick me with some fancy smells and special effects?"

I cursed silently. "Look, it's a long story but I can't Change. Trust me, I'm just like you. And I want to…"

The young boy charged at me, roaring with both arms outstretched.

So much for talking him down.

I stepped to one side just at the right moment,

dropped and swung my leg around, catching him in a vicious trip. At the speed he was going it would be a miracle if he didn't snap his neck.

Which he didn't, thankfully. Instead the kid skidded several feet in the muck and mire, landing in a jumbled heap against the wall about twenty feet from where I stood. He was precariously close to the main street and exposure as a Felis in broad daylight.

It was a stupid move, a child's move, and one that any experienced fighter could have dodged or avoided. Except this kid was running on adrenaline, hormones, action movies and as many video game moves as he could memorize. In the fantasy world you don't end up face down in a pool of piss. Well, at least not too often.

He sprung to his feet and spun around to face me again, angrier than ever. His face glistened, the fur highlighting every bit of moisture. The T-shirt was soaked, clinging to his muscled form along with his faded jeans. If nothing else, I had managed to make him smell even worse.

A figure appeared behind him, silhouetted in the daylight.

"What's going on?" The policeman stepped forward, one hand on his belt and the other outstretched into the darkness of the alley. "Both of you, hold it!"

The boy spun around, still partially in the shadows. His hands flexed open and shut once, twice.

"I said, hold it right there!" The cop was young, blond and just started to shave. His eyes were wide and blue and I could smell his fear. Great.

His hand fumbled with the small strap covering his holster. "I said, hold it!" His voice rose with the last word, edging into squeaky girl mode.

The rogue stepped toward the policeman, his face

still in the shadows. He'd reach the policeman first unless I did something.

I dashed toward the front of the narrow alley as the
cop pulled his automatic pistol free, the barrel shaking
in the daylight. His other hand went to the radio mike
secured to his right shirt epaulette. "C234, I need some
backup here at McDonald Street, near Sanderson. Two
people fighting in an alleyway, attempting to put them
under arrest."

My hand dipped down into a thick pile of something-I-didn't-want-to-think-about, coming up with a
baseball-sized mess. I tossed it at the policeman, trying hard not to breathe as the stinky, slimy mess left
my hand. It soared past the rogue's head and splattered
dead center on the cop's chest.

The astonished man looked down at the soggy stinking garbage soaking his uniform shirt—ignoring the
kid for a second. "What the…" His nose wrinkled, the
smell of the alley's debris almost overwhelming him.

The kid turned around and glared at me. I could see
his mental wheels spinning, going over his options. Stay
and fight and get shot and arrested or flee.

He charged down the narrow lane past me, slowing
down just enough to scoop up his jacket. He leaped to
one side, bouncing off the walls to get enough height
to clear the fence at the far end.

I watched as he dropped back down onto the pavement. He looked back at me, shook his head and sprinted
off into a side alley.

The policeman wiped his shirt with his free hand,
the pistol still pointed at me. "You…"

"Hey." I raised my hands. "I'm good to go."

An hour later I sat on the wooden bench at the booking area of Station 14, beside a Parkdale hooker who hadn't been able to tell a cop from a potential customer and a drunk with a bloody nose who kept falling asleep on the prostitute's shoulder.

Hank Attersley appeared at the front counter, his face beet-red while he talked in a low voice to the sergeant. A lot of hand-waving ensued, with more than a few references to "that woman" being made. I suspected they weren't discussing the one next to me with more false parts than the Bionic Woman.

Finally the sergeant threw up his hands and pushed a piece of paper over to the detective, which he signed and pushed back. The older man approached me, his hands on his hips.

"I'm not sure whether to be upset or laugh," he rumbled from deep in his gut. "That poor fellow is going to spend a fortune getting that uniform dry-cleaned."

"He'd be better off tossing the entire thing out." I offered my handcuffed wrists. "Please?"

He didn't move. "We're going to go back to my desk to talk."

"You can talk to me." The young woman next to me batted her eyes at the police detective. "And I won't even charge ya for it."

Hank rolled his eyes as he reached down and undid the cuffs. "Follow. Now."

The old desk was scratched and battered, at least ten times older than the computer it held. Off to one side a snapshot of Hank and his wife riding horses sat in a stainless steel frame, one I had sent him at Christmas.

Hank dropped into the wooden chair with such force the wheels screamed for mercy. "What the hell are you doing?" He rubbed his temples. "Actually, don't tell me too much. I don't really want to know."

"Look, I'm sorry about messing up the kid's uniform." I sat down in the interview chair next to the desk. "But geez, Hank—are you getting them out of high school these days? That kid's barely old enough to shave!"

He closed his eyes again then opened them. "Right now I wouldn't push your luck, Reb." His gaze focused in on the two riders. "Assaulting a police officer is still a crime." He looked at me, putting the full intensity of his twenty years of experience behind those steely blue eyes. "What was that all about?"

I drew a deep breath, feeling an ache in my ribs. Not as young as I thought I was. "The teen's involved in a case I'm working on."

"The Winters case?" Hank motioned for me to continue.

I stayed silent.

"Reb, if this kid's a suspect and you let him go…" One hand reached over to open a desk drawer. "I'm trying hard not to hear this."

"It's only a lead." I watched him grab a plastic bottle of warm water. "If anything, your officer interfered in our discussion and enabled him to escape."

"As I understand it, you two were tussling in the dirt and he wasn't sure who was attacking who." His forehead furrowed. "Or is that 'whom'? I always get that screwed up." He twisted the small blue cap off and took a deep swig of the clear liquid. "Look, tell me what you know about the kid. Let me put that into the Winters file and get it re-opened." The portly detective held up the bottle and let out a deep sigh. "If you had ever told me growing up that I'd be paying a buck a bottle for water, I'd have said you were nuts." He turned back to me. "So…what's going on?"

"It's a possible lead. I don't want to turn over the info to your boys right now because it may be nothing."

"We don't want to check out 'nothing'?" His eyes narrowed. "This doesn't have anything to do with that scummy reporter downstairs waiting for you, does it?"

I sat back in the uncomfortable metal chair. "He's here?"

Hank gazed at the ceiling. "Yes, he's here and he's waiting to see if he has to bail you out or not." He picked up a well-chewed pencil from the desk and gnawed on the pink eraser for a minute before continuing. "You're not seriously working with this jerk, are you?"

"What if I am?" I knew better, but wasn't in the mood to play the submissive today.

Small bits of eraser landed in my lap. "I can't believe this. Reb, you could do so much better than…" His lips pressed, he could do nothing but gesture at the door. "Working for that rag? Girl, if you had started a few years younger you could have gotten on the force, easy and be here, with me, instead of selling yourself out to some idiot thinking he's found the Holy Grail and wants to sell tickets to touch it!" His voice rose until everyone in the room was staring at him, quite the accomplishment considering he wasn't the most interesting attraction. That honor went to the drunk goof in the corner who was alternating between vomiting on himself and expounding on his views of the Canada-U.S. Free Trade Agreement.

"No offense, but that's really none of your business." I tried to soften my tone, seeing the pain and annoyance in his eyes. "Look, I'm working the case, and you know that I can't share some information with you. I was hired by the family and I answer to them first."

"This is a murder case, Reb." Hank lowered his voice

to an angry whisper. "I know you've never worked a murder case and there's a reason for that—it's our area of expertise. We don't have private investigators running around here like they do in the U.S. or on film getting into everyone's business and screwing up a good case." A worried look came over his face. "You know how much trouble I could be in just for listening to this and not putting those cuffs back on you?"

I leaned forward. "Hank, I'm not trying to cause trouble. All I'm doing is following a lead. That's what the family hired me for, to investigate Janey Winters's death 'cause you're overworked and understaffed." I arched a brow. "Unless I missed something in the last couple of days."

He let out a huff of agreement. "If you only knew how bad it was." A quick glance around the room. "Half the horror stories aren't that far from the truth. They're talking budget cuts and I'm not ready to retire."

"Which is why I'm doing what I'm doing." I beamed my best smile at him. "And I really don't have anything to connect this kid with the case other than a rumor he was in the area. He got pushy and we got into a tussle. Honest."

"Honest." He looked at me. "Reb, I can't let a killer go free. You know that. This isn't some movie where we all dance off into the sunset and the killer joins a monastery 'cause of his injured spirit." One thick finger tapped the wooden desk, hard. "Winters's killer needs to be dealt with. And not with some freakish vigilante justice."

"I swear." My right hand landed on my heart. "If he gives me reason to believe he's got anything to do with Janey Winters's death I will hand him over to the

proper authorities. Swear." I left out the part where, by
Felis law, it would be the Board.

He stared at me for a long minute without blinking
before pulling away. "Don't make me a liar, Reb." A
sad look crossed his face. "Don't make me regret our
friendship."

"Who the hell else would put up with you?" I sighed
dramatically, drawing attention from the prostitute who
had now been moved to a desk not too far from where
I sat. "I mean, Hank...those fuzzy handcuffs only go
so far, ya know?"

The detective let out a chuckle, dismissing the curious stares from both police and criminals. "Right.
Well, I don't think the rookie wants to press charges.
Be too embarrassing, I figure. So you're free to go. But
don't get in over your head with this, Rebecca. Your
rep isn't so good that it can take a hit from hanging out
with street scum like that photo dog." Attersley shook
his head and slid another of his business cards across
the desk. "Just be careful, girl. I don't want to be visiting your grave 'cause some nutcase figured you were
standing too close to him and popped you."

"I'll be fine." I picked up the new card and placed it
in my back pocket.

"Now get out of here before I change my mind and
lock your ass up for a month!" Hank stood up and
roared, shooting a sly wink in my direction.

I strutted out through the swinging wooden gate, letting it snap against my butt with a resounding crack. I
could have let it miss me, but then who am I to pass up
a chance to make a dramatic exit?

A short elevator ride down into the main lobby led
me into the crowded main floor where people were
being sorted, deported and contorted into various

groups depending on what they were there for. I spotted Brandon, sitting on a wooden bench far in the back with a relaxed look on his face while he watched one particularly endowed woman juggle her bosom back into the smallest tank top in history.

"Hey." I strode to him, making a point to ignore the flamboyant woman next to him. Maybe a hooker, maybe not—who was I to judge? Besides, she probably made more in a night than I did in perhaps…a month.

"Hey." He jumped to his feet and swung a knapsack over his shoulder a bit too quickly, his face flushed. "No bail?"

"No bail." I glanced at the woman next to us. "They decided to let me go until they find the body."

The floozy's face dropped like a rock as she turned away from ogling Brandon. I hooked my arm into his and escorted him through the crowd out into the cool night air.

"That was interesting." Bran chuckled, maneuvering me away from the police station down a side street. "I thought they'd toss the book at you."

"Nah." I smiled. "Hank's a good cop, but he's not going to toss me to the wolves unless I can give them something. And right now, we've got less than nothing." The brisk air shot into my lungs with a cold burst, flushing out the sweaty stink of the police station. "He got me to promise that I'd turn the kid over to the authorities if I found he had anything to do with the murder."

"Which, of course, in your interpretation would be the Board." Brandon was as smart as he was sexy. Damn.

I grinned. "You're catching on to how we work."

"He won't get in trouble?" Brandon opened the door of a Starbucks and motioned me in. "Get a coffee and a snack. We'll pretend it's a nutritious lunch and boost our caffeine levels."

"Right." I strutted up to the corner and placed my order, adding a thick slab of carrot cake. Taking a seat at the far end of the café, I glanced out the window at the traffic crawling by.

Bran put the tray down in front of us. "Again, and your cop buddy won't get in trouble?"

"I hope not. It'd be nice if the kid worked his way through the system and did his time but…" The carrot cake was moist and sweet when I took a bite, buying a second of thinking time. "You can't put a Felis behind bars. Might as well just slit his throat and be done with it."

"And Felis justice is…" Brandon stirred his own light brown coffee with a wooden stir stick. "More of what I saw last night?"

"It may not be pretty, but it's what we've done for years." I wasn't ready to go into a discussion about the Pride and what passed for law in the family. I'd been on both sides and wasn't sure I could explain or defend it.

"So what was the deal with assaulting the cop?" He lowered his voice to a whisper, glancing at the other patrons. "That's all they told me."

"Had the kid in an alleyway. Couldn't let the cop see him in full Change." I added sugar to my coffee and took a sip. "Better to let the kid go."

Bran shook his head as he reached over and pulled off a small bit of my carrot cake. "I'm still not getting what all the secrecy is about. Why not come out to the world?" He sat back in the well-worn faux leather chair and tilted his head toward the window and the pedestrians outside. "Do you really think their world is going to change that much if they find out there's Felis out there?"

I almost gave myself whiplash looking around to see if anyone had overheard Bran's statement. "Scream it a bit louder, why don't you…"

"No one's listening." He grinned before reaching over and grabbing my hands. "I could tell them I was a vampire and you were a zombie and no one would care. Or they'd try to sign us to movie contracts. So, back to my question—why won't you consider coming out?"

The carrot cake fell apart under the white plastic fork, making me even more envious of those who could cook. If it didn't have the baking instructions "just add water" it wasn't in my cupboard. I tried to corral my thoughts as I chewed on another delicious mouthful.

"Think of it this way—are you willing to stake the lives of innocent children on it? Because there's always going to be someone who'll try to use our differences to justify violence. One screaming xenophobic madman, one bomb, one group of Felis kids on a playground somewhere." I jerked my thumb out the window at the passing pedestrians. "Heck, we can't all get along just based on skin color. Imagine adding that some of us get darned furry whenever we feel like it." I lifted the paper cup to my lips. "I imagine there'd be a slew of lawsuits from freaks wondering if they can claim paternity because they're furries on the weekend or some lunatic demanding we all be sterilized to keep the gene pool furball free." A shoving match began just outside the coffee shop, as if on cue—a pair of teenage boys posturing for a larger group waiting for the streetcar. We watched the game act out over the next two minutes until everyone had saved enough face and the streetcar arrived.

I took a sip of coffee. "That's why. And I've yet to hear a good argument against it."

Brandon nodded. "Okay. So what's our next step?"

"We go back to the school and see who the kid was. Get a name from his friends or bluff the school into giving it to us, start tracking him that way." I grimaced, thinking of the footwork. "Take a few hours but I figure we can browbeat the info out of someone."

"Or..." Bran pushed the knapsack he had been carrying over to my feet. "We check his book bag." He grinned as my eyes went wide. "What, you think I just stood around when you ran off?"

EIGHTEEN

I TOOK THE bag from him and flipped open the leather flap. "You walked into the cop shop with this? Are you nuts?"

He put his hands together with a twinkle in his eye. "Wise man say, walk with attitude and never blink."

"That's awful." I pulled out a handful of binders. "However, I'll forgive you this time." I opened the first book and read the name carefully printed on the cover. "Tony Kolanski."

"Definitely not his mother's name." Bran stole another piece of cake. "Guess she got married. Or remarried."

"Whatever." History, physics and one battered mathematics book that must have dated back to the 1980s. "Nothing else here—guess he keeps his electronics on him." I pushed the books back into the bag. "Finish up and we'll go visit his mother."

"What?" Bran frowned. "You think she knows about him going wild?"

I nodded and took another sip. "She's his mother. She knows something's wrong, I'm sure of that. But she probably doesn't know how bad things have gotten. Right now he's a kid on the run and probably pretty pissed off." I pulled out my cell phone and hit Jess's number. "But we can at least start a hunt for him and his home is as good a place to start as any."

Bran reached over and took the phone from me. "I

don't think that's a good idea. You really want to put a citywide hunt out for this kid?"

"Uh…Yes." I didn't snatch the phone back from where it sat on the circular table, but I was close. "Jess's going to be able to throw down a roadblock and track this kit wherever he's hiding. If he tries to leave the city by bus, plane or train we'll know long before the cops do, and it'll be a lot more quiet than screaming it over the airwaves."

"And that's for the best?" The edge of Bran's mouth twisted up in a sarcastic smile. "Having him hunted down like a dog?"

"Like a cat, if you want to continue the image properly." The coffee was cooling quicker than I could drink it. "Look, this 'kid' has killed one woman, and attacked me. Twice." I held up two fingers to emphasize my point. "So I'm not really thinking that he's going to roll over and ask for a tummy rub if we meet him again. Throw down the net and we'll pick him up somewhere down the line."

Bran shook his head. "I can tell you from experience that if he slips into the runaway underground, you'll never find him."

"Never say never." My gaze remained on the phone.

"Look…" His hand landed atop mine. "I'm not bullshitting you on this. He could be in a whole other city by lunchtime if he makes the right connections. Hocks his toys and hits the road and then where will you be?"

"And this talks me out of calling Jess because…"

"He's not going to split without trying to get some funds. Beg, borrow or steal from family and friends." Bran held up a hand, marking off the points on his fingers. "First stop's going to be his family if he knows he can get something out of them. Advance on college funds, whatever. Next, places where he's got buddies or where he hangs out a lot. Scrape up enough for travel expenses." He stared at me. "If you launch one of your hunts, I can guarantee there'll be bloodshed. The kid's not going to go down quietly. He's not going to bow down like a good little boy in front of one of your alphas. He's going to brawl like a world-class fighter right there in the middle of the street at high noon and he won't care who sees it. That generates press and that's not going to be good if you want to keep your secret.

"And…you've got me." He grinned. "I'm the one he sent the photo to so he should want to talk to me." He puffed his chest out. "Mano a mano."

I poked him in the chest. "So macho."

"Hey!" The chair wobbled dangerously as he tried to regain control. The wooden legs finally succumbed to gravity, dumping Bran on the floor with a thump so loud the other customers looked over, some with annoyance that we had dared to disturb the tranquil setting. He scrambled to his feet, ignoring the glares.

I dropped my head onto the table, resting it on my hands. "I need to move out of this city. I need to move out of this life."

Bran reached over and patted my head. "Maybe. But right now let's go over to this boy's house and see what's up before you pack up and leave, 'kay?"

There were only a handful of Kolanskis in the phone book and only one within walking distance of the school. It was one of Toronto's older streets, townhouses squeezed onto every square inch of earth with a floor mat's worth of grass in front and back.

The Kolanskis's house had been built on a postage stamp-sized piece of land on the corner of two small side streets, probably bringing up the house's value. A small picket fence, no higher than my waist, ran around the front of the house. The porch was filled at one end with plastic storage boxes almost totally obscuring the view out the front window. The house needed a paint job badly from top to bottom.

Bran swung open the gate. "Nice place." The brown grass stood ankle-high with a few stepping stones leading up to the porch steps. We picked our way through to the front door. I reached out and poked the doorbell with my index finger.

A woman opened the door. Life hadn't been good to her, not by a long shot. Her blond hair was long and stringy, sticking to her face and neck. Her bloodshot eyes stared at us as if we were plague carriers.

"Yes?" Her voice wavered up and down the scale with that one word.

I brought out my official identification. "Hi there. My name's Rebecca Desjardin and this is my partner, Brandon Hanover. I'm a private investigator looking into the death of Janey Winters. May we come in?"

Her eyes darted to Brandon's face then back to mine, then out to the empty driveway. "Maybe. Yes." She stepped back. "We have PIs in Canada?"

Bran snickered, silenced with a sharp jab in the ribs from yours truly. I stepped inside the narrow hallway, a sickening sweet smile plastering my face.

"Yes, yes we do. Certified and everything." I showed my license again. "Seriously legit."

"Oh, my." She pushed by me, motioning us into the living room. "Please, sit down."

The living room was quaint and comfortable, from the hand-knit afghan lying over the back of the dark-green sofa to the family pictures hanging on the wall. I spotted Tony up there—a sweet baby rolling on a carpet with a wide toothless grin, a shy child glancing at the camera as he struggled to keep his balance on a bike and a pre-teen with a sullen look standing between his mother and a gruff man who had to be his stepfather.

None of them involved fur.

Brandon nudged me with a glance over to a side table. The Toronto *Inquisitor*, at least three months' worth of copies, neatly stacked. We now knew where Tony had gotten the idea to contact Brandon.

"I'm not sure what I can help you with." The blonde woman sat down and wiped her hands on the stained apron at her waist. Her voice quavered as she looked back toward the door. "My husband'll be home in a few minutes, maybe he…"

I sat on the sofa beside her. Another time, another place I'd have been more tactful but we just didn't have the time to spare. "Kathy. We know about Frank. And Tony." I showed her the small scars between my knuckles. "We know."

The whisper shocked her into silence for a few seconds. Her thin hands, the skin dry and flaking, moved to touch mine. "You're…like Frank?"

"I'm a friend of Frank's." It was the truth, in a way. "We're worried about Tony. We're worried that he might be…out of control."

She rose from the sofa and walked around the chair where Bran sat, her attention on the family photographs.

"Frank never told me about," her hands fluttered in the air, "his disability. I only figured it out when Tony was a baby and, well, was different."

I flinched at her choice of words.

"I called him, told him I'd had the baby and it was a boy. I waited for him to say something but he didn't."

The strangled sigh tugged at my heart. "He didn't want to talk about it."

"So you raised him on your own. With his..." The words jammed in my mouth. "With his differences."

"I never told Henry about Frank. I told him that Tony's father had been killed in an industrial accident, made it feel right." A deep whiffling breath, punctuated by sobs. "We got married when Tony was six. The worst of it was over by then."

"So you taught him how to control himself," I prompted.

She sniffled. "I tried." Her reflection in the picture glass was distorted and warped. "The first time he... went furry, I freaked. I thought about taking him to the hospital but then I realized they'd poke and prick him to death."

I nodded. "Yes, yes they would have." Inwardly I winced at the image. It was one of the Pride's biggest fears, to lose a kit to the wonders of science. "So you didn't take him."

"I couldn't do that to my boy, let them treat him like an animal. So I did the best I could." She wiped her eyes and stared at me. "Did I do okay? Did I do all right by him?"

I smiled. "You did the best that you could. I doubt many women would have been up to the task." This was the truth. There was a reason why Ruth had been so valued by the Pride. "It must have been hard keeping the secret."

"As soon as he was old enough to understand I told him to never do it again." Kathy wiped her nose with one sleeve. "I told him that if he had to do it to go into the bathroom and do it away from anyone else."

My jaw tightened. Putting Changing in the same

category as masturbation wouldn't have sat well with any Felis, much less a hormonal teenager with his emotions in flux.

"Frank should have told you." I stood up. "He should have helped you with this."

Brandon, to his credit, sat there in silence. His gaze kept darting to the front window and the dim light allowed in by the storage boxes. I sensed the tension building in him. Any minute now Henry could walk through that door and we'd lose any chance at privacy.

It was time to start dealing with the future, not the past.

I moved to touch Kathy's arm. "We need to talk to Tony."

Her moist eyes shot up to meet mine. "Oh my God... you think he had something to do with that teacher's murder? I mean, I read about it but when I asked him about it he just shrugged and said it was a crackhead looking for money." The words tumbled out in a panic. "I didn't push it. I knew he was acting strange but I thought it was just part of being a teenager, wanting to be alone so often." She stared at me, a sad smile on her face. "He's such a boy. You know."

I nodded. "I know, and trust me, teenage Felis can be a handful."

Kathy opened her mouth, stopped then continued. "Felis? Is that what you call yourself?"

"It's what Frank was. And what I am." I didn't care right now about confidentiality or keeping the family safe. My eyes went to the family pictures hanging above and around us. "It's rough growing up with these...skills."

"It's hard for all of us at that age. I guess I didn't realize how much more for him." Kathy picked up the ends of the apron and began to wrestle it into knots. "Now he's hurt someone and has to answer for it."

"Yes." I couldn't lie to her. "We think he's involved with the murder and we need to find him."

She shook her head, the light greasy strands sliding back and forth. "I haven't seen him since he left for school this morning." A tear broke free and ran down her face. "You think he killed her, don't you?"

"Yes." I was being way too honest but there was no time to be subtle, to cushion the truth. "He lost control, we understand that. But we need to get to him before the police get on his trail. We need to help him before he kills again." I began to speak faster, my fingers clenching together in loose fists. "He needs to learn about himself, his heritage and how to control himself. He needs to..."

Bran came to his feet. "Trouble."

The front door swung open, admitting a giant who filled the lobby. Henry Kolanski strutted into the living room with a scowl on his face and hands thick enough to fit around my neck and Bran's with room to spare.

The beefy man fell into the chair Kathy had vacated only a few moments ago. His stare took in the three of us. "Kathy. Beer, please."

The woman trotted into the back, the kitchen presumably, and dashed out with a bottle, cap already off. She put it into his hand and moved to stand by his chair. He looked at us. "Who are you?"

Before I could speak, Brandon leaped forward, shaking the hand that didn't hold the beer. "Brandon Hanover, investigative reporter." In a parody of what I had done only minutes before, he dug out his press identification from his wallet and placed it in Henry's view.

"Hmph. Who do you write for?" His eyes narrowed

as he scanned the small print under the photograph. "Hey, I recognize you. You write lots of good stuff for the *Inquisitor*." His tongue darted out to wet his lips. "I like that rag." The lips twisted into a smile. "Good paper. Fun reading. Only newspaper I have in the house, home delivery every week."

I let out the breath I had been holding, slowly.

"So whatchya here in my place for?" Henry said. "I work hard all day in a warehouse hustling boxes. Ain't no alien bodies here or crazy flying squirrels carrying off babies."

"Well…" Bran's eyes met mine as he grinned wider than a cat with a mouthful of bird. "We're here because there's been a sighting of a monster cat in the area and wondered if you or your wife had seen anything."

The tired man's eyes lit up. "You gonna quote me?"

Brandon's fingers flew inside his leather duster, coming out with a notepad and pencil. "You speak, I write." He nodded toward Kathy. "Your wife here hasn't seen anything, but if you have…" His eyebrows waggled upward. "It's a hot story for our next issue."

"Hmm." Henry nodded, his eyes studying the beige carpet. "I've seen some mighty big cats in the backyard. But I'm not sure if you'd call them 'giants.'" One meaty hand scratched his pate.

The pencil scribbled across the empty page. "But you have seen some large ones, yes?"

Henry shifted in the chair and took a deep swig from the bottle. "I've seen some nice big pussies in my time." He leered at his wife beside him, who shifted her weight from one foot to the other. "And you can quote me on that."

Bran returned the wide grin. "I hear you, man. I hear you." He matched the man, leer for leer. "Great quote."

Bran looked around the room, casually zoning in on the pictures. "You got a boy? Any chance of talking to him? Maybe he's seen something."

Henry shrugged. "Don't know if he'll have anything to add. He's always shutting himself up in that room of his." He turned to his wife. "Where is Tony, anyway?"

"He's at school still, honey," Kathy said in a soothing tone, as if to a child.

Henry looked at his watch and tapped his forehead. "Twelve-hour shifts fuck up your mind. I keep getting misplaced." He looked up at us, pride in his eyes. "He's a good boy."

"I'm sure of that." I nodded toward Brandon, edging to the door.

"That all you want?" Henry got to his feet with a groan. "Sorry I can't give you more, but these damned dogs are killing me." He pointed downward. "On my feet all shift and I ain't getting any younger, and if I pull these off you'll be writing about a lethal gas attack."

We all chuckled at the joke. I glanced at Kathy, seeing the relief on her face. Her secret would stay safe, at least for the moment.

"I just need to know how you spell your last name." Brandon continued the charade, boldfaced to the end. Damn, the man had charm to spare.

As the weary man began to recite the letters, I pulled Kathy aside. "If Tony shows up, please call me." I handed her my business card. "Don't call the cops, don't call anyone but me."

She nodded. "Please." A fast glance toward her husband brought out a sigh. "Henry's a good man but if he thinks Tony is in trouble he'll just…" The sentence trailed off.

I smiled. "I hear you. We just want to get Tony some

help. Call me." I raised my voice as Brandon stepped toward me, flipping his notebook closed. "And be sure to call if you see that large cat again."

Kathy nodded as her husband stepped beside her and wrapped his meaty hand around her waist. "We sure will." The pair escorted us out the door onto the porch and left us standing next to a stack of boxes and a short step away from the dying grass.

"That was smooth." I exhaled.

"Thanks." Bran beamed as he walked down the steps and offered me his hand. "I figured that he'd be more likely to be happy talking to a reporter than to someone looking for his kid." He hefted the knapsack back up onto his shoulder. "Sad thing is that they didn't even recognize their kid's bag. Sort of disconnected from the boy's life."

"Well, it's sort of obvious to me that there's no time in that household." I shuffled along the dry grass toward the gate. "I can't imagine growing up and hitting puberty without having someone around to help deal with being Felis."

We walked through the small fence and back onto the street. Bran turned toward me. "Is it really that tough?"

I shrugged while we walked down to the corner. "It's just rough going through that time of life regularly—there's a whole lot of hormones fluxing around."

I spotted a small park nearby and steered us toward the single empty bench. The two of us sat down near a passel of mothers watching their kids scramble over monkey bars and a playground that didn't resemble anything I had growing up. The mixture of faux wood, bright plastic and various rope nets had me wondering if they would handle my weight.

"So now what?" Bran stretched out his arms along

the wooden back. "We've got the parents aware, we're not calling in the dogs, so to speak, and now we're here in a lovely quiet spot." The knapsack sat at our feet.

I opened the bag and began stacking notebooks on Bran's lap. "Maybe there's something here that'll tell us where he hangs out."

"Definitely not his bedroom," Bran said as the stack grew higher. "Every kid has some hangout to go to when life gets rough. And if anyone owes him cash he'll be looking to collect it before he leaves town."

"Exactly." I dug deeper, coming up with a well-worn business card. "Bingo."

Bran grinned as I turned the card around and pointed it at him. "Brad's CyberCafe. About three blocks from here."

My heart skipped a beat. "And within spitting distance of the alley and his school. A perfect place to watch the cops and watch me."

Bran winced. "Saw you go in under the crime tape and followed you home after that. Probably figured you were a police detective."

I rolled my eyes. "Of course. Why would he think I'd be a private investigator or worse yet, another Felis."

Bran let out a sigh. "All this is going to make confronting him a hell of a lot harder. Are you going to be able to sell the idea of going to the farm and handing himself over to Jess instead of turning himself in to the cops?"

"I'm not sure," I said. "Part of me wants to thrash the kid into snail snot…"

"And part of you wants to hand him over to the Pride for proper training and teaching him how to understand his gifts."

I sniffed the air. Something was wrong.

"Stay here." My lips pulled back from my teeth in a snarl as I spun around, seeking the source. "I think there's a plan here." I pushed him down onto the seat and tossed the book bag into his lap. "A really, really bad plan."

NINETEEN

I SPRINTED ACROSS the playground, headed for the shadow behind one of the low hedges.

A cigarette dangled from Jess's mouth like some sort of Western flashback, matched by her cowboy boots. The kids scattered in front of me, mothers snatching their precious cargo out of danger—probably thinking I was chasing down some terrorist or child abuser.

Jess smiled as I pulled up. She took a deep drag on the cig and blew it over us. "Good senses, Reb. I wasn't sure you'd catch me. I'm still upwind of you."

My teeth were still bared. "Don't ever spy on me again." I grabbed hold of her light-blue blouse, my mind automatically labeling it as expensive and thus a prime target. "I mean it."

Jess laughed and brushed my grip off with a swipe of her right hand. "Girl, you really don't want to get into it with me." Her eyes flashed. "I went easy on you the last time."

Brandon chugged up, still carrying the knapsack. "Ah, the cavalry. Or at least the horse." His eyes went to the lit cigarette. "Those things'll kill ya."

"Thanks," Jess said dryly. She turned her attention back to me. "Did you really think we would let you handle the hunt on your own? Just give me his name and we'll be done here. Leave it to us to bring him in. We'll take care of him."

"You'll kill him."

The older woman pursed her lips. "Maybe. Maybe not. Not your decision to make either. Belongs to the Board."

I moved into the shadows, feeling the tension in my shoulders. "You want him? You work with me to get him."

"Why?" The question slapped me across the face as if I were a kit again.

"Because that was the contract we agreed to. I find the one who murdered Janey Winters."

"And you did." Jess took another long drag and blew smoke rings toward the crowded playground. "Now we'll bring him in for you. Not a bad deal. You'll still get paid." The end of the cigarette shone a bright red as it bobbled from her lips. "Look, this isn't the way we thought it'd go. We thought you'd find some crazed family member who hated Janey or some crackhead who managed to get past her defenses. We're dealing with a rogue male, a wild animal who took out a full-grown woman." Her eyes scratched over my body. "He'd take you out in the right circumstances, and you know it. You've gotten lucky twice—do you really want to go for the trifecta?"

I swallowed past the sudden ache in my stomach. "He's good, but he's had no training."

"He was still good enough to toss you down the stairs." Jess nodded to Bran. "You know I'm speaking the truth. You want to protect her, as do I." A smile twitched the edges of her mouth upward. "Don't need Felis senses to tell that much."

Bran looked at me. "He can Change, Reb. You can't. I know you're good but why not leave this to the experts."

"Because it's my job." I shook my head. "I don't leave

a job half-done. I promised Mike Winters I'd find who killed his wife and bring him in."

Jess chuckled again then dropped the cigarette on the ground and ground it under her heel. "You're even more stubborn than you used to be. Didn't think that was possible." She licked her lips. "Okay, go get your kit then but I'll be around for backup." One salt-and-pepper eyebrow rose. "Don't push it."

I nodded. "Done." It was still early afternoon, the children racing around with seemingly endless energy. I envied them. "Just don't let him scent you. He knows me, but another strange Felis is going to send him skittering underground and then we'll never find him. He's a kid, a scared, lost kid. Emotions all mixed up, a mess inside. Let me at least try to do it nicely before you call a hunt."

Jess took a step back, blending into the growing shadows. "Your way first, because you asked so nicely. But if he blows you off or tries to get away—our way."

Then she was gone. I sniffed the air but she had blended back into the darkness and the cigarette smoke had effectively blinded me.

"My, she's a charmer when she puts her mind to it," Bran said while we walked back across the playground. "Sort of like the big sister who beat you up in the back yard whenever your parents weren't watching."

I felt like someone had punched me in the chest, the memories of the Challenge and of Jess beating me rising from the backwaters of my mind. "I don't want to talk about that right now." Mentally I slapped the rush of emotions and images surging forth. This wasn't the time to dissect that mess. "Not right now," I repeated, using the mantra to complete the cycle. "Not now."

Bran stopped on the sidewalk, the book bag hanging from his right shoulder. "Okay." The words held a sense of sadness, pain and more than a little affection. "Let's go get this kid before someone else gets hurt."

Brad's CyberCafe sat between a flower shop and a corner market. Two floors held enough neon lights to put Times Square to shame, with a handful of computers available for rent. A few kids were there, already playing the latest first-person shooter game, screaming and swearing while getting blown away by some crack shot in Taiwan. Adults were restricted to the guy behind the counter selling overpriced coffees and herbal teas, and a pair of lovebirds sitting in the far corner cooing to each other while their respective sons and daughters played the video games at the far end of the café.

"Nice place." Bran glanced around the first floor. "All it needs is a jukebox."

I laughed. "And a pinball machine."

"Bah. These kids don't know what they're missing with their newfangled video games and fancy-dancy music tunes." He winked at me, putting a smile on my face.

A waitress appeared within minutes of us sitting at one of the rare empty tables. The menu was simple, a photocopy stuck in a plastic holder. Bran let out a low whistle while he scanned the words.

"Fried mac and cheese. Yum." He beamed at the waiting woman. "I'll have an order of that. And a diet cola."

"Just a diet cola for me." I couldn't help letting out a sigh as the young woman disappeared into the back. "Diet soda? With fried mac and cheese? You do see the silliness in that, right?"

Bran shrugged. "Sue me. Besides, I find the regular

stuff too sweet." His eyes went to the bar. "Heads up. Guess he didn't see or smell you on the way in."

A thin young man swung the door open, almost smashing it into the wall. Without looking around, he strutted to the counter and rapped his knuckles on the faux wood. The barista got to work in silence and a minute later a tall latte with plenty of foam appeared in front of the teenager. He pulled a cell phone out of an inside pocket and began texting, his fingers flying over the tiny keyboard at a furious rate.

"Probably calling in all his IOU's." Bran leaned in, whispering. "Tell you what—let me go and see if I can chat him down. Too many civilians around for you to start something here."

I pressed my lips together. The café wasn't packed, but full enough that a fight wouldn't go unnoticed or without some casualties—to people or furniture. "Go." I grabbed his arm as he started to get up. "Sit on his left side."

"Why?"

"Because that's downwind. He'll smell me on you if you don't stay downwind." I couldn't help feeling sheepish. "It's sort of obvious."

"Ah." Bran grinned.

"But don't forget who and what he is." My nose twitched. "Don't forget."

"I won't." Bran patted my arm and grabbed one of the small macaroni bites that had just been dropped off at our table. "Damn, those are good." He picked up his soda and took a sip, carrying the glass with him.

He strode to the counter and sat down on the stool next to Tony. The teenager turned slightly to assess this newest entry into his world. His nose twitched—he'd learned fast how to assess a potential enemy. As long as Bran stayed downwind he'd be safe.

"Hey." Bran nodded. "How's it going?" The conversation was so low that if I hadn't been concentrating and had a bit more skill than the average human, I wouldn't have heard anything.

Tony glared at him. "What's it to you?" With a sneer he turned away and took a sip of the fancy coffee.

"You know who I am. You came to my penthouse and slipped that picture under my door," Brandon said.

Tony put the cell phone down. "Did I?"

"Brandon Hanover." Bran stuck his hand out. Tony didn't return the gesture. A second later Bran rubbed his chin, ending the attempt.

"Whatever." Tony took another sip.

"Before we go any further I know who and what you are." Bran kept his voice low, neutral. Tony's head snapped back as if he'd been slapped. "I know what you did. A helluva lot more than just taking a picture."

"You printed it." Tony reached back and pressed his greasy dark hair back down with the palm of his hand. The kit needed a shower badly, with a shave and a new set of clothes. "You thought it was real."

"I know it was real. I know you're real." Bran shifted his weight to one side, taking yet another submissive pose. The bastard must have spent a lot of time watching *Animal Planet*. He was working it like a pro. I fluctuated between feeling proud of his survival skills and terrified that he'd pegged it so quickly.

Tony slurped more coffee. "Nothing's what it seems."

"I know you sent that photo to me to expose what they are. What you are." Bran continued, not allowing Tony to interrupt. "What I want to know is how you ended up in the alley with your teacher in the first place."

Tony shrugged. "Got lucky. She wanted it and I gave it to her."

"No, you didn't." A sad smile touched Bran's lips. "You didn't rape her. You couldn't do that. But you were hot for teacher, weren't you?"

Tony's cheeks went scarlet. Bran continued, "Hey, it's cool. Listen, there isn't a man alive who hasn't gotten excited seeing some hot woman up at the front of the classroom."

The rogue replied with a short laugh. "Mrs. Winters, she was a good lady. Really good legs, you know?"

"Sure." Bran playfully dug his elbow into the teenager's ribs. "Bet you liked it when she kept her back to you, you know? Get you all thinking about what she'd be like, eh? Bend 'er over the desk and do her right there in the classroom."

I knew Bran was just trying to be smart and sympathetic to the kid, but I was about to walk over there and crack their heads together like a pair of coconuts.

Tony nodded again. "She was one sweet looker." He stared at his hands, placing them both on the countertop, palms down. "But I never thought…I mean…"

"You caught a whiff of her scent and went nuts, didn't you?" Bran took a swig of his cola. "Tell ya, it's not just you Felis who get it going at the smell of a woman. There's nothing like it, that delicious sweet 'come and get me' smell." He let out a low wolf whistle. "Let me guess. You know she's like you and you follow her for a bit and then decide that day, that day you want to talk to her about maybe getting together. No one needs to know, just you and her." The words tumbled out of his mouth as if he were sketching a picture. "You call her over, she comes to see you in the alley."

Tony let out a weary sigh, almost a sob. "Do you know what it's like growing up…growing up like this?" His fingers flexed on the table and scratched the cheap varnish. "My mother told me it wasn't from my father, my stepfather, that is. Some dumb fuck she screwed a few times and never to speak of it again. Told me to keep it inside, keep it secret and don't talk about it to anyone, ever." The right hand lashed out and gripped Bran's wrist so tightly the skin started to turn white from lack of blood. "Told me to do it in the bathroom if I really had to go furry. Like I'm some sort of pervert."

I sighed. Kathy might have meant the best for her son but she'd gone about it all wrong, turning Tony's Felis abilities into something dirty and shameful. I wasn't sure how much Felis he had in him but I knew it couldn't be denied and shut up forever.

"Mrs. Winters figured out I was like her as soon as we started talking. She hadn't realized it before 'cause I sat in the back and away from her. She barely remembered my name. I went furry for her. I wanted to show her it was okay, just the two of us. She was the first woman I've ever felt close to." The fingers increased their grip on Bran's wrist. "She didn't understand. She told me that I needed to get help, that there were rules we had to follow. Said we had to stay secret, stay silent," he growled. "Like I've been told to do all my life."

I spotted a thin line of blood working its way down the side of Bran's hand onto the counter. Every instinct screamed at me to get up, to launch myself at Tony right then and there, and hang the consequences. But I had to have faith in Bran's ability to defend himself and I knew my time would come.

"I hear you." Bran nodded. He looked down at the hand pressing his wrist into the counter. "Dude, I ain't going nowhere. Lighten up."

Tony looked down. He lifted his hand up a fraction, keeping Bran's left wrist trapped.

"So she said no," Bran continued. "And you got mad."

"She shouldn't have said no, not like that." Tony shook his head again, the greasy strands flying around his face. "I want to talk to her, find things out and she's all 'no, I have to go' and babbling 'bout rules and how she can't tell me anything, can't tell me nothing 'bout what I am, what she is. She starts heading out of the alley and I know I'll never see her again. She's going to turn me in to the cops, to the docs, to whoever wants a piece of me."

"You grabbed her." Bran nudged the conversation forward.

The teenager grunted. "Look, it wasn't supposed to go that way." He pushed the coffee cup around in a circle. "She was scared and in a rush and I was pissed and angry and knew if I let her just go, just go like that, I'd be fucked." He brushed away a thick lock of hair and released Bran's hand. "I don't know what happened. I mean, we were just talking and then…" Tony shook his head again. "I just grabbed her neck, just wanted to show her that I was serious, that. I was worthy, you know? And then I just, I just lost it." The last few words came in a soft whine. Part of me ached for his lost youth, ripped bare in a second of fury against Janey, against the system keeping our secret.

"Why'd ya take the picture?" Bran prompted.

Tony tapped on the cell phone screen a few times

before laying it down in front of Bran. I could imagine what they were looking at.

"My mistake. Their mistake."

"Them who?"

"Whoever made me like this." Tony held up his free hand, wriggling his fingers. "I know someone knows who I am, what made me like this."

"So you dropped this at my place in a cry for help?"

He shrugged. "You're a reporter. I figured you'd report it and there'd be some sort of follow-up story, someone investigating what she was, digging up the truth. What I am. Give me some answers 'cause I didn't have any."

"I know you feel bad about that. Guilty as all hell. Wasn't what you wanted." Bran's voice carried through the air as I popped one of the macaroni bites into my mouth.

Kolanski's head bobbed slowly, reminding me of those small glass birds that were all the rage years ago. The red fluid went only so far up the neck then the bird would fall forward, bounce for a second or two, returning to his original position, going on as long as you let it.

The breeze abruptly shifted, the front door flying open with the arrival of a gang of teenagers yelling and cajoling each other about some high score on a video game. Right back at the two men.

Tony's head lifted, nose skyward. His eyes widened as his hand pressed down on Bran's wrist. The first small tufts of fur began to spread across the back of his hand, the claws protruding from between his knuckles. He jerked his head to one side and stared at me, then turned back to Bran.

"You're with her." It wasn't a question.

Brandon nodded. "Yes. Yes, I am." He continued to

speak, his words carefully chosen and slowly spoken. "She wants to help you. We want to help you." A long pause. "Why did you attack her? You wanted help and she's like you."

Tony growled, his attention going back and forth between the two of us. "She can't change. I told her to and she can't change. She ain't like me."

"You know she is. You smelled her when you broke into her house and assaulted her." Bran kept his tone neutral. "She's not a cop, she's a P.I. investigating the murder.

"She's still a cop, just a private one." Tony looked down between his legs at the tiled floor. "I'm not going into a cage for the rest of my life for an accident. I don't care what she is, I wanted to scare her off."

"She doesn't scare easily." Bran glanced over in my direction with a smirk.

"She tried to kill me in the alley."

"I doubt that," Bran murmured as if he were smoothing ointment over a fresh wound. "She wanted to help you find out who you are. Your real father, your heritage."

Tony drew a sharp breath. I could see the emotions running through his face, one surfacing to rule the others.

Rage. Pure Felis rage.

Tony's face began to shift, the skin reshaping itself to allow the flatter nose, the small facial hairs sprouting free and turning a light tawny color as they travelled across his jaw and neck.

"I know what I am now. And I don't need anyone's help."

Kolanski let out a leonine roar, pushing the stool back from the counter and standing up. He grabbed

Bran by the trapped right wrist and tossed him at me with all his strength, picking him off his feet and throwing him like a rag doll.

Bran slammed into my table, and by default, me, like the classic ton of bricks. We crashed to the floor in a pile of kindling and soda, a few mac and cheese balls scattering around us like chaff.

Tony raced out the door as I struggled to get back on my feet, pulling Bran with me. Bran shook his head. "Guess that class in negotiations really wasn't worth the B I got." His eyes went to the spilled snack. "Oh, man…I was looking forward to those."

"We'll be back." I scrambled over the debris and raced out, not looking back to see if Bran was behind me. Tony was now fully Changed and in public view— Jess would kill him for that alone.

The long shadows stretching across the street signaled the approaching evening, something I was grateful for while I sprinted after the teenager. If we were lucky someone would take him for a costumed clown on his way to the latest birthday party or some sort of frat prank—not one of Brandon's "freaks" wandering the streets of Toronto.

Tony cut the street corner so sharply I almost skidded off the cement into traffic, my running shoes screaming to try and keep their traction on the sidewalk. At the back of my mind I noted that he was heading, of all places, for his house. No matter how old you are or where you are or what you think, there's no place like home. Except in this case it wasn't going to be the sanctuary he was hoping for.

Sure enough, as we reached the edge of the playground I caught Jess's scent, fresh and nearby. As if I didn't have enough to worry about.

The playground equipment stood in the center of the sand-filled oval, the faux wood and garishly colored plastic pipes warped and shaped for safety. A varnished rope net hung off of one side of the turret for children to climb up and play on. Tony leaped up onto the shiny metal slide and scurried to the top of the tower. He spun around and glared at me as I pulled up just short, my toes digging into the sand.

"Don't you judge me." His eyes were wide as he pointed at me. "Don't you even try to judge me."

I put up my hand. "Dude, you are so not talking to the right person about that." Out of the corner of my eye I spotted Jess, a slim shadow in the patch of trees to my right and behind the frazzled teenager. "You've got to get some help." Putting my hand up, palm out, I continued. "Just calm down, pull it together and we'll talk. There's nothing here that can't be fixed."

"I'm a fucking freak." The plaintive cry tore at my ears. He bent backward and let out a cross between a roar and a scream.

I winced. There was only so much the neighbors were going to put up with before they called the cops to report the disturbance and, well, we knew where that was going to lead. Even if they didn't link him to Janey's death, yelping something like that was bound to get someone's attention.

"Tony, come on down." Bran appeared behind me, breathless. Seems he wasn't in as fine a condition as he thought he was. "Let them help you." His hair was askew, his face scarlet from the short run. "They understand. They're just like you. Give them a chance to make things right before it's too late."

Jess stepped out of the darkness, still in human form. She took a long drag on the half-burned cigarette in her hand and blew smoke rings into the air as she walked onto the playground. Her cowboy boots reverberated on the old railroad ties before sinking into the sand.

She looked up at the teenager then over at me, and Bran, before returning her attention to the kid. "Turn it off, Tony." The low rumbling tone came from the bottom of her toes, sending a shiver up my spine. "Get skin again. Right now."

Kolanski stared at Jess for a second, a thin string of drool running out of one side of his mouth. It ran out onto the end of one of the fine whispers before dropping down into the sand. "Who the fuck are you?"

Jess shrugged. "Someone you should listen to." She took one last puff on the cigarette before bending one leg and putting the stub out on the bottom of her boot.

"Littering. It's not good." She tucked the dead butt into a front pocket, not taking her eyes off of the teenager. "I said, dump the fur. Now." The last word wasn't a request. I remembered the tone from many a training session back on the farm.

"Damn, she's good," Bran whispered in my ear, one hand on my shoulder. "I'm trying to Change back right now, I'm so scared." I could tell by the tone in his voice he wasn't joking.

"You should be," I said in a stage whisper without taking my eyes off the young man perched at the top of the turret.

"Who the fuck are you?" Tony was still in full Change.

Jess shook her head. "Kid, you need a lesson in control. You need a lot of lessons, but we'll start with this one." She pointed a finger at the ground right in front of her. "Down. Now. And Change back."

Tony laughed, a purring tilt to his voice. He crouched

and pointed a furred finger at the older woman with claws fully extended. "You want to go, bitch? I don't think you'd be much of a challenge." He nodded toward me. "You want to put me in a cage. Not gonna happen." His lips peeled back, exposing bright, white canines. "Not gonna happen."

Jess shrugged. "Your call, kit. But don't say I didn't warn you." She glanced around the playground. Time wasn't going to be on our side forever and each second Tony stayed in full Change was a second closer to the Felis being discovered.

Jess rolled her shoulders back, closing her eyes and let out a long hiss of air. Then she Changed, faster than I had ever seen before.

The white hair on her head blended perfectly with the light fur on her face, her hands furring up with claws shooting out so fast I winced at the pain. Her nose retreated into her face just slightly, enough to accentuate the long fangs pressing out against her lips. She pulled them back in a vicious smile at the teenager.

The shocked look on the kid's face was, in a sad way, welcome. Here was one of his own family, one of his extended bloodline. The question was, would he accept Jess's authority without a fight?

The answer came as Kolanski launched himself off the top of the tower with a half cry, half roar. His leather jacket flew open, flapping in the air and exposing the threadbare T-shirt covering his chest.

TWENTY

JESS TOOK UP a defensive position, not moving an inch. She bent her knees slightly, dropping a fraction with her hands at her sides—palms up and claws ready, her fingers half-closed to allow the sharp nails total freedom. Her pupils had changed to the slitted feline view with her nose twitching as the musky scent of the attacker crashed over the two of us.

Bran took a step forward. I slammed my forearm into his chest, pushing him back and behind me. I exhaled, feeling the blood start to pound loudly in my ears.

Tony crashed into Jess at about shoulder level, reaching out to grab at her. Jess turned to the left as if it had been choreographed, tossing the kit to the ground with a resounding thump.

He rolled to his feet with astonishing speed. I'd forgotten how fast we could be when we're young.

Grabbing Jess with an angry yell, he grappled with the Board member, both of them searching for a good grip to toss the other to the ground. The claws ripped into Tony's leather jacket, matched by his return attack through Jess's jean shirt. Blood began to show through the tears. The smell hit my nose like a firecracker blast, ratcheting my senses up another level.

Jess wasn't a fool. You didn't get to her age and level in the Pride without having a few tricks up your sleeve. Tony's claws were now firmly imbedded in her arms and trapped there as she pulled and shoved, not letting him pull them out. It must have hurt like hell, but it effectively neutralized the kid's attack.

Tony's eyes went wide as he felt himself losing control.

Jess hit him three times, smashing his nose hard. She didn't gouge his face, instead letting the raw power of her punch do the damage. "Surrender now. Give it up," she hissed at the startled Felis.

In response Tony yanked his claws free, ripping long gouges in Jess's skin.

He jumped to one side, landing behind Bran. I turned toward him but he was too fast, too hyper in his anger and rage.

Tony pushed me to the ground and grabbed Bran. He put his bloody claws to Bran's throat.

Jess's pounce stopped in midair. She landed beside me in the soft sand, dropping to one knee as she stared at the kid.

"Don't do it." Her voice was strangely soft and still threatening. "There's been enough killing."

Tony had one hand on Bran's forehead, yanking his head back as a push brought Bran to his knees. I could see the jugular pulsing, fractions of an inch from Tony's claws.

"What are you going to do, eh?" The kid glanced down at Bran and then back at the two of us. "I'll tell you what you're going to do—you're going to let me walk out of here." He tugged at Bran's hair, hard. "Unless you don't care about another dead body."

"Come on, Tony." Bran's hoarse whisper reached our ears, barely decipherable. "You're smarter than this. You know this isn't going to work."

The teenager shook his head, yanking back on Bran's short hair again. "I don't know nothing other than I'm a

freak." The sharp nails danced dangerously close to the
pulsing skin, scraping across the top layer. "You don't
know anything about me."

"Tony." I stepped forward, keeping my hands at my
sides. "You're a Felis. Jess here is the leader of the Pride
that your father belongs to. Your real father." I drew in
a deep breath, watching the two closely, Tony's eyes
locked with mine—still defiant.

My fingers pulled into a fist, my nails digging into
my palm as I continued. "You need help." I glanced at
Jess for a fast second. "She's the one to give it to you."

"She's going to kill me." Tears began to flow down
Tony's furred cheeks. "She's going to kill me. I killed
Mrs. Winters and now she's going to kill me."

"No," Jess replied. "If I wanted to kill you you'd
be dead already." She nodded sideways. "Ask her. She
knows."

The ancient scars on my back sent off phantom
waves of pain. "She's right. You're not all that, kid."
I shuffled forward an inch. "Come on, let the guy go.
He's been nice to you. Don't do something else that
you're going to regret."

"Don't move," Tony screamed, his eyes as wide as
they could go, the pupils flashing an eerie green in
the dying daylight. Confusion was written all over his
furred face. Here he'd found his family and he was
caught between fearing us and needing us.

My claws begin to slip out slowly, edging through
the newly healed skin between my knuckles. My jaw
clenched as I tried not to show the pain. Bran looked at
me, giving an almost imperceptible shake of his head.

"Don't move or he dies," the rogue screamed again,
the claws now pressing hard on Bran's throat. A thin
scarlet line began to form as the blood trickled down,

disappearing under his shirt. My nose twitched, processing the new scent.

I drew in a sharp breath, letting it out as a growl. Bran's eyes went to the size of saucers as he stared at me, a mixture of pride and fear in them. Glancing from Jess to me to Jess again Tony came back to look at me with a strange expression on his face, one of fear and curiosity.

The world changed. Colors became clearer, the brightness of the playground equipment singing to me. The shadows beckoned me into the cool safety and calmness of the night. The scents of the people around me jumped into vivid clarity. Someone was cooking a cake two blocks over, hot dogs burning on a grill nearby, a couple making love in an upstairs bedroom.

I had Changed. For the first time in over twenty years.

And I was pissed.

I let out a roar and leaped at the startled teenager. In my mind's eye I knew this was what Janey Winters had done in the last few minutes of her life. She fought for what she loved—her kids and her husband, to get back to them.

I was fighting for Bran.

Tony released Bran as I crashed into the pair. He turned to run but I grabbed the kid by the shoulders and slammed him to the ground, moving in to take control. As I straddled the kid, Bran scrambled away, one hand on his cut neck.

"Fuck you." Tony yelled as he swung at me in an eerie reversal of our first meeting. His paw landed on the left side of my face, the nails digging into my cheek.

I slapped it away before he could get in too deep and clubbed him in the side of the head. His left ear began to swell like the proverbial cauliflower, throbbing red through the greasy black hair. I landed another punch to his already sore nose.

He bucked his hips, trying to unseat me, except I had been here too many times before and I wasn't going to be tossed off that easily. I dug my knees into his ribs and continued to smack him around, letting my nails just scrape the skin.

Kolanski continued to flail back and forth, grabbing hold of my leather jacket in the same way that Jess had his own—but it wasn't working out the same way. Instead of trapping my arms, he was instead tying up his hands and kept taking my blows to the face.

"Reb." A hand landed on my shoulder. Jess. "Stop. He's not going anywhere now." The grip increased. "Rebecca. Look at what you're hitting."

I glanced down at the battered and bloodied face under me, both of us panting. Tony had Changed back. He blew scarlet bubbles out of his nose and mouth as he stared at me, his eyes now fully human. His hands fell away to the ground and dug into the sand.

"He's a kid, Reb. You told me that. Let's take him away from here and get him some help." Jess's soothing tone ran over me like a cold shower. I closed my eyes and exhaled, the blood rush leaving me as quickly as it had come on. The sights and smells of the playground returned to a dulled state, the muted tones of the city overwhelming the base feral odors and images. I didn't need a mirror to know I had Changed back.

I got to my feet, leaving the kid on the ground. He didn't move, glancing back and forth between Jess and me. A low whimper came out every few seconds from between his cracked and swollen lips.

"First lesson, kit." Already finished Changing back,

Jess leaned over him and pointed a single index finger in the air. "Know when to stay down. There's no shame in being beaten by a woman." She gave me a sideways look. "Especially that one."

Kolanski rolled on the ground, shifting his hips around in the sand. "What are you going to do to me?"

Jess held out her bare hand. "We're going to take you home first. Then we're going to teach you how to be more…" Her lips twitched. "More human."

The teenager took a firm grip on the hand and pulled himself to his feet. Turning to one side, he spat out a mouthful of blood before wiping his nose on the sleeve of his torn leather jacket. "Yeah. I guess so." Tony looked up at Jess. "My parents?"

"We'll take care of it." She kept hold of Tony's hand, turning the handshake into a test of strength. "But if you try to run or do anything without asking me…" A burst of anger shot through her blue eyes. "I will rip your throat out. And no one will be able to stop me." Jess's eyes flashed to mine then returned to locking with the kid's. "No one. Understand?"

"Yes, ma'am," Kolanski muttered, breaking the lock to stare at the ground, both hands tucked into the top of his jeans. At least he'd accepted Jess as an alpha. That'd take a bit of the edge off the training.

Jess offered me her hand now, a wide grin on her face. "Suppose it goes without saying that you're welcome back at the farm, no questions asked."

"What?" I spat into the sand, covering the detritus with a kick of my sneaker. "You toss me out on my ass and now it's all forgiven 'cause I managed to Change?" A pain started in my chest, something that could have been a panic attack. It burned and throbbed, stretching out tentacles to shred me from the inside out. Then it began to die down, leaving only a ball of nausea in my belly and a headache that demanded quick and heavy medication.

"I never doubted that when push came to shove you'd have it in you." Jess nodded to the kid who was busy brushing sand off his jeans. "We're going to the farm. You go find your man."

I spun around. Brandon was nowhere to be seen.

"He ran off. That way." Jess shrugged. "Hope he can handle it. Not a bad guy." She took hold of Kolanski's arm and began to walk away, keeping a firm grip on the leather. "I'll call you with an update."

"Wait." The throbbing in my chest began to expand, threatening to steal my breath. "You...me..." I swallowed, my throat bone dry after being so full of saliva and blood only a few minutes ago.

"If you're going to challenge me it's a damned bad time to do it." She smiled. I could see the weariness in her eyes. The fight had taken more out of her than she wanted to admit.

"I'm not coming back."

"I didn't expect you to." She licked her lips. "I guess I could apologize for screwing things up all those years ago but I'm not sure if it'd make a difference."

"It would." Every cell in my body ached.

"Then I do." She extended a hand. "I'm not too big to say when I've screwed up. I could tell you that it was all tradition but I think we've had enough of that lately." Her eyes went to the kit next to her. "Times are changing. Either we adapt or we're going to end up with more problems than we know what to do with." Jess tilted her head to one side and smiled. "Good to have someone with a firm grasp on the outside."

I rubbed my eyes. "Yeah, just make sure the check

doesn't bounce. I'd hate to have to come up there and cause trouble."

Jess chuckled. "I'll make sure of it. Your dad, he'd be proud of you." There was a flash of something in her eyes, something like regret. "He'd be real proud."

Before I could pursue that line of questioning she turned away, yanking on the kid's arm. "You so much as twitch and I'll give you a beating you won't soon forget."

The two stumbled off the playground leaving me alone. I limped over to sit on one of the benches, letting the cool night air wash over my heated skin. My hands were sore and the scratches on my cheek still oozing enough blood to remind me I needed to get cleaned up—you'd be surprised how much crap you can catch from a cat's claw, never mind a Felis's. I took a deep breath, searching.

Bran's scent was long gone and I couldn't find it on the wind now sweeping up the street from the evening commuter traffic. I sat there for a while, letting the shadows cover me and the cool night air clear my mind.

A street cat yowled at me as he took his position atop the wooden tower. I got the message and stood up, feeling the burning start in my muscles.

Save the man, lose the man. No wonder superheroes stay single.

The taxi dropped me off at the condominium on King Street. Dan grabbed the front door's metal handles with a wide grin as he opened it. He touched the brim of his hat.

"Pleased to see you again, Ms. Desjardin." His left eyebrow twitched once, twice. "Are you all right? Your face…"

I held up a hand. "I'm fine. Just need to clean up a

SHERYL NANTUS275

little bit." The smile on my face was extremely forced. "You know how kids are."

The eyebrow twitched again. "Mr. Hanover hasn't returned yet."

"Figured as much." I forced a smile, knowing the older man wouldn't fall for it. "I need to get my cat out of his apartment. May I request your attendance for same?"

He let out a soft sigh. "I usually don't allow admittance to anyone's apartment without the express written permission of the owner." One side of the moustache came up. "But I can understand your position. I'll escort you upstairs."

"Wouldn't have it any other way," I replied. Not that I couldn't have broken in and retrieved Jazz on my own, but I figured Bran deserved better.

The doorman opened the lock with his passkey and stepped aside to allow me to walk in. Jazz, ever the attention-whore, sauntered out to curl her whiteness around Dan's legs where he stood.

"Stay." I waggled a finger at the cat. "Let me get your food and litter box and we'll be off." Making sure Dan had me in full view, I grabbed the necessities, with the travelling container for Jazz. Within ten minutes we were back down at the front counter, the bright lights of the security camera monitors flashing on and off as they cycled through their routine.

"Can you call me a cab?" Jazz mewed pitifully from inside the dark blue plastic box, sticking her paws between the metal bars. I reached in with one finger and stroked her soft white fur.

"Of course." The elderly man picked up a phone and tapped in a number. "Shall I take a message for Mr. Hanover?"

I paused for a second, weighing my options. "No. He'll know where to find me. Or not." I offered my hand to the doorman. "Thank you for your help."

"Thank you." The man smiled broadly, showing off a set of perfect teeth. "You've brought a bit of...excitement to these old bones. Can't say that I haven't enjoyed it."

"Good. Just stay safe." I grabbed the handle of the cat carrier as the cab pulled up. "And thanks again."

THE HOTEL'S MANAGEMENT was understanding, at least after I promised to pay any damages caused by Jazz sharpening her nails on the furniture. True to her innate ability to tell my emotional mood, she spent the two days we were there lying either on my lap or curled around my neck, purring softly while I worked on the paperwork to get the house repaired, the cheap bandages from a store-bought first aid kit helping the cuts on my cheek heal.

Hank was right about the contractors. They were in and out so quickly I was able to move back in and re-open the business before the hotel got uppity about the cat.

I was sitting behind my desk, working on yet another set of insurance papers when I heard the front door creak open. Jazz lifted her head from the couch and let out one of her enquiring trills before returning to her usual position. My pulse began to race when I tracked the familiar scent and then slowed as I placed a name with the smell.

Jess stepped through the hallway into the small lobby. "Hey." She stood there, her hands tucked into the front pocket of her jeans, a smile on her face.

"Hey." I didn't get up. "How's it going?"

"Pretty good." She pulled out a small envelope from the inside pocket of her leather jacket. "Check for your services. Thought I'd deliver it personally." The woman walked forward, stopping just in front of the desk. She didn't move to sit. I didn't offer.

"Thanks." I got up and took the envelope, placing it on the desk atop the stack of unpaid bills.

One eyebrow rose. "You're not going to open it?"

I shrugged. "I know you're good for it."

"You should." She sat down in the empty chair and looked around the office. "They did a good job."

"Sure did. Still looking for a new Brown Betty, but beggars can't be choosers." I rocked back in the squeaky wooden antique chair. "How's Tony?"

Jess let her breath out in a low whistle. "He's working. Hard. Got him putting in so much time on the chores, he barely has time to think."

"And Mike? The kids?"

"They're...coping." Jess nodded to Jazz who returned her look with a quiet purr. "I let Mike and Tony slug it out once already. Mike held back but still bloodied the kid up. Not going to close open wounds but it's a good catharsis for everyone. Mike understands it's partially our fault. Shouldn't have happened. Calamity of errors and all that."

"Moving forward and all that," I said, trying not to sound too sarcastic.

"Figure the best option is to keep Tony in custody for years, maybe let him out on a short leash if he earns it. Killing him ain't no proper solution."

I nodded. "How about the kids?"

"The younger one's still confused. The girl's going back and forth between swearing a blood oath to kill him and falling in love with the bastard." She shook her head. "Teens."

"Tell me about it." I rocked forward again. "And Tony's real father?"

"Kelly beat Frank up pretty badly, and now she's smothering Tony with so much affection that I think she's going to offer to bottle-feed him next. Frank's falling over himself with trying to take over as a father to Tony and groveling to Kelly, to say nothing of trying to make amends to Mike. It's not perfect, but it's a start." Jess shook her head. "We screwed up. Can't take it all out on the kid."

"Right." I glanced at the sealed envelope. "As long as the kids and Mike can live with it."

"They're more understanding than I'd thought they could be." She flexed her fingers, knuckles popping with a loud crack. "Tony's been pretty contrite. I think he's getting his emotions under control."

"His...other parents?"

"They've agreed to send him to our 'special school' for the time being." Jess grinned. "Dad didn't care as long as the kid was out from underfoot and Kathy, well..." Her face softened, suddenly reminding me of my mother. "She knew this day was coming. She's just glad he's not going to jail for the rest of his life. Tony's spoken to her a few times. A bit of crying but they're both coping with it."

"So everyone wins in the end." I pushed papers around the desktop.

The woman shrugged again. "Best we can come up with given the circumstances. It's not only Tony's fault or Frank's or Kathy's, it's everyone's."

"Best you can do." I tried not to sound judgmental but it rang through.

Jess leaned in, her voice low. "Look, no one's perfect. No system's perfect. This is all new to us. We never had this sort of kit before." She let out a sigh. "Wish we still had Ruth around. She'd be able to sniff the kid right straight up."

I nodded and twisted the metal clip straight. "Except she's dead, and you've still got Davis to deal with."

"It's all a mess." Jess sighed again. "And it'll take a while to clean up. We nominated Harry Wheaton to the Board, just so you know."

Now it was my turn to shrug. "I'll make a note."

"You know you're welcome to come home. I made that clear to everyone." Her eyes went a steely blue. "If they had a problem then they'd have to deal with me."

"Yep." I raised my head to meet her gaze. "But that's not my home. Not anymore."

Jess cleared her throat. "I understand. Still, it's good that you're all right again." She paused, staring at me.

I looked away. I'd never been a good poker player. Too many tells, as they call it.

"You can't do it again, can you?" she asked, a bit of sadness creeping into her usually neutral tones. "You've tried and you can't Change again."

My tongue rolled into my cheek and around to the other one before I responded. "Would it make a difference?"

"Not really." She shrugged. "Not now."

"Not going to beat me up again? Revoke my status?" I felt my blood pressure rising.

She put up her hands. "Don't put words in my mouth. I didn't say that."

"Then what?" My voice rose. "What happens now?"

"You do what you do. We do what we do," Jess said. "Hey, we all screwed up on this one." She got to her feet. "Can't say that I'll be any wiser in the future, but at least we can start making things better."

I glanced at Jazz who tilted her head to one side and rolled onto her back. "Guess we're all learning."

"Ain't that the truth." She put out her hand. "You've caused quite a stir, by the way. Between your...change of status and Tony's existence things are changing quickly and furiously. Tell you the truth, it's sort of exciting. Been a long time since the Pride's been rocked with this sort of news. Suddenly people are thinking and talking and asking questions, and wondering what else is out there that we've ignored or missed along the way."

I returned the smile, forcing myself to stay silent on that particular interpretation of "exciting."

"Well, keep me in the loop." I stood up.

"Sure will." Jess turned as if to leave, then paused. "I'm sorry it didn't work out with him."

I was grateful she hadn't used his name. "Thanks. So it goes."

"He's a good man, just so you know. I liked him." Jess stepped away, stopping to pet Jazz's exposed tummy. "Dating humans, well, some people just can't deal with it."

"I guess not." I didn't move out from behind the desk.

Jess smiled as she reached the hallway. "You never know what you can handle until you try, Reb. Never underestimate yourself."

Suddenly I caught it on the air, the faintest of scents carried in from the street.

The woman grinned like a Cheshire cat before stepping out of sight. "Or others, it seems." The words hung in the air for a second. I had to get her to teach me that trick.

Bran appeared in the doorway. He was wearing his

black leather duster, as usual, with a white T-shirt and jeans. A small bandage covered the cut on his throat. He shifted his weight from one foot to the other while staring at me.

"Hey." I exhaled the word, still standing behind the desk.

"Hey." His hands moved to sit in his coat pockets, then to his jeans pockets then to flop around in front of him like fish out of water. "Jazz okay?"

"Well, she misses all the extra treats." The white cat let out a full-strength yawn, letting everyone know she knew we were talking about her. "Other than that, she's fine."

He shuffled his way into the lobby. "They did a good job cleaning up the place."

"Yep. Hank said they were good and they were. Expensive, but good." I floundered through the conversation. "Jess was just here."

"Ah. Good news?" Bran moved closer to the couch and Jazz.

"Depends on your definition." I watched as he reached out and began to stroke Jazz's soft fur. Ever the traitor, she rolled over and let out a wide yawn, exposing her tummy for even more attention. "Tony's in rehab, or what passes for rehab up on the farm. Cops aren't any the wiser and have closed the case. Mike's coping, so are the kids."

"And you?" Bran left the cat and moved closer to the desk, standing opposite me. "How are you doing?"

"I'm…coping." I couldn't lie. "Jess told me I could come back to the farm if I wanted." I pushed the thick envelope with my index finger. "Don't think I'm going to take her up on the offer. Been out here in the world too long. Besides, I'm not sure if the rest of the Felis will be as forgiving as she is. Right now they're trying to deal with the concept that we can breed with humans and the possibility of other lost kits out there. It's a lot for them to deal with."

"And you?" Bran moved around to the right side of the desk, coming closer. "How are you coping now that you can…" A puzzled look came over his face as he waved his right hand as if he were brushing away flies. "You know."

He was right in my personal space again, his scent sweeping over me. "I don't think I'll do it anytime soon." I lifted my hands and showed him the healed skin. "Besides, it's too much trouble. No offense to my kin, but I've learned how to live without it."

"Oh." Bran moved even closer to me, his eyes meeting mine. "I mean, I was sort of hoping to see what it's like at night." One hand flopped between us. "That is, when it's cold. And I need to stay warm." A sigh escaped his lips. "Am I making any sense here?"

"You're okay with this?" I breathed in deeply, wallowing in his musky smell. "I thought…when you left…" Now it was my turn to flop around like a fish out of water.

Bran reached down and pushed the envelope across the desk. "Honestly, I was scared." A sheepish look crossed his features. "I guess it's a sort of fight or flight thing. I just wasn't ready to see you…you know, like that."

"Understandable," I mumbled.

He moved his hand along the wooden desktop.

"There's a reason why Felis stay with Felis." The words felt stale.

His hand landed atop mine and squeezed it lightly. "I'm sorry about what I did. And I can't say that I won't be a bit surprised and off-kilter at times when you do things in your own…special way." Dark, deep eyes met mine as he leaned in towards me. "But I can say that I'm willing to give this a try if you'll let a mere human share your bed."

I moved in for the kill and captured his lower lip with my teeth, nipping lightly, not enough to draw blood. "Yes. And yes."

Bran drew back. "To what?"

"To everything." I got up from behind the desk and walked around to face him. Wrapping my hands around his waist, I glanced toward the couch and Jazz, still on her back and watching us intently. "If you lock the door I'll move the cat."

He smiled broadly. "Deal. Just don't scratch me up too much. I've got an image to maintain."

I frowned. "What?"

Now it was his turn to smirk. "Got me a real freelance assignment. With the *National Post*. A respectable newspaper with a good reputation." Bran nodded to my shocked expression. "Time for us all to start something new, eh?"

I grinned as I pulled him in again for another long kiss, releasing him in time to let out a growl loud enough to scare Jazz off of the couch. "I guess you can always teach an old cat new tricks."

* * * * *